Murky Shallows

The lagoon that surrounds the city of Venice and more than thirty other islands besides, barely covers the mud-flats beneath it though high tides may flood the city streets. It can be a murky and sinister place in autumn and winter when drifting fog slows water-traffic to a standstill, but no more murky and sinister than some of the characters in this novel.

The sensitive Stefano, son of the aristocratic Chiara, has returned with his Finnish wife and two children to make his home on the Lido. Chiara bitterly resents the presence of an alien daughter-in-law and schemes to regain sole possession of her son and grandson. Meanwhile her powerful Sicilian husband, reared by the Mafia, is furthering his own unsavoury ends by organizing a publishers' and writers' conference in a prestigious hotel, when matters take a totally unexpected turn. Fortunately Arvo Laurila is already on the scene, the Finnish detective who made his bow in Ona Low's delightful first novel, *To His Just Deserts*. In a world where polluted air and water are rivalled only by the corruption and decadence of local society, fear, hatred, revenge and sudden death are as much at home as in the Venice of the Doges.

by the same author

TO HIS JUST DESERTS

ONA LOW

Murky Shallows

A Story of the Venetian lagoon

COLLINS, 8 GRAFTON STREET, LONDON W1

William Collins Sons & Co. Ltd
London · Glasgow · Sydney · Auckland
Toronto · Johannesburg

First published 1987
© Ona Low 1987

British Library Cataloguing in Publication Data

Low, Ona
    Murky shallows.—(Crime Club)
    I. Title
    823'.914[F]   PR6062.O87/

    ISBN 0 00 232125 4

Photoset in Linotron Baskerville by
Rowland Phototypesetting Ltd
Bury St Edmunds, Suffolk
Printed in Great Britain by
William Collins Sons & Co. Ltd, Glasgow

My acknowledgments and thanks to:

Signor Franco Nogara
President of the Federation of European Guides
Associations and Chief Guide of Venice; and to
Signora Sheila Rodighero,
both of whom read and commented on this book.
And to Signora Pat Liani
for her help in arranging interviews.

CHARACTERS

CONTENTS

CHAPTER 1

DIRTY WEATHER AHEAD

Smoothly the *Marco Polo* moved from embarkation channel into lagoon, turning her back on the quivering fringe of factory chimneys and oil tanks on the Marghera skyline, directing her course sedately towards the Most Serene, the Queen of Cities. To starboard loomed the gaunt disused flourmill on Giudecca Island, louring sullenly across the water at fancy cruise ships and idle cargo vessels lining the Maritime Station. The ferry kept her distance, ignoring too the busy small fry; motoscafi, vaporetti, barges, speedboats, gondolas: darting, chugging, gliding in and out of the mouth of the Grand Canal.

With the rush for Coke, canned beer and crisps satisfied during the first ten minutes, the barman propped himself against the counter and gazed into the distance, gnawing at some insoluble problem of his own. Around him at tables in the saloon, lorry-drivers aired their grievances lethargically, with long somnolent pauses, even gesticulation too much of an effort. Outside on the sun-scorched deck, large red-faced men, surrounded by a harem of grannies in sunglasses, skimpy cotton blouses and tight scarlet or gamboge slacks, slumped on benches, laid low by jungle-heat humidity, amid a clutter of empty tins and ice-cream wrappings. A plague-stricken galleon returning from a rather less success-ful Crusade, on its way to sanctuary on one of the more distant lagoon islands.

Until one of the large gentlemen mopping his lustrous cheeks with a paper tissue chanced to raise his eyes to the scene before him, leapt up and charged to the ship's rail, overturning an intervening can with a clatter that aroused those who were nearest to him.

'What do you know?' he yelled. 'Just take a look at that!'

Sated with the cloud-capped towers and palaces, lofty

peaks and soaring spires, masterpieces of art, architecture and natural splendour of nine European countries, his companions nevertheless responded obediently to the call. They clustered round him, examined, considered and found favour.

'Now isn't that real pretty! What is it?'

'Old, isn't it. Looks like some kind of palace. Hey, Joe. What would that be?'

Respectful attention was turned on a bespectacled youth, uncomfortably swaddled in a conventional suit, who might have been anyone's grandson but was in fact their guide, mentor, guardian and comforter.

'That's St Mark's Square with all those people,' he informed them, 'and the building's the Doge's Palace, where their ruler used to live. On the far side of it there's St Mark's Basilica.'

They digested this in silence for a moment till a voice inquired, 'What's the name of this town?'

'Venice,' said the young man, unsurprised.

'Venice,' the voice repeated as its owner turned in triumph to inform the lady with him: 'There, I said it was Wednesday today, not Tuesday. Rome Saturday, Florence Monday, Venice Wednesday, so it must be.'

The ferry glided on, inured to the vision of churches, Gothic, Byzantine, Renaissance palaces and lesser buildings staring across the lagoon. Inside the saloon voices were momentarily raised on the subject of wage-indexation but even that contentious issue could not compete with a temperature of 36°C and a humidity of 95. Under the watchful eye of her parents, a solemn-eyed two-year-old investigated and finally greeted as daddy a benevolent round-faced monk, who grinned and shook his head decisively. A most potent, grave and reverend signore turned another page of his Mickey Mouse paperback while a nondescript woman of uncertain age, a likely spinster and indubitable Englishwoman, wrote a final word in her crossword puzzle, closed her book and went out on to the deck.

On the starboard side a sandy-haired man was reloading an obviously expensive camera while his freckled companion looked up from her guidebook, eyed the newcomer and, with a strong Hamburg accent inquired, 'Are you speaking English?'

'What would you like to know?'

'This beautiful church on the right. How is it called?'

'Oh, that's the church of San Giorgio on its own lagoon island.'

'Thank you. Excuse me. My name is Dagmar Frick. My husband is there but I must not disturb him when he makes photographs.'

'I'm Iris Lawton. Is this your first visit to Venice?'

'Almost. We passed here five years before only one day. Are there many islands of the lagoon?'

'I suppose about forty in all. The lagoon covers a wide area.'

'You know this area well?'

'I live here.'

'You live here? That must be wonderful.'

'Maybe. It has its drawbacks.'

At this point, Iris's companion was summoned away to be positioned strategically against the background of a rapidly-retreating San Giorgio while the camera clicked several times. Iris moved further along the rail, her eyes wandering over the opaque sediment-clouded lagoon, the drab shapes of small islands doing nothing to relieve the monotony of its mirror-flat surface, the passing vaporetto huddled low in the water, its cargo of crammed perspiring humanity threatening to burst asunder constraining rails and sides, the pallid sky bearing down and suffocating from a few feet above the mast.

On her return journey from more northerly bearable climates, she had spent the previous night in a quiet friendly Austrian pension, driving at leisure along country roads that morning towards the frontier. The humidity had closed in on the autostrada north of Udine, had blanketed the featureless Veneto plain with its nondescript townlets and had clamped down inexorably as she circled Mestre and crossed the two-mile causeway linking Venice to the mainland. A not-unexpected twenty-per-cent rise in the price of

11

a ferry ticket but mercifully no more than half an hour's wait. She meditated mistrustfully on what might lie ahead.

The ferry was now apparently racing an orange bus along the Lido strand as they both made for San Nicolò. For a moment Iris imagined herself on the deck of a cruise ship leaving San Nicolò and the Lido behind, swinging to the right at the end of the island, past the two-mile-long breakwater into the Adriatic and south into the true blue Mediterranean. She joined the movement of lorry-drivers and motorists down to the car-deck. Doors slammed, engines revved and as the flat ship's prow clanged down on to the landing-stage, the game of who-goes-first, with victory to the most unscrupulous, got under instantaneous way.

Only a short distance separated Iris from her residence in a quiet tree-lined street divided in two by a homely canal. She parked alongside a grassy bank, rummaged for her keys in her handbag, grabbed two cases and made for the fortress-strong outer gate. In the small garden beyond, a bevy of multi-coloured cats gazed heavenward, heaven being represented by one of the balconies from which manna was wont to descend. One key for the gate, another for the heavy outer door, a third and fourth for the two locks on her own door. With the last of these open, she found herself in darkness and clicked on the hall switch. Nothing happened.

With light provided through the open door she located and mounted a step-ladder and flicked the fuse-switch above the door. The darkness continued. As a last resort she sought the line of switches in the communal storeroom corridor below. Noting her extended absence, some kind soul had apparently turned off the switch, unaware of the freezer left operating above.

Back in her kitchen, recalling the carton of peach-flavoured ice-cream and packets of fish and lasagne she had cheerfully committed to deep-freeze on departure, she postponed the evil hour by setting about the ceiling-high blind covering the kitchen window. A hoist on the lifting braid separated the slats and raised it some two feet where it jammed immovably. Another job for some elusive carpenter. Like a rabbit emerging from its burrow she crawled nervously beneath it on to the balcony to turn on the gas from the meter located there.

That panacea of all British ills, the nice cup of tea, being now indispensable, Iris prostrated herself on a very hard floor and crawled under the kitchen sink cupboards to reach the water-cock. Somewhere above, her industrious neighbour, who had moved in a year before and was still renovating and repairing, scraped what sounded like a broad-bladed ploughshare over his tiled floor, setting every tooth on edge. But the kettle was humming contentedly as Iris edged open the freezer door and was powerless to stem a richly-scented orange flow surging down the main fridge door like lava from Vesuvius. An indescribable stink of rotting synthetic peach and decaying fish and meat vastly outclassed the results of cleaning operations on one of the more neglected Venetian canals. A tingling sensation reminded her of a friend's warning: 'At their worst the mosquitoes are in September.' A final suicidal urge directed her trembling hand to opening a wall-cupboard door, only to release a cloud of mothlike creatures which scattered in all directions. It was then she noticed the corpse blobs enlivening at intervals the join between apple-green walls and whitish ceiling.

A shrill whistle from the boiling kettle almost drowned the low repeated menacing purr of the telephone. A wrong number, surely: nobody yet knew she was back. She turned off the gas, went into the hall and cautiously lifted the receiver. It was her habit to answer with her number in English, on rare occasions thus avoiding the fruitless exchanges and explanations over wrong numbers. But her mind was by now a blank: just what was her number? It was still too dark in the hall to see the small reminder on the apparatus and there was something odd about the uncomplaining silence at the other end. And then the breathing started: violent, rasping, insane, punctuated by unintelligible mutterings. It wasn't the first time and she was able to counter with her own menacing silence until the breathings and mutterings gave way to stuttering indignant questions in Italian: 'Why don't you answer? Who's there?' and the receiver was slammed down, a signal for Iris to do likewise. A sick mind in which muddy thoughts like polluted muddy waters stagnated and decayed. Revulsion rather than fear sent Iris charging across the kitchen for a bucket which she filled from the boiling kettle, cooled with clear tap water, and supplemented with cleaning powder and cloths. Having expelled three evil-smelling packets, she set vigorously to work on the noxious freezer. That would do for a start. Tea could follow later.

CHAPTER 2

CLOUDING OF THE WATERS

In most countries of the world, the weekly day of rest may combine opportunities for paying due respects to one's creators, divine and human, though nowadays more worldly distractions may replace the first of these occupations and distance apart limit the frequency of the second. In traffic-free Venice, however, parents and children, more casually dressed than of yore but with every hair in place and shoes immaculate, plod purposefully along narrow streets and over humped bridges to their obligatory Sunday rendezvous. Some hardy souls may even undertake the twelve-minute boat journey to what is for the average Venetian that infinitely remote island the Lido, that divides Venice and its lagoon from the Adriatic Sea.

Saturday in contrast is a normal day for school and shopping, the latter mainly in family-owned bakeries, butcheries, dairies, groceries and greengroceries, where customers jostle for attention under the stern eyes of the proprietor and his wife, who well know (but sometimes ignore) whose turn it is for attention before they ask. Personal service has its compensations for some, but it takes time, so it was not until half past two that, in a second-floor flat confronting the lagoon not far from Malamocco, some four miles south of the Lido boat terminus, Italian-born

Stefano finally corked the half-empty bottle of Piave. Simultaneously his wife, Finnish-born Tania, started to deal with the abandoned dessert plates while eight-year-old Rosa with brother Toni, a year and a half younger, slipped quietly from the table to resume the building of a space-station in a corner near the bookcase.

Even before Tania had finished clearing the discarded orange peel on to a single plate, Stefano had extracted a grappa bottle together with a couple of glasses from a cupboard behind him and carried them to a low table near the window with the suggestion, 'Let's have a coffee with some of this. No need for you to start on the washing-up yet. Today's a holiday for once.' His English had the fluency of a ten-year residence in London.

He sensed and countered his wife's unspoken, 'It may be for you,' by adding quickly, 'After all, last night's performance didn't finish much before eleven. Let's drink to today's strike. How could we survive without them?' Having filled the glasses, he picked up a local paper, raised slippered feet on to the sofa, leant back and turned to the sports page. For once in harmony, the children's voices, still attuned to the sounds of the London suburb they had spent most of their lives in, supplied the culminating touch of serene and satisfying domesticity.

Tania had abandoned the half-cleared table to embark on coffee-making in the kitchen, returning momentarily for her treasured Finnish Arabia coffee cups stored in the sideboard for rare moments of relaxation. As the water started to filter through the coffee, she gazed out across a grey lagoon. A still, melancholy day with a mist lurking off the Marghera shore and no contrast of sun and shadow to enhance the drabness of the abandoned island of Poveglia, brooding on the lagoon to her left, its deserted hospital buildings gradually decaying. So much talk now about revitalizing the islands: would it come to anything? And would sudden brash modernization, the creation of a so-called 'Lagoon Park', be much more appealing than the overgrown desolation and decay of the present?

She switched off the coffee-machine just as her meditations were interrupted by the sound of thumpings and a boy's voice yelling resentfully, 'That's my bit. I was going to do that. It's not fair. You always do the best parts. Shan't play any more.' Sounds of violent demolition followed, accompanied by kicking and stamping. At least, Tania mused resignedly, lagoon islands crumble and decay silently and are not shattered by sudden human assault.

'Please, Stefano, do something about Toni,' she called through the door, as she put cream jug and sugar basin on the tray and reached for a biscuit tin. But the noise continued unabated and she carried the tray into the room to discover Rosa already curled up in a chair, serenely absorbed in the book she had left there earlier, apparently unaware of an enraged Toni punching her, stamping on her feet and trying to tear the book from her hands. As his mother appeared, he returned to his work of violent demolition.

Having safely deposited the loaded tray, Tania seized the hysterical child by the shoulders, turned him to face her and held him in silence while he kicked and bawled. Gradually the storm died down and he faced her passively, his mouth opening and shutting with words he dared not say aloud. 'Now you will first apologize to your sister,' she said eventually, her voice quiet but steel-hard. 'And then you will pick up and put together every piece just as they were before you started pulling them down.'

She released him and he stood rigid for a moment or two glaring defiantly while she regarded him without expression. Finally he burst out, 'I'll tell Grandmother about you and you'll be sorry then. You'll see. She's on my side.' Over his shoulder he tossed a contemptuous 'Sorry' in Rosa's direction before crouching again to gather up some of the scattered pieces. Reluctantly he assembled the first two or three before being caught up in the fascination of construction, sparing a brief lofty, 'I can manage better without your help,' for his sister. For a brief interval peace returned.

By now Tania had poured out the coffee. An arm appeared to take the cup from behind Stefano's paper when she called his name and she was able to sink into a chair with her own cup. Almost immediately she was up again. 'Mother's

16

letter,' she exclaimed. 'I'd almost forgotten it.'

She fetched from the hall table an envelope postmarked Finland, tore it open and started reading. Almost immediately she gasped and after a whispered 'Oh no!' her eyes raced along the lines. Alerted by her cry, Stefano waited until she raised distraught blue eyes at the end, before he inquired gently, 'Bad news?'

'Yes. Father's had a serious heart attack. He's got over it but the doctor's warned him to take things easy. Imagine telling Father that! There could be a recurrence at any time. She begs us to come and see them as soon as possible—with the children, of course, and specially for Christmas, though that won't be for more than two months. Arvo's been off on a police job in Lapland and when she wrote this letter they'd only just managed to contact him.' Arvo was her brother and a detective-superintendent in Helsinki.

She was aware of Rosa standing quietly at her side, blue eyes very like her mother's, wide and anxious. 'Grandfather won't die, will he?' she asked.

It was now two years since the family had last been in Helsinki and Tania wondered how much of the vigorous kindly old farmer the children remembered. Quite a lot in Rosa's case, she suspected: the little girl always asked specially about him whenever a letter came. 'No, dear,' she replied, 'not if he's careful and he will be now, I'm sure. Don't worry.'

Toni had joined his sister. 'Are we going to Finland for Christmas?' he demanded. 'By aeroplane to see Father Christmas and he'll bring us lots of nice presents and we'll go tobogganing and skiing? Mummy, I want to go to Finland like we did before.'

'That was two years ago when we were living in England,' his mother reminded him, 'and we were able to go by special cheap charter flight. It would cost very much more for the four of us to go from Italy.'

'Nonno Angelo can pay: he's got lots of money. I'll telephone and ask him. Now.' Anticipating opposition, he darted swiftly to the telephone on the hall table.

With a sudden violent movement, his father threw down

17

his newspaper and leapt up from the sofa to dash after him, grabbing hold of him as he dialled a well-remembered number. 'Oh no you don't,' his father snapped. Hoisted out of reach of the telephone, Toni drummed his feet against his father's thighs and wriggled round to punch the spectacles on his nose in a wild attempt to shatter the thick-lensed glass. 'I will, I will,' he shrieked, pulling now at the horn sidepieces until two hard smacks silenced him in momentary astonishment before he gave vent to a bawl of impotent fury. A squirming resistant armful of rage, his father carried him to the children's room, threw him on to the upper bunk and left him there screaming, firmly closing the door behind him.

Tania sipped her coffee in silence, isolating herself from the conflict, vaguely thankful that her normally lethargic husband had at last taken a share in disciplining the boy, who since their arrival in Italy a year before had become increasingly unmanageable. Despite the many years abroad, Stefano had never questioned the Italian male axiom that housekeeping and the upbringing of children were solely the woman's responsibility. Self-centred, a dreamer without ambition, the pampered son of an over-indulgent mother, he regarded his home as a refuge, his wife as a second mother and his children objects for self-congratulation perhaps, but more of a pleasant distraction than a responsibility. And ever-present in his consciousness was the looming figure of his father, tyrant, ogre, dynamic forceful public figure, who despised his younger sensitive flute-playing son and, ashamed of having him around, had packed him off as soon as convenient to study music in England. Later, by a word in the right quarters, he had assisted him to remain there, playing his flute in the orchestra of a London opera-house.

In London Stefano had met and married the beautiful Finnish au-pair assisting the British family he boarded with and there the two children had been born.

With his elder son firmly established in New York, Father Angelo Vescovo suddenly decided to recall his lacklustre younger offspring, who had at least gained sufficient of a musical reputation to be offered a job with the Venice opera-house, La Fenice. What this overgrown schoolboy, still tongue-tied and apparently half-witted in his father's presence, thought of him, had never crossed Angelo's mind to discover.

Now Stefano made his way back to the sofa, shaken by his own unexpectedly violent reaction and uneasily aware of the real spark that had set it off. He sat down awkwardly and remained rigidly upright, glaring fixedly at the Turner interpretation of the Grand Canal facing him. 'We'll go to Finland for Christmas,' he said grimly. 'We've got enough money saved for the flight. There'll be no need to ask him for anything.'

Tania had discovered that the envelope from Finland still contained a slip of paper. She drew it out, read the message on it and unpinned the cheque attached. 'Look at this,' she said, holding the cheque up for Stefano to see. 'Two million lire available from the Banco di Roma and signed by Father. There's a message here that it's to help with paying our fares and Father's added—his writing's very shaky— "Please come".'

'We'll go for sure,' Stefano told her. 'They won't need me then at La Fenice and if they should happen to, Giorgio will stand in for me. It's a long time since . . .'

It was at this point that the heart-rending howls from the bedroom—with occasional pauses to determine what effect they might be having—were interrupted by the ringing of a bell, signifying the arrival of a visitor at the condominium gate, who identified herself to Tania as Chiara 'just dropping in for a moment to see you all'. Tania pressed the release switch, informing Stefano over her shoulder, 'It's your mother.' There was a hurried rustle as he folded his newspaper and placed it neatly in the magazine basket before rushing into the bedroom to don tie and jacket and replace slippers with shoes. True devotion, Tania wondered, or the old feeling of inferiority?

She opened the door and listened to the staccato tap of high heels on the two flights of stone steps that separated their home from the outer door. Chiara's newly-tinted hair —a russet red that called to mind a vixen in autumn woods

—slightly over-made-up sharply-etched features between pearl-studded ear-rings, ivory blouse at the neck of a charcoal-grey jacket over matching skirt and finally dark-grey suede shoes, revealed themselves successively as she climbed, slowly but even so a trifle breathlessly, the shallow treads. No longer so slim as she appeared in the photographs Stefano had shown Tania soon after they had first met, but careful attention to dress and diet, together with regular visits to hairdresser and beauty specialist, had kept figure, face and hair reasonably attractive. What had once been a sweet appealing voice had however acquired a brittle quality which in Tania's presence at least she made little attempt to soften.

Confronted at close quarters by her mother-in-law, Tania groped nervously for the appropriate Italian words to greet this rarely-encountered vision of sophisticated elegance: a complete lack of interest by the locals in newcomers had limited linguistic practice and her husband preferred to forget his own language in the home. Hesitatingly she ventured in basic Italian, 'It is nice to see you. We do not expect you today. Please come in.'

'Good day.' Chiara greeted her contemptuously in strongly-accented English, pecked her cheek and swept into the living-room to fling her arms round and kiss dramatically her son advancing to greet her. 'My darling boy, 'ow are you?' she continued in English, presumably for the ignorant foreigner's benefit. Having moved further into the room, she stopped in exaggerated horror before the still-untended dinner table. 'You 'ave not washed the dishes yet? At three o'clock? And why are you 'ere, my boy? Ah yes, I remember, I see it on the newspaper. The orchestra is in strike at the La Fenice—is it again for more money?—and the public is not seeing this afternoon the *Aida* it 'as paid for. Why you not come to 'ave lunch with your mother, Stefanello? I eat —ate—at twelve o'clock, not in the middle of the afternoon. Ah, Rosa, 'ow are you, child? You are a good girl at the school, I 'ope. But where is my . . .?'

A door opened and a small tear-stained figure rushed towards her and threw himself into her arms, sobbing uncontrollably. 'Granny Chiara. Granny Chiara. I love you so much, Granny Chiara.'

Chiara stroked his curly black hair tenderly before lifting his head to survey his face. 'Little Tonino,' she murmured adoringly, 'you are crying. Tell Granny Chiara, Tonino darling. What is the matter?'

Toni glanced momentarily at his mother with a wild gleam of triumph. 'Mummy slapped me,' he whimpered pathetically, 'and I hadn't done anything. She's horrible: she's always smacking me. She loves doing it.'

Clutching the child to her, Chiara turned to confront Tania. 'Is this true,' she demanded, 'that you beat this innocent child?'

'He's lying.' Stefano's voice was unnaturally harsh. 'I smacked him and he thoroughly deserved it.'

'You didn't! You didn't!' Toni screamed. 'It was Mummy and horrible Rosa. She knocked down my beautiful space-station I'd built all by myself and I cried and Mummy smacked me for crying. She always takes Rosa's part. Daddy's only saying that because he likes Mummy better than me. Please, Grandma Chiara, take me home with you. I hate Mummy and Daddy and Rosa and they all hate me. Take me away, dear Grandma Chiara.'

Ignoring the amazement that transfixed the faces around her, Chiara turned to Tania, her face sharp-drawn with rage. 'You dared to use violence on my grandson,' she spat out. 'My son's child! What kind of foreign devil has my Stefano for a wife, I ask myself.'

A small figure confronted her, blue eyes glittering with indignation. 'Mummy didn't smack him. Daddy did. Why don't you believe him? Toni knocked down our space-station we'd built together but Mummy didn't smack him for it. Daddy did later when he tried to telephone and then he kicked Daddy and tried to break his glasses.'

Rosa was interrupted by a second attack from her brother, who, sensing that justice might be closing in, was determined to create as much havoc as he could before he lost the opportunity. He was immediately grabbed by his father who made him face his trusted protector before demanding icily:

21

'Now you will tell your grandmother the truth. Who was it smacked you?'

'Mummy, Mummy, Mummy.'

Stefano's grip tightened and his tone became icier. 'Who smacked you?'

The contest was suddenly abandoned. With untroubled confidence in the omnipotence of his guardian angel, Toni admitted with feigned remorse, 'You did, Daddy. I'm sorry.' His eyes sought sympathy in those of his grandmother.

'Why?'

'I was a naughty boy. I . . .' His voice broke in sobs.

'What did you do?'

'I kicked you when you stopped me telephoning to Granny Chiara. Nonnina Chiara, I'm sorry. I was afraid you'd be cross with me. Please, dear Nonnina Chiara, say you're not cross with me.'

She bent and kissed him tenderly on his forehead before raising her eyes to plead with her son. 'He's such a sweet little boy,' she reproached him. 'He needs affection so much: he gets little enough of it from his mother. *Poverino, carissimo*. Don't cry little Tonino. Nonnina Chiara isn't cross. Look, little one, she's brought a nice present for you.'

His crying ceased as she got up from her chair and he followed her eagerly to the leather bag she had left in the hall from which she extracted a square package in brightly decorated gift paper. 'Don't tell Mummy and Daddy. They're chocolates with lovely liqueur centres, just for you, my darling. Hide them quickly.'

She was too late; Stefano was already beside them. 'Give those to me,' he ordered Toni, who, despairing of creating a further scene, and realizing that his father was in no mood for any kind of opposition, surrendered them without resistance. 'Now go to your room and stay there until I tell you to come out. You understand?'

Toni crept away with a last heart-rending glance at his grandmother who was equally aware that the present odds were against her. In stunned silence she moved back to the sitting-room where she sat down white-faced and remote in a chair near the window. Rosa watched her, longing to give comfort to this unhappy old lady however much she disliked her. Tania completed the clearing of the table and started to prepare fresh coffee.

'You'll have some coffee, won't you,' she suggested in an uncertain voice, having difficulty in keeping out of it her dislike and anger. 'We've been having some grappa,' she added. 'Would you like some?'

Apparently returning from some lofty and distant retreat, Chiara responded indifferently, 'I feel I need a little of both —in the circumstances. Of course, you 'ave not cigarettes 'ere, and will not like that I smoke. In this moment, 'owever, I 'ave the need for one.' She duly extracted from her handbag on the table in front of her a gold filigree-adorned cigarette-case with matching lighter, took out a cigarette and, after looking in vain for some assistance, lighted it herself.

An uneasy silence followed while Stefano put the television on and located a football match on one of the many channels and Tania laid out fresh cups and poured grappa into two of the glasses. She had no great liking for the spirit and couldn't have faced a second glass but like tea for the Englishwoman, coffee is a sovereign Finnish restorative.

Tapping ash from her cigarette, Chiara waited until Tania had returned to the kitchen, before suggesting plaintively, 'Stefano, my dear, please close the television. Is not often that I 'ave the opportunity to come to see you—and when I see the disorder you 'ave to live in and your un'appy family life, I am no more surprised that I am not invited. But surely when I find the courage to come, you can talk to your mother. Please, I 'ave important things to say to you. Come and sit near me.'

He obeyed reluctantly, perching on the edge of the sofa, his arms stretched forward over his knees, with his long sensitive fingers clasped in front of him, a means of defence it seemed against the emotional assault he knew was to follow. Chiara paused significantly, regarding him with bitter intensity, her already half-consumed cigarette directed like a weapon towards him.

Aware that Tania, now out of hearing, would return at any minute, she opened the attack. All sharpness had disappeared from her voice: it soothed and coaxed and yearned as she lingered over the melodious syllables of the pure Italian of Tuscany.

'Stefano, my son, you trust me, you've always trusted me and I've defended you against the hard world, against your clever brother, against your father above all. I've been the only one who's understood you: your sensitivity, your imagination, your wonderful talent. And Toni is your son, not hers: he is sensitive and talented like you: he and I understand one another as you and I have always done. You love your wife, I know: she is a beautiful woman but she's hard and cold like the country she comes from and she has no feeling for you and even less for your son. And she is ruining him as you have seen today. He longs for affection and understanding and he turns to me for it, not her. Stefano, you must leave her before she destroys both of you.'

There was an impatient movement from her son but before he could speak, she uncovered his clasped hands with one of her own and continued:

'No, I understand, you don't want to live in your father's home, but I can arrange a comfortable flat near us in Venice: you can eat with me whenever your father is away. And Toni can stay with me and you'll see him every day. She can have the girl and Angelo can allow her something, so she'll have nothing to complain about. We'd even pay her fare back to Finland where she'd probably be happier.'

Stefano tore his hands away, stood up, and, short in stature though he was, managed to give the impression of towering over her, as he burst out, 'Leave me alone and leave Toni alone. I'm quite happy as I am and so is Toni, or he would be, if you didn't interfere. I've had about enough . . .'

He was interrupted by the summons of the telephone, strode into the hall and picked up the receiver. She listened hard-faced to his '*Pronto*' followed by a pause, during which Tania appeared with the fresh coffee. After a brief '*Si. È qua*,' he looked into the room. 'It's for you,' he informed his mother, passing the receiver to her when after a startled 'For me?' she had joined him.

24

As he returned to the sofa he was aware that her voice had changed: she was using the sibilant Venetian dialect which he, brought up in Rome and after years abroad, understood almost nothing of. He wondered momentarily how she had picked it up. She spoke only for a minute before returning, a new animation in her voice.

'I'm so sorry,' she explained in rapid Italian. 'I'll have to leave immediately. It was one of your father's assistants in the tourist conference they're planning for next spring. I forgot to tell you your father's in Rome today: there's only my maid in the house and she let him have this number. He needs some papers urgently, addresses I think he said of some of the participants he'll have to contact and I'll have to go at once and find them for him. Stefano, can you call a taxi for me?'

'There's a bus to the boat stop passing here in five minutes that will be quicker,' he told her. 'The taxi may well take at least ten minutes to get here.'

'No, no. A taxi will be better. I can telephone myself perhaps if you don't want to.'

Stefano rarely used a taxi and had to look up a suitable number. Ignoring the coffee and grappa awaiting her, Chiara briefly informed Tania, 'I 'ave to go suddenly,' and disappeared into the bathroom, emerging as the bell below announced the arrival of the taxi, her face newly furbished.

''Ow do I look?' she asked, almost skittishly in English. 'Toni seems to sleep, the angel, so I don't disturb 'im. I am so sorry I cannot spend a longer time with you both but we see ourselves again soon. I must not keep waiting that busy gentleman.' Whether this applied to assistant or taxi-driver not having been made clear, she kissed Stefano lightly, pecked at Tania's cheek and called back, 'Be a good girl and 'elp your mother, Rosa,' as she disappeared through the door.

Stefano moved back across the room to open a window. He watched her emerge and, without looking up, get into the taxi which moved off in the direction of Malamocco village.

'That's odd,' he commented, 'the taxi's going in the other

25

direction. I suppose he's going to turn back farther on where the road's wider.' He picked up his own grappa and drained it immediately, reaching for the one poured for his mother and holding it meditatively while he reflected:

'There are times when one drink isn't enough. One of her slightly hysterical days. Let's forget it.' He sipped at the glass and then put it down. 'Rosa, go and wake Toni and get him to put his coat on. We'll drink the coffee you've poured, Tania, and then we're all going for a long walk. I need some fresh air.'

CHAPTER 3

SOUTH SEA ISLANDER

On entering his overheated study, Angelo Vescovo removed his jacket, expensively tailored to make the least of his unflattering bulk, and arranged it over the high back of a newly-acquired adjustable chair, paired incongruously with a massive mahogany desk created by eighteenth-century Italian master-craftsmen. He lowered himself on to the chair, switched on an angled metal lamp and riffled through the correspondence that awaited him, slitting open the flaps with a silver Toledo-dagger paper-knife and scanning each letter rapidly. Two envelopes in pastel shades, one of them scented, he cast aside contemptuously, but gave prolonged attention to a booklet extracted from an envelope bearing in a lower corner the embossed inscription The Manuzio Printers' and Publishers' Corporation with the towns Rome - Florence - Venice - Milan - Naples discreetly spaced below. An Italian version occupied the corner at the far side of the envelope.

He leaned back, switched on a parchment-shaded standard lamp a short distance to his right and in its softer glow examined the booklet approvingly, having himself played a considerable part in its production. The broad glossy cover displayed a picture-map of the world, dotted with stylized coloured thumbnail miniatures of its wonders, both of natural and human achievement. Printed in gold across the wastes of Northern Canada, Scandinavia and the Soviet Union were the glowing words:

INTERNATIONAL TRAVEL WRITERS' AND PUBLISHERS' CONVENTION
Venice 1st–5th May

Angelo paused and spat out a dismayed obscenity. The dolts—his Italian appellation was considerably more expressive—had omitted the year. Already four months behind schedule after a series of printers' strikes, postal freezes, endless procrastination in the provision of material which had had to be amended repeatedly, interminable correcting of appallingly set-out and erroneous proofs (while he had seethed and fumed like his native Etna), the two thousand copies at last awaiting dispatch should by now have been drawing in at least a quarter of that number of applications.

It was too late now to make the necessary insertion and the omission might well escape notice. He turned over the pages, which detailed the numerous distinguished patrons, the illustrious sea-front hotel that would welcome the delegates, the aims of the Congress, and the instructional and social programme. Block hotel bookings had been made months before, speakers from areas of special interest engaged, and less prestigious brochures circulated to publishing concerns, authors' unions and well-known travel writers in various countries. An encouraging number of applications had already been received; with the help of this glamorous production, many more should follow.

So far as Angelo was aware, the Congress would be an unusual one. The writers were to be treated to information about the less well-trodden but still intriguing areas of the world together with local advisory services, transport, accommodation and interpreters, while publishers could extend their knowledge of distribution chains, translation rights, publicity and advertising services together with potential new markets. Above all, exploiters and providers of travel literature could benefit from mutual contact and make their own discoveries about developments and achievements elsewhere.

The administrator and manipulator of an assortment of business interests at various levels of respectability, including (in their higher reaches) the proprietorship and financial control of both a publishing house and a large printing concern, Angelo had all the cynicism of his kind, but even so he was truly dazzled by the brilliance of his inspiration. Not only would his involvement in the Congress add to both fortune and reputation: he would be able to take advantage of this assembly of the influential and knowledgeable of five continents for his own private and even more profitable purposes: existing connections could be checked and extended and new possibilities sounded.

Angel Vescovo had been born some sixty-five years previously in a Palermo slum and had since made good use of his early education there. No one had wondered or cared about the non-Sicilian surname (its English equivalent was Bishop): presumably some soldier or seaman had married a local girl a century or so before and after a couple of generations the family had become accepted and received into the protective arms of the district Mafia. A bright and hard-headed boy, Angelo had taken pains to win the approval of schoolmates with influential Mafia connections and as a reward was maintained at school longer than most and on leaving set up in a job with a local newspaper. He proved so astute and amenable to his benefactors that a transfer to a national paper in Rome over which they exercised a certain control was arranged for him before he was twenty. Again he proved amenable, though increasingly more personally motivated. He rapidly established a reputation in the press and also the publishing world, with a directorship by the time he was thirty. He was by then an honoured and active member of the organization that had befriended him and, with help from this quarter in return for services rendered, he was soon in a position to establish his own company, to be known at first as Manuzio Publications after the two early Venetian printers of that name.

At that age he was strikingly good-looking: jet-black hair with an inclination to wave, and worn slightly longer than that of most men of his age and position, brooding dark eyes which he had learned to hood magnetically, and the aloof tragic air of the Byronic outcast. With a wide circle of friends of his own careful choosing, including a number of fashionably adventurous Roman wives, he nevertheless cultivated a public image of a solitary, brilliant, romantic dreamer.

When pert, pretty and spoilt Chiara, only child of a father of aristocratic Venetian ancestry, was introduced to him, it was obvious that the sixteen-year-old was enthralled. Until now Angelo had skilfully avoided matrimony but as the gold-lashed green eyes gazed spellbound into his own, he recalled all he had heard of the family fortunes and calculated that now was the time to hazard all. With a father in frail health, this desirable girl would soon own not only a palazzo on the Grand Canal but, even more important, the millions needed to maintain it in first-class condition and ensure a standard of living in keeping with its splendours. Moreover she was young enough to be malleable and looked astute and hard-headed enough to develop the social skills that would help him on his way. In due course she might be left to follow with discretion her own inclinations, leaving him to pursue his.

A few days' acquaintance confirmed him in his assessment of her eligibility and he now had to produce evidence of his own. His birthplace need not be revealed until official documents had to be signed and any withdrawals out of the question, and his respectable non-Sicilian surname proved an unexpected advantage, influential Roman acquaintances being persuaded to supply a fictitious pedigree. They had married within three months, Pietro, a miniature of his black-haired aggressive father being born a year after and the dreamy blue-eyed Stefano, with a slight resemblance to his now-departed maternal grandfather but to nobody else, had arrived two years later.

By now a businesslike understanding could be agreed upon between the partners: a family of sons had been established and each parent was free to go his or her own way, provided care was taken, at least on Chiara's side, to avoid open scandal. Increasing interest in the pleasures that money could buy soon dispelled Angelo's mystery and magnetism: the Byronic tragic outcast was rapidly losing his physical, though not mental, agility together with his slim and supple figure. But a retreating hairline, pouched eyes and a thickening voice resonance apparently had little effect on success with well-disposed Roman ladies and money was not only fast begetting more money but its owner was discovering ever more unobtrusive though none the less interesting ways of increasing his fortune.

With a sigh of self-approval, Angelo bent forward to extinguish the desk-lamp and replace the booklet before again leaning back in his chair, a pudgy hand sliding over the glistening skin dividing by several inches the scanty dark hair on either side of it. He tilted the chair back as far as it would go so that his eyes rested momentarily on an unlit chandelier, thence travelling over the ornately-carved oak ceiling and finally coming to rest on a bust of the Venetian playwright Goldoni, gazing down upon him sardonically from the top of the high mahogany bookshelves lining the opposite wall. Wedged tightly on the shelves, gold-tooled leather-bound volumes in sombre browns, crimsons and greens brooded in shadow, having gathered dust there for decades.

With its serene self-assurance evolved through the centuries of comfort and scholarship it had sheltered, the room both irritated and gratified him. Between gold-brocade curtains, still undrawn, Gothic-arched windows surveyed the Grand Canal, shrouded now in clammy fog so that all traffic had come to a standstill. It was here that his in-laws: father, grandfather, great-grandfathers for a dozen generations and more, had browsed and prepared monographs, discussed trade, politics and the arts and admired the now almost invisible Guardi prints set against magenta damask wall-covering. An appropriate setting for the exclusive Seicento nobility, ousted three centuries later by a new species of baron, Sicilian-born in a tenement who had clawed his way to power and wealth by means only slightly more disreputable than those of his aristocratic Venetian predecessors.

Goldoni having provided inspiration, he pressed a button within reach of his hand, before unfolding the booklet for a further admiring perusal. After an interval long enough for him to start fidgeting irritably, the door opened a slit and a girl's heavily made-up face peered round it uncertainly. At the sight of him glaring at her ominously, she gasped 'O Madonna!' in appalled confusion, resisted an impulse to take to her heels, and finally inserted into the room the rest of herself, conspicuous in a carnation-pink low-necked blouse above skintight faded blue jeans. Apologies started to pour out in incomprehensible dialect, of which he could make out only something resembling 'Oh, Signore, I had no idea you were in. Forgive me. I . . .' at which point he roared in his native tongue, '*Basta*—enough. Why are you decked out like a floozy? Where's your uniform? Where are you intending to go?'

She hesitated before gabbling, 'I bought them this afternoon. I was trying them on,' but was interrupted by a repeated, 'Where were you intending to go?'

'To the disco.' She lowered her head, forcing a few tears into her eyes and looking as abject as a bold face would allow. Mascara started to smudge her cheeks.

'Aren't you on duty now? Where's the signora?'

'She is out, signore.' The words were almost inaudible.

'When did she leave?'

'Soon after lunch. At about one-thirty.'

'Did she say where she was going?'

'To see her grandson Toni.'

'And she isn't back yet? Surely she will expect to find you here.'

'Yes, signore.'

'But you were going out.'

'Yes, signore.' The tears were flowing faster and with possibly more cause.

'So the signora had other plans for this evening?'

'I don't know, signore. It's possible because she does not

31

usually stay so long. Perhaps a dinner-party.'

'But she would have returned to change for that.'

'I don't know, signore.'

Mingled with her fear of him, there was a hint of malicious enjoyment, almost of complicity. He shrugged his shoulders and let the matter drop. What his wife did in her spare time concerned him as little as his own activities concerned her. The girl before him—what was her name?—Beata was it? —continued to sob, though with sly speculative glances at him as she mopped her eyes with a pink paper handkerchief. A faint resemblance to Chiara, he reflected, though with none of her social know-how. He eyed her coldly. As if speaking to a rebellious child he said, 'You will change back immediately into your uniform and resign yourself to spending the rest of the evening indoors. You understand?'

She nodded her head in submission before widening damp smutted eyes coquettishly in his direction. 'Does the signore need something?' she asked humbly.

'Yes. A pot of coffee and some sandwiches.'

'What kind of sandwiches, signore?'

'Smoked salmon, pâté, chicken: whatever is available. All three, perhaps: I'm hungry. Tell Roberto I shall need the boat to get to the station at 10.30 whatever the weather: I have a sleeper reservation for the 10.48 train to Rome. On second thoughts, I'd like some hot soup, minestrone if it's available, as well as the sandwiches. And a large beer with it. And if the signora comes home, she need not know I'm here. I want to be undisturbed.'

She lingered a moment as he turned away, wondering if this was all, finally asking somewhat pleadingly, 'There will be nothing more then, signore?'

'Nothing more now, signorina, thank you. Apart from bearing in mind what I said to you earlier. Unless of course you are tired of working here.'

'No, no, signore.' Her hands flew to her face, covering her cheeks with dramatic exaggeration before she closed the door silently behind her. Angelo had already turned to the pearl-grey telephone on a table in a corner across from the door and was composing a familiar six-figure number.

A pleasant woman's voice greeted him. *'Pronto.'*

'Ciao, Cristina, my dear. Camillo must be home if you are, for sure.'

'I will call him, Signor Vescovo.' The tone of her reply was not welcoming and there was little warmth in the man's voice that followed.

'Camillo here, Good evening. You wanted to speak to me, Signor Vescovo?'

'I want also to see you, Camillo, as soon as possible. I'm just back from Milan and will be leaving again soon after ten and there are several things to discuss. It's quite foggy now so you'll have to walk. I'm mainly concerned with certain allocations and appropriations, so bring any records you have with you.' He replaced the receiver promptly to forestall any attempt at protest and turned to a computer keyboard, which, with a component screen and an electric typewriter, occupied the rest of the table. He touched some keys and a name, address and telephone number appeared on the screen. He again lifted the telephone and tapped out the number shown, this time a considerably longer one. He waited for half a minute, reflecting meanwhile that the time in New York should now be around half past three. A smooth masculine voice announced in American English:

'This is the residence of Mr Peter Vescovo. Who is speaking, please?'

Angelo responded in heavily-accented English. 'Angelo Vescovo speaking from Venice, Italy. Is my son at home?'

'I'm sorry, Mr Vescovo. He's usually at the Solarium at this time. Shall I try to locate him and ask him to ring you back?'

At the Solarium on what was probably a fine Saturday afternoon! If he wasn't hard at work, he could at least have been on the golf course or at some ball game. Maybe he was entertaining clients, though. 'Please do that,' he replied. 'And let me know yourself if you can't locate him.'

'I will indeed, sir.' The receiver was replaced.

Angelo returned to the desk, gingerly knelt down just inside the space between the extensive drawers and began fumbling underneath the back of it. He located a hidden button that he pressed upward and at the same time steadied a back panel which was moving downward towards him. A space just wide enough to accommodate a number of books was revealed: he sought for and finally extracted two ledgers and a couple of smaller volumes which he placed on the floor beside him and replaced the panel. It was at that moment that the telephone rang.

He scrabbled wildly, bumped his head on the desk surface above it, clutched at the desk edge and, groaning and cursing, heaved himself to an upright position. Out of breath and slightly stunned, he hobbled to the table and grabbed the receiver, grunting '*Pronto. Chi parla?*'

A startled silence followed, ending in a tentative, '*È Signor Vescovo?*'

'Who the hell's speaking?' was the Italian response.

The reply was immediate and in English. 'Oh, it's you, Pop. Now I recognize your voice. I called as soon as I got your message. How're you doing?'

'And it's you, Pietro. Just knocked myself out but it doesn't matter. How are you, boy?'

'Fine, Pop. You're all right, are you?'

'No, I am not. Shall we stop wasting time and get down to business. I want you to listen carefully. Have you got a notebook handy?'

'Well, no, Pop. I'm in the Solarium. But you know me. Memory like a computer. Shoot.'

Angelo winced at what even he recognized as an outworn Americanism, reflecting as it did the lingering immaturity of his elder son, now in his early thirties. When he thought of himself at that age . . .! He proceeded curtly in Italian. 'I have at last received a copy of the full Congress prospectus that I told you about: four months behind schedule but there's nothing now that can be done about that. Everything's in English, naturally, translated by a competent American, with summaries of aims, arrangements, programmes and the like in Italian, French and German. I sent you a cable about this a week ago but so far have had no reply. Distribution will get under way on Monday. How many do you estimate you can place effectively?'

Pietro had forgotten the cable, delivered when he had been more than usually under the weather, so was forced to make a wild guess. 'I could find a home for some thirty or forty,' he suggested hopefully in English.

'Absurd. With the whole of the States, together with Canada and Mexico within your area, you must already have listed two or three hundred possibilities. Not only publishers, remember: clubs, unions, writers, even journalists might be interested. How about advertisements in newspapers and journals?'

'Those appeared months ago.'

'They've had little enough effect. Try again and get advice from an agency.' Crisp Italian punctuated lethargic Eastern-seaboard drawl. 'Sunday's the best day when people have got time to think about things. And bear in mind the literary and travel pages of the heavies. List the organizations and individuals you'll be sending the prospectuses to and send a copy of that list to me as soon as they've been sent off. I can then do some checking myself. We've had plenty of applications from all other areas and I'm only asking myself what is happening in yours. Where are you now?'

'In the Madison Solarium. It's Saturday afternoon, Pop. I can't keep my nose down all the time.'

'With clients?'

'Er . . . yes. With some folk from Chicago as a matter-of-fact.'

'What's their business?'

Pietro spoke unguardedly. 'I didn't ask them.' His blunder dawning on him, he added quickly: 'Didn't need to, of course. They're a couple of TV executives. There's a possibility of their serializing one of our titles.' Pietro marvelled at his own ingenuity.

'Don't forget your monthly report is due at the end of the coming week, so make sure it's on time. How are Monica and the girls?'

Had a rumour about the break-up already reached the old slave-driver? It had been only a few days since his long-suffering wife had finally reached the end of her tether and walked out. Ample grounds for divorce and crushing

35

alimony existed. Hardly the moment to break the news to the whip-swishing old patriarch. Pietro swallowed the loathing brewed from years of inadequacy to respond cheerfully, 'They're fine, Pop. I'll tell them you've called. When you telephoned home, they'd have been er—on a visit to Monica's sister in Brooklyn. Is there anything else you'd like me to do for you?'

'Just what I've already asked would be a miracle on your part. Don't forget I'll be checking.' Angelo's voice expressed his weary contempt as he added, 'You'd better not keep your . . . clients waiting. Goodbye.' His slippered feet moved noiselessly over the priceless though now slightly faded eighteenth-century carpet to his abandoned chair, its back still shrouded by a charcoal-grey jacket, and he resumed his earlier position of meditation, his head now bowed slightly as he brooded over his disappointing family. Was it always so for a man of outstanding ability like himself that the spark of genius could not be handed down?

In a rare moment of imagination he travelled back over the centuries to the splendours of the late Quattrocento, the early flowering of Renaissance achievement. What part would he, the leader and adventurer, have played in that age of turmoil, magnificence, challenge and above all intrigue? The age of the superman to whom nothing is forbidden. A brash dominating condottiere with the services of an army to sell to the highest bidder? Hardly a painter or poet: he had little artistic taste or ability, though possibly a banker or even more fittingly a merchant prince. Surely though, for one with a name such as his, a career as a Church dignitary would have been inevitable, with opportunities for worldly pleasures less restricted than in the present era: a bishop indeed, a cardinal, eventually the Pope himself. Family disappointments forgotten in this vision of celestial supremacy, Angelo was abruptly dragged back to earth by a knock at the door and the appearance of Beata, more seemingly attired and bearing a loaded tray.

'Where would you like it, signore?' she requested humbly, her newly-washed and adorned eyes seeking contact with his.

Ignoring her gaze and shuffling together opened envelopes, letters and the cherished prospectus, Angelo made
room for the tray. She paused after depositing it to whisper
seductively:

'Would the signore have need of me again this evening?'

He returned her gaze now. 'Thank you, Beata,' he said.
'This evening definitely no. Camillo will be arriving at any
minute now: he will of course have his key. But you will be
available to attend on the signora when she returns. That
is understood, I assume.'

'Good night, signore.' The whisper was now somewhat
plaintive and she lowered her eyes momentarily before
raising them again to meet his. But Angelo was already
pouring beer from the opened bottle and she slipped away
unregarded.

Briefcase in hand, Camillo arrived some ten minutes later
to find tray, with empty glass and bottle and crumb-strewn
plates, already deposited on the floor outside the door.
Inside his employer was studying ledgers while drinking his
coffee.

The secretary was one of the many clerical functionaries
born and bred for their role in an Aldous Huxley *Brave New
World* laboratory. A passport would have referred to medium
height with no mention of the medium build, weight and
seemingly intelligence that accompanied it. A passport
photograph would have emphasized the large-lensed,
heavy-rimmed spectacles over dark eyes contrasting with a
sallow complexion and doing nothing to relieve an expression of vague anxiety mingled with resignation. Of
Camillo's secret dreams, emotions, opinions, Angelo knew
nothing, though he suspected a deep affection for his lively
wife Cristina. All that mattered, after all, was his scrupulous
efficiency.

The following hour was devoted to the elucidation and
discussion of matters financial. Finally Angelo closed the
ultimate ledger, moving away to select a bottle of sherry
from a cupboard while his assistant replaced the contents
of the secret compartment. Angelo uncorked the bottle to
fill two cut-crystal glasses. He raised his own glass.

'To your health, Camillo, and accept my sincerest compliments. You have arranged things magnificently. I have had wind of one or two recent queries relating to the utilization of the $50,000 donation received from the—let me think—Preservation of Renaissance Ecclesiastical Sculpture Society: PRESS as they call themselves. But your highly intelligent dispositions will inevitably deflect any pertinent inquiries in other directions and we shall have no difficulty in disclaiming even the least knowledge of the matter.'

Camillo shook his head deprecatingly as he fitted his own records into his briefcase ready for departure. He accepted his glass gratefully and was then dismayed to learn that Angelo had not yet finished with him.

'I hope that Cristina is in good health,' the latter said patronizingly. 'There is no prospect yet of a son for you?'

'We should have to find a larger flat before we could start a family,' Camillo reminded him, not for the first time. 'And I am sure you will be aware of the impossibility of any hope of that here in Venice.'

'Indeed. And, as my representative in Venice, I would earnestly dissuade you from considering a move to Mestre. Buying your own flat here might not present too many difficulties, though.'

Camillo limited his reaction to a look combining reproach with scepticism.

'Oh yes, I well understand,' his employer went on. 'The cost of any kind of flat in Venice would indeed be prohibitive. But it is not unlikely that I could assist you, Camillo. In return for special services, naturally.'

Camillo continued to regard him in silent distrust.

'Nothing very demanding or time-consuming, though with possibly a trace of risk. Mostly merely taking possession and arranging dispatch and distribution of small packages and of course taking responsibility for all payments. The arrangements would apply only to Venice and its surroundings: other useful areas are already provided for.'

'I am sorry, signore. You will remember you mentioned the matter once before. And my answer remains the same.'

'But you are already a criminal, Camillo. An accessory in robbing individuals, organizations, the State.'

'But not in murder, signore, in destroying minds as well as bodies and in suffering and heartbreak for those close to the victims.'

'You're far too sentimental, Camillo. The victims ask for what they get and those close to them should have brought them up more intelligently.' A sudden horrifying suspicion blazed in Angelo's mind at his own words as he recalled the lethargic evasiveness that had irritated him just a short time previously. He stifled the idea and continued:

'All right, Camillo. It's up to you. I can easily find someone else. But naturally you will not breathe a word of my suggestion to anyone, including Cristina. Because any hint of a suspicion I might have on this matter would have most unfortunate results for her and your need for a larger flat would no longer exist. You understand me, of course.'

All expression faded from Camillo's face as he put down his glass, picked up his briefcase and made for the door without a word.

He hurried home through murky streets that for the first time in his life held lurking shadows. Cristina was absorbed in a TV newscast when he entered his small sitting-room. He alarmed her by turning off the programme without saying a word and then staring down at her fixedly.

'Earlier this week,' he informed the frightened brown eyes, 'I saw an advertisement about a Self-Defence course at a local sports centre. I didn't much notice which but I can easily find out. You and I are going to enrol for instruction at the earliest possible moment. I can't tell you why but it's related to Angelo Vescovo and I think that explanation will be enough.'

CHAPTER 4

FAIR WEATHER SAILOR

On the night of Hallowe'en, with a full moon dimmed behind restless clouds, sirocco-driven storms swept up the Adriatic, piling up before them the massive high tides that at such times appear to threaten the complete and final immersion of the mudbank-supported city of Venice. Sirens announced the imminence of 'high water' during the evening of the All Saints holiday but on the following day of mourning for the dead, All Souls, the early sirens were duplicated, thereby signifying a potentially grave emergency.

Most Lido-dwellers forced to visit the city at such times get no such warning but they make a habit in autumn of checking their almanacs, sniffing the wind direction and watching the water level at the lagoon edge. When moon, wind direction, tide and water level combine to suggest cause for concern, they pull on high rubber boots (kept handy at this time of year) and reach for their raincoats and umbrellas before sallying forth.

Rosa and Toni had been enrolled at a private English school in Venice on the insistence of Grandfather Angelo, who paid their fees. Ostensibly, as he himself made clear, his generosity was motivated by concern for the children's welfare: they could master Italian gradually and painlessly as part of the school course rather than suffer the bewilderment of a classroom environment in which they could understand little of what was going on around them. He had on occasion, however, been heard to admit to the advantages both to the children and himself of the early friendships they were likely to make with the offspring of certain prominent Venetian families who were likewise aware of the value of an English-type education.

This being a Wednesday and therefore a school day, Tania prepared the children with boots and mackintoshes before setting out for bus and boat to San Zaccharia, a stone's throw from St Mark's Square. Here to the children's delight they mounted the long line of trestle tables which connected boat stop with the Piazzetta, the 'Little Square', and the main square beyond. They tramped along in single file, narrowly avoiding the long line of walkers moving towards them, watching in fascination the two showmen rowing their boat across 'St Mark's Lake' and at intervals glancing upwards at roof and cornice to locate the thousands of pigeons forced to take refuge there. Compelled at last to descend to street level, they had waded and splashed through swirling brown water and in due course reluctantly climbed the staircase to the school. The rapid rise in the level of the water had been worrying Tania, however, and with a dismayed group of other beleaguered mothers, she had spent a couple of hours by the first-floor window, soothed by the reassuring babble and hum of young voices making and memorizing new discoveries. A perceptible fall in the water level tempted her out again to slosh through a city that had become one with its canals, her legs and feet clammy from the overflow into the tops of her boots.

The rain at least had stopped when she reached the Lido and the wind appeared less boisterous. With a bus about to leave, she was home in little more than ten minutes and was greeted as she opened the door by the sound of Stefano's flute, this Wednesday being a free day for him. She slipped into the bedroom to change into dry clothes and shoes and then went to the kitchen to make a cup of coffee, imitating with raised eyebrows the motion of pouring water into a coffee-pot as she passed Stefano, his lips and brow puckered as he concentrated on mastering the trills, glides and arpeggios of a composition new to him.

A few minutes later he joined her in the kitchen. 'I suppose you were caught by the aqua,' he said. 'Mother telephoned you.'

'What time?'

'Oh, about nine. I was still in bed.'

'She'd know I wouldn't be in then. So what did she have to tell you?'

'She might have forgotten. She seemed to think it important to get in touch with you at once.'

'And she didn't leave a message?'

'She did. Give me a chance. Though I don't know how you'll take it.'

'Oh?'

'She said they're organizing a special children's day in Burano this Saturday. There's a small fair arriving for a day or two and they're going to have a fancy-dress children's parade and competitions and the like.'

'What? In this weather? And at this time of year?'

'I asked that. She said they wanted to avoid too many tourists surging in all over the place. Apparently they'll be putting up a marquee in case it's cold and wet. But this sirocco weather never lasts more than three days and the forecasts are quite good.'

'What's all this got to do with us?'

'It's Toni she's thinking about, naturally: she thinks he'd enjoy it. And she's got Angelo to promise to take her and you and the children to Burano on Saturday in his motor-boat: I'll be working that day, thank goodness.'

'I'm not going.'

'She's phoning Toni today at his school to tell him about it so you can guess what to expect from him. And I will say she did apologize for the way she behaved when she was here. She asked me to say she'd been having a lot of trouble with her nerves recently. And she's worried about Angelo: he's overworking and has got a lot on his mind, she says: I suspect he's playing her up one way or another. Anyhow she really does seem to want to make amends and who knows, you may be able to—'

'Stefano, I can't face it. You know what I think of Angelo: to have to put up with the pair of them with Toni around for a whole day would be unbearable.'

'You know, I think Angelo genuinely likes you: it's just his way.'

'He likes any woman below the age of forty, and I don't happen to fancy his way. No, I can't. You'll have to tell her: make up some excuse, if you like. Toni's a bit off-colour.'

'She'd be here at once to check. Look, couldn't you get Iris to go with you?'

'Iris? With them? She'd loathe it.'

'You said the other day the two of you had talked of going to Burano before the winter gets under way.'

Tania paused to consider. The two women had been friendly for some months, the original connection having been made through Arvo, Tania's brother, whom Iris had once taught English to in a summer school, later following up the acquaintance by visiting his family in Helsinki during a year she had spent teaching in Finland. If only she could persuade Iris to gatecrash and turn up with her unannounced, her parents-in-law would hardly dare to turn away a highly-respectable English teacher. The atmosphere would certainly be frigid but there'd be no emotional outbursts and scenes.

'I've told her quite a lot about them: she'd know what to expect,' she meditated aloud. 'I've told her too about Chiara's last visit. And she said then in an amused way that she might rather enjoy meeting a woman like that: it would be quite an experience. It might be a way out, if she hasn't got another arrangement and if I can appeal to her protective instincts.'

Thursday was a golden day, *tempo sereno* as the weather forecast had aptly described it. Iris was bashing at her typewriter, haphazardly as always, much of her attention directed to the opposite bank of the canal visible through the glass doors on to the balcony. A flurry of multi-coloured cats was bearing down on a white-haired fur-capped gentleman who was removing a newspaper-covered package from the back of a motor-scooter he had parked on the bank. Ripples of delighted anticipation—nothing so vulgar as pushing and shoving—galvanized the throng as the wrapping was unpeeled and, together with its contents, set down beside the scooter. The benevolent feline philanthropist disappeared (probably for his own refreshment) into an unpretentious wineshop nearby, while newcomers, flashes of black, white and gold, sprinted to join the feast and help

43

to maintain their evident sleekness. A sudden jolt as Iris's own tabby, comfortably sleek from tinned rabbit, fish or liver, bounded on to the table to spread herself over hand-written copy material and start lazily to wash herself, purring contentedly. Purring sounds, Italian-style, from the telephone announced a caller.

Back from the first of her two daily trips to Venice the following morning, Tania had gathered courage to make her appeal. Iris wondered at the hesitation in her voice as they greeted one another and the pause before Tania came out with:

'Iris, I've got a special request which you won't like but I need your help badly.'

Another pause, long enough for Iris to ask, 'Is this a guessing game?'

'Well, you remember we talked about going on an outing to Burano with the children before the winter closes in if we had a fine Saturday?'

'Something I'd obviously enjoy, so that can't be it.'

'No, not exactly.' Again a pause. 'I told you what happened a fortnight ago, Chiara's visit, I mean.'

'And presumably she hasn't been pouring oil on troubled water since. Probably flicking the water on to the sizzling oil, if past form is anything to go by. And it's got something to do with outings or Burano or the children, like enough.'

'Well, yes.' Tania went on to explain Chiara's invitation and her own reluctance to accept it.

'And you want me to think up a good excuse for your not turning up.'

'I'd like you to come with us.'

'Without an invitation?'

'Well, yes. But if you turned up with me and I said brightly—well, that I'd already arranged to go with you that day in the ordinary boat and what a wonderful idea to bring you along—a highly-distinguished English teacher in Venice.'

'Tania, no. I'm already shivering at the ice-cold reception awaiting me. With my primitive Italian landing me deeper in the mire with every word I fumbled to utter.'

'She always speaks English to me so that doesn't matter.'

'So she speaks English, does she? No, Tania. It'd be unbearable and they'd never forgive me, or you.'

'She's never forgiven me for having been born, so it wouldn't make any difference to me. And you're unlikely to see either of them ever again.'

'And you can't refuse? No, I suppose not. What does Stefano say?'

'He understands how I feel but he can't see any way out without really landing me in the doghouse. She'll spread it all over Venice how her callous daughter-in-law, that foreign woman who's taken her son away from her, was now deliberately trying to turn her own grandchildren against her. And at the same time depriving the poor little dears of a treat that had been specially arranged for them. Please, Iris. I've got to go. It could be rather uncomfortable for you but think of how much worse it will be for me if I'm alone, with her taking a sadistic pleasure in turning Toni against me and Angelo full of fatherly affection pawing me.'

'Does he indeed?' Iris commented. 'And how does she respond to that?'

'It delights her. She can see how much I loathe it. And she's used to it: it happens all the time with him. Anyone that's the least bit pretty.'

'That lets me out, at least. You know, this is beginning to intrigue me. I'm starting to dislike both of them so much that I wouldn't care what they thought of me. All right, Tania, I'll be there. Where and when do we meet?'

Two days later as Iris unlocked doors and gate to let herself out, the few leaves the gales had left clinging to the trees lining the canal were glistening in sunlight, though the air felt decidedly colder. She was leaving early to make a few purchases on the way and she arrived at the rendezvous by the lagoon to find Tania already waiting for her, looking unexpectedly cheerful. The children, warmly dressed in scarlet Finnish-made tracksuits, greeted her with an excited and jumbled account of the day's programme, with Tania having to wait to pass on her news.

'I tried to telephone you half an hour ago,' she said, 'but you must already have left. Chiara called late last night, from Florence apparently. Angelo had had some arrangement there and had taken her with him. So I'm let off the hook, it seems. For the moment anyhow.'

Irish paused a moment before expressing their shared relief, 'Thank goodness for that.' A vivid image had flashed through her mind of a beautiful desirable fish to be lured and trapped at leisure before being finally disposed of. Tania continued:

'She insisted I should go anyhow, for the children's sake, of course. According to her there's a boat from the Fondamente Nuovo at 12.35. What do you think? We're all set to go, with packed lunches for the four of us. We've got just about enough time to get there. And it's a lovely day.'

Burano without in-laws would be a delight and they were soon on the Number 1 accelerato, the slowest boat on the lagoon, which carried them on its sedate way to the Arsenale stop where they boarded the Circular motoscafo. A keen wind from the north met them as the boat turned into the lagoon which spread lethargically like a trapped and tamed sea. They boarded the Burano boat with only seconds to spare and soon they were leaving the buildings, towers and domes of northern Venice behind them, with San Michele, the island of the dead, to starboard and glass-blowing Murano to port. Tania took refuge in the saloon with its slippery seats, Iris following close behind, but the children remained on deck: they were warmly dressed and unlikely to come to any harm. Through the windows Iris watched the boat they had just left docking at San Michele and a scatter of mostly elderly women disembarking on their way to pay their respects to the dead. Creamy-pink walls embellished with single or triple white-trimmed arches and surmounted by clustered cypresses suggested a fantasy Disneylike park, and inside the walls a chapel could be glimpsed with shining monuments and angels beyond.

On arrival at Murano, Tania's conscience prompted her to check on the children's whereabouts and she left Iris to wrestle with a large-scale map of the lagoon she had with her, refolding it against obstinate resistance to her immediate requirements. A commercial traveller jotting entries in a file glanced at her pityingly: an obvious woman unable to fold a newspaper in a crowded train. Men who had probably been shopping in Venice for clothes, do-it-yourself equipment and other sundries gathered in a familiar group and set to playing cards: heavy burly slow-moving men, whose growling slurred speech, with little colour or intonation, resembled a half-drunken chanting, though the men were sober enough. In contrast, the voices of an unseen group behind her rose and fell excitedly in a choral ensemble of Germanic, Scandinavian and Gallic varieties of English. With the appropriate map panel now uppermost, Iris settled to a topographical survey of her more distant surroundings.

Emerging from the staircase on to the deck, Tania stood aside to allow the sprinkling of new arrivals from Murano to descend. From her position by the rail, Rosa caught sight of her mother at once and ran to meet her, drawing her towards the group standing alongside. A man with his back to her was explaining something about the island, his hands circling and stabbing through the air, adding drama and suspense to his tale, while Toni and a lank bespectacled boy of his own age listened enthralled.

As she approached the group, the man turned and regarded her with friendly interest. A tallish strongly-built individual in pale grey sweater and slacks, his crinkly hair touched with grey, his eyes a startlingly dark blue: in his mid-forties, she decided.

Toni took it upon himself to perform the introductions. 'Mummy,' he announced, 'this is Giorgio's uncle—he goes to our school. This is our Mummy. He speaks English.'

Giorgio's uncle smiled down at his sponsor, briefly ruffling his wind-blown hair, before inclining his head politely to Tania. He raised it with a gentle smile on his lips, his blue eyes holding hers as if there had long been a mutual understanding between them.

'Giovanni Fedele,' he informed her, extending his hand, 'though I must be a very slow pupil when I am still in Toni's school. Giorgio has spoken often of Toni's mother. I think you are coming from Finland where the glassmakers try to surpass our workers here in Murano.'

The English was fluent though imperfect and slightly accented: the voice had repose and suggested a cultured background. She paused, uncertain of a suitable reply and he continued unhurriedly:

'Are you content in your new home in Venice?'

Again she paused. A short conventional 'Yes, I am,' would be untruthful and would add little to the conversation: a longer and more accurate answer would be out of place in a conversation with a stranger. She temporized.

'In fact, I am only ever a visitor to Venice: I live on the Lido.'

'So you prefer sunshine, green trees and a view of the sky. I think I too could not be content to live in Venice. I inhabit Pellestrina, an island next to the Lido, so we are neighbours. And I work in Chioggia far at the south end of the lagoon beyond Pellestrina. Do you know it?'

She shook her head. 'I've heard the name,' she said, 'but I've never been there.'

There was a silence between them while the boat drew away from the landing-stage, its engines throbbing noisily, and turned north on course for Mazzorbo and Burano. The children slipped away to seek a better vantage-point while Giovanni looked down reflectively at his powerful but carefully-groomed hands spread before him on the rail.

'Is not important to visit Chioggia,' he meditated. 'You have seen Venice in its right place in the centre of the lagoon. In Venice is much decay, many buildings in bad condition. But are many beautiful buildings also and fine shops. Chioggia is a shadow of Venice: what is the right word?' A hand detached itself from the rail and an impatient snap of his fingers suggested exasperation before the hand was returned firmly to the rail, as if, Tania reflected, it were being disciplined for unsuitable behaviour. 'Now I have it,' he continued, in a spurt of triumph, 'a run-down Venice. The beautiful buildings are all in decay and are no fine shops. Is all completely run-down.' His voice had resumed

48

its earlier detached calm. 'But perhaps if you are interested in boats and fishing and you have a camera or you paint ... Chioggia is still alive in her fishing but Venice is alive only in her tourism.' He spat out the last word with a downward gesture on the rail of a freed fist. 'Fish aren't so profitable as tourists but they are less trouble and need not so much space.'

'Do you work as a fisherman?'

An upward jerk of his chin and a brief, slightly mocking smile. 'No, I work as policeman, carabiniere if you know what they are, though not many Italians can tell you exactly. But I play as fisherman in my free time which is why I go now to Burano.'

'Do they fish in Burano?'

'Yes, they fish, but is different from Chioggia.' He pointed to a small boat some distance away in which a man was standing facing the prow as he rowed. 'He is a Burano fisherman, perhaps taking up mussels which grow in the mussel beds here. Chioggia boats are much bigger and fish in the open sea for many kinds of fish.'

'And are you going to fish here this afternoon?'

'No, I am going to get my motor-boat. It does not function right so I have taken it to my friend in Burano who is good in repairing motor-boats. He has telephoned me to say that is ready today. Do you visit Burano or Torcello? Or perhaps both islands.'

'I've been told there's a special children's day in Burano with a fair and other entertainments.'

He frowned and shook his head slightly. 'I have not heard of it. But I can ask about it for you.'

For a time they stood side by side in silence looking out over the water while the boat ambled placidly along the deep-water channel providing passage through the mud-bank shallows and marked by the double lines of bricole, stalwart logs leaning together conspiratorially, clamped together by metal collars and topped by lanterns. Gulls flapped and glided and came to rest in alert meditation like vagrant statues seeking a handy plinth. Slime-grey water heaved and sank as a blue-black wave-furrow retreated from the bow's cutting edge and patches of matted weed slopped restlessly on the liquid surface.

She was conscious of Giovanni regarding her gravely. 'Do you feel that you are in Finland here?' he asked quietly. 'I have heard that is a country of much inland water, of many lakes and islands.'

Tania realized with some surprise that this was the first time any such similarity had occurred to her and considered for a moment before answering.

'No,' she said at last, 'but I don't know exactly why. Forgive me, but if I answer truthfully, I must say that the Finnish lakes seem more alive, perhaps because they always have forests and grass near them—in summer that is, of course. Winter is clean and white and somehow perfect. Our lakes are beautiful and serene. But this water seems dead: it's murky and polluted and horribly stagnant: it suggests to me only evil and corruption just below it.'

He half-turned towards her as if she had opened his eyes to a new discovery. 'You feel that,' he said quickly, and then after a brief consideration added, 'I think I understand what you feel. But is not stagnant, this water, is tidal and is changed two times daily from the sea. Polluted, yes, from industry and from people. Evil and corrupt, no. It has protected the people of this region for centuries and now provides a living for some of them.'

Rosa appeared at Tania's elbow, pulling her coat sleeve as she pointed to the far side of the boat. 'Mummy,' she said, 'look, there's an island with an old house on it.'

They moved with her to the other side of the ship just as it was leaving behind a decrepit patch of land. Its protective wall had disintegrated into a dishevelled heap of rubble and tumbled stones littering the shore mud and tangled decaying weeds. The buildings it had been constructed to protect crouched dejectedly here and there, their roofs still more or less intact, their empty rectangular window sockets staring bleakly into desolation. 'Once a busy prosperous island with a monastery and a hospital. Now, as you see, abandoned.'

The island they were approaching was in worse decay. 'That is small,' he told them, 'but also it had a monastery at one time.' The remains of buildings stared back at them: two rows of gaping windows, cracked and rotting brickwork, at one end skeleton rafters groping into nothingness above crumbling walls that for many years must have been unable to support any kind of roof. 'You are right,' he continued. 'Here is indeed death and decay and there is so much of it in our lagoon.'

With his eyes travelling over the dark water, his hands now inert on the ship's rail, he launched into a description of the creation of the lagoon by three great rivers, the arrival of the present-day Venetians and the wealth and bustle of the region centuries before, when every island had had its monastery, convent or fortress, now almost all crumbled into decay. As the boat approached Mazzorbo with its new housing estate, he continued, 'And this to replace the decay. Better or worse, I wonder. The island of Mazzorbo which joins to Burano. Soon we are almost there.'

Tania looked ahead, startled. 'I didn't realize we were so near,' she exclaimed. 'I must go and find my friend who is alone in the saloon.'

'Your friend?' Giovanni looked at her sharply, disbelievingly it seemed. 'You have a friend with you?'

Tania was already on her way and turned back to say hastily, 'Yes. Please excuse me. And thank you for all you have told me,' she added before disappearing down the stairway.

She need not have worried: Iris had not been alone. One of the group behind her had spotted her map and he and the others had gathered around her. The map was now wide open again and held up by two pairs of arms for all to study while a species of lecturing competition appeared to be under way, fingers jabbing and voices uplifted in question, exposition and speculation.

'Hello, Tania,' Iris greeted her friend, as she joined the throng. 'These are students of the art of restoration who've recently arrived for courses on San Servolo, near us on the Lido. They're really on their way to Torcello but just at present they seem to be a bit lost in all those shallow bits to the far north of the lagoon. Oh dear, we aren't there, are

51

we?' The boat was slowing down with an assortment of roarings and shudderings and her companions deserted her to peer through the windows.

'No, it's only Mazzorbo, the stop before.'

'Mazzorbo,' Iris repeated, trying to get the map under control again. 'Let's see. No, perhaps I'd better start folding it up again if we're so near.' With Tania to help, the operation went a little more smoothly than previously. 'Did you notice the two islands we passed,' she continued. 'They'd need quite a bit of restoration, wouldn't they?'

The boat was moving again along a green shoreline, past a long bridge connecting islands and then alongside colour-washed houses. Iris joined the student-restorers at the window and glanced back at Tania. 'But this looks a bit better, at any rate,' she commented. 'Ah, there's our stop.'

Having exchanged goodbyes with her recent acquaintances, she followed Tania on to the deck where they were joined by Rosa and Toni. They followed the crowd of Buranese shoppers and international visitors moving on to the landing-stage and along a path with old ladies displaying lace mats along its edge. Where the crowd thinned somewhat, they found Giovanni and Giorgio waiting for them. Tania had an impression of momentary relief on Giovanni's face as he caught sight of Iris tagging behind a bit, and as she introduced her to him, he inclined his head respectfully. 'An English lady, clearly,' he remarked, smiling warmly. 'Are you visiting Venice?'

'No, I live here. I'm an English teacher. You speak English well. Have you been in England?'

'Unfortunately, no. I have learned English in the school and I have spoken sometimes to American—and also English—visitors. But now I must ask about the children's festa. Ah, that young lady who sells the lace. I think she is mother with young children so she must know.' He hurried across the street towards a woman in charge of a table spread with lace, and was soon engaged in a rapid interrogation. The others ambled across towards him and he turned at their approach, tragedy intensified in eyes, head, shoulders, hands and voice.

'Signora, what can I say? We are one week too late. Is a mistake. The festa has been last Saturday. I am sorry, especially for your little Toni and for Signorina Rosa.'

Toni turned furious eyes on his mother. 'You were wrong,' he muttered, his voice growing in intensity as he spoke. 'You always make mistakes. We could have come last week if you hadn't been so stupid, stupid, stupid.'

He was screaming by now and attacking Tania with fists and feet but was cut off in mid-onslaught by being hoisted on high by a powerful left hand gripping the back of his tracksuit while an even more powerful right hand slapped him across each cheek before returning him to earth.

'That is what we give boys who hit their mothers,' said Giovanni.

After a five-second silence of stunned amazement, Toni blurted out, with the shocked outrage of a Tsar molested by an uncouth mujik: 'You slapped me.'

'So you noticed it. That is good,' Giovanni assured him unrepentantly.

'You'll go to prison for that. It's against the law. My grandmother in Finland told me so.'

Tania and Giovanni exchanged a smile: of amusement at the pronouncement of sentence by the criminal himself, of complicity, and on Tania's part of relief at the short sharp shock administered to the offender. She eyed the rebel almost benevolently as she informed him:

'We're in Italy now, Toni, not Finland. And Giovanni's a carabiniere, that's a policeman who's a soldier at the same time. He can arrest people who behave badly as you did and it's they who get sent to prison. Oh, Toni, what have you done?'

Thwarted in every way, Toni gave voice to an ear-piercing wail which turned all faces in his direction: what kind of mother could this foreign woman be who did not rush to comfort her unhappy child? Giovanni again saved the situation.

'Rosa,' he inquired, 'do you like animals, dogs and cats maybe?'

Rosa's face lit up. 'I love cats,' she said. 'I had my own

53

cat in England but we had to leave her behind with a neighbour.'

'And you were very unhappy, of course. I understand it. But Toni doesn't like animals, I think.'

Rosa was about to reply when Toni, who had been achieving the extraordinary feat of wailing and listening at the same time, broke in excitedly, his voice now completely normal.

'Cats are silly. They're only for girls. I like dogs, big dogs, and they're for men, like me.'

'And would you like to go and see some dogs as there isn't a festa today?'

'Yes,' said Toni, 'now at once.'

'We can't go now. They are not here in Burano. They are on another island and just now there is no boat to take us there. But Giorgio and I are going to get my own boat and if I hear you have been a good boy, I take you there later. That is if Mamma, Iris and Rosa would like to come.'

Glistening tear-washed eyes implored: the infant fiend of malice and all uncharity transforming itself into a radiant newborn cherub. 'Please, Mummy,' he begged.

Tania raised an eyebrow as she glanced at Iris, who nodded. 'If it isn't going to give you a great deal of trouble,' Tania said humbly, 'we'd all love to come.'

'It will be the greatest pleasure for me.' With equal humility Giovanni gazed admiringly at Tania before glancing at his watch. 'Now you want to see Burano. Is the happiest island of the lagoon and you will like it very much. If I am not soon at my friend's house, he thinks perhaps I don't come. We must arrive to the island before it is dark. If I am there—' he pointed to a spot on the lagoon edge a short distance from the water-bus landing-stage—'after two hours from now, can you find me all right? Burano is small but easy to be lost in.'

Rosa suggested a trail of pebbles and breadcrumbs like Hansel and Gretel: Toni asserted he never got lost. With a half-salute that became a wave to the children, Giovanni strode off down the path, the studious and silent nephew at his side. Tania watched him for a moment, compact, erect, head held high, the sunlight glinting on the grey of his hair, disregarding, but alert to everybody and everything in his surroundings, a disciplined man well aware of his own potentialities, a man who knew exactly and was fully in control of where he was going. A recollection of Stefano sprawled on the sofa with the sports pages flickered through her mind: indolent, uncertain, living from day to day. Reproaching herself with disloyalty and recalling Stefano's sensitivity and imagination, she joined in the noisy discussion about which way to go.

Iris's map showed a pattern of black buildings on a yellow background which could provide no help with local topography so she could only suggest, 'We've got a fair amount of time so let's just relax and go wherever our feet take us. Toni will be able to guide us back,' she added, with slight malice.

And that indeed is the way to get to know Burano, which presents a succession of camera targets in every ten yards. Even on a melancholy day it is an island soaked in colour, with house-fronts each apparently newly-painted in ochres, browns, greens, powder blues, lilacs and golds, all set off by white door-frames, green shutters, shining brown doors. After a succession of rain and storm, Saturday had perforce become the general washing-day. On lines crossing streets, patches of grass, spaces between shutters flung wide, on clothes-horses outside front doors and on supports jutting from windows, the household drapery and apparel displayed themselves: tablecloths, sheets, bed-covers, tea-towels of variegated decoration, bright-blue dresses, drab-blue jeans, a grass-green pullover with scarlet collar and cuffs, a coffee-brown coat. And sunshine had brought out the bird-cages hung outside doors or on open shutters, trilling, cheeping, twittering from the bright yellow or green canaries and budgerigars inside them.

This was a day of sunshine and movement, with the leaf-patterns of tree clusters in streets and squares restlessly adorning house fronts and crazy-paving below, and fishing-boats, as multi-coloured as homes, rocking gently and nudging the stonework beside canals. A few painters had set up easels at street corners or within visual range of an arched bridge or the leaning church tower. Men worked on boats or nets while women gathered in washing for ironing, exchanged gossip or browsed in senior-citizen black alongside their lace-stalls, alert for lingering late-autumn customers.

The quartet sauntered contentedly along a canal-side street to the far shore of the island where nets were drying and finally settled on a bench to dispose of their picnic before inspecting the centre.

The lace-making school being temporarily closed, they were trailing along one of the main streets, pausing to examine window-displays of lace mats, tablecloths and blouses, when Toni, who seemed to have the impression that his was the responsibility for shepherding the flock, caught sight of the monster cornet. It sprouted just ahead of them from the side of a café-bar, set slightly above the eye-level of a ten-year-old, rose for about a metre and was crowned with a tapering convolution of raspberry-pink, apple-green, primrose-yellow and ivory, utterly repulsive to the discerning, irresistible to the young. 'Mummy,' he squeaked, a quivering forefinger directing her attention, 'can I have an ice-cream like that one? Please, Mummy. Rosa wants one too, don't you, Rosa?'

Rosa's eyes spoke for her. 'I wouldn't mind a coffee,' Iris contributed. 'Let me treat you.'

Realizing he had a useful ally, Toni clutched her hand convulsively and led her firmly to a table on the café terrace before she could have time to change her mind. Tania and Rosa followed and they had hardly got settled before a short black-haired swarthy-faced waiter in white coat and black trousers approached them, smiling companionably.

'What you like?' he asked.

Cornets alas were not served at the tables but their contents in four splendid colours could be provided in small dishes. Tempted by the ice-cream, Iris finally ordered coffees for herself and Tania. Toni did his own ordering in the fluent scraps of Venetian he had picked up from Italian fellow-pupils, his hands outlining a large circle rising to a high peak. His protests at the less spectacular portion were cut short by his mother.

The waiter continued to hover within earshot while they sat there, whether by chance, to offer further service, or out of curiosity, not immediately apparent. Iris became aware of his attention while she was relating an anecdote about one of her less predictable language pupils and put it down to the fact that at this late season, he had little else to do. Having scraped every last remnant from his dish and thoroughly licked the spoon, Toni lifted a finger to summon the waiter in the manner of his elders and demanded in regal tones: 'And now I want the toilet.'

'I show you *subito*—at once, signore,' the waiter responded, with mock obsequiousness. 'This way, please. Very clean, signore.' He retreated within the café, followed by Toni, Tania and Rosa, while Iris relaxed over her half-empty glass of caffè latte, holding out an ingratiating hand towards a splendid tortoiseshell cat who was investigating hopefully the surroundings of the tables. She became aware of the waiter seeking her attention and automatically reached for her handbag to pay the bill. His mind, however, was clearly on other matters.

'Please, madam,' he inquired, 'you are English teacher 'ere in Venice perhaps?'

'Yes, I am.'

'Can I take English lessons?'

'But I teach in a school and don't have much time for private pupils. And I live on the Lido. It would take you a very long time to get there.'

'My brother—that is, the brother of my wife, 'as a motor-boat. I can use it. I come direct to Lido, not by Venice. Is not far.'

'But why do you want to learn English?'

'My uncle in England 'as restaurant. If I speak English, 'e give me a work. But for London must speak much English. I not find a teacher 'ere in Burano.'

'When are you free?'

'Now are not much tourists, can be free most times. The

57

father of my wife is boss of this restaurant. I can arrange. Two times in the week.'

Iris considered a moment. 'You understand you must learn and practise a lot in your free time as well, if you want to speak well enough to work in London,' she said.

'I understand, madam. My wife speaks better. She can 'elp me.'

Iris fished out a pen and wrote carefully on a piece of paper which he provided from his order pad. 'There,' she explained, as she handed it back, 'that's my name, telephone number and fee for an hour's lesson. Think about it carefully and discuss it with your wife and father-in-law and if you all agree you can telephone me and make some arrangement. And now let me pay the bill.'

The other three reappeared as this transaction was being completed, with the ensuing argument about financial liability cut short by Toni's darting into the middle of the traffic-free street, ready for instant departure. 'We've only got eight minutes to find Giovanni,' he reminded them, pointing to the watch he had been given for his last birthday. Without further concern he turned to the right along the street, leaving the others to scoop up belongings and hurry after him.

By now, in mid-afternoon, the streets seemed oddly deserted and partly as a result of their earlier meanderings, there were several uncertain pauses at street corners, all ignored by Toni, who within five minutes had delivered them, as instructed, at their rendezvous.

CHAPTER 5

RESCUE OF A CASTAWAY

Giovanni was awaiting them, camera at the ready and was already extracting a finished print which he handed with a grin to Tania. 'For you, signora,' he said, 'I will make another later for the Signorina Iris and an enlargement for myself, naturally.' Tania glanced at the print and laughed before passing it to Iris. It presented a Napoleonic Toni striding before the troops, Iris rummaging in her bag for her own camera, Rosa looking up at her mother to ask a question and Tania, serenely beautiful and remote, however hurried, worried or uncertain her real feelings might be.

Giorgio had a small telescope trained on the cathedral on Torcello and ignored Toni's demand to be allowed to use it himself. As Giovanni was escorting the others towards his boat, Toni snatched the telescope and began to adjust it. A scuffle started; the telescope was laid aside for full-scale combat. Giovanni stepped aboard and as he extended a hand to help Tania on to the boat, she turned back and called: 'Toni. Come along. We can't wait for you.' Rosa and Iris followed on board, all three trying to attract the attention of the boys who were now rolling on the grass.

They settled in the cabin where Giovanni produced a small map of the lagoon and handed it to Tania. 'Now,' he said, 'I give those young tearaways (a good English word, that) a shock.' He moved to the wheel and set the engine pulsating. The boys suspended the fight to stare at the boat as Giovanni set it into motion, moving off in the direction of Treporti and the mainland.

Of those on the boat only Rosa was momentarily distressed and her worried appeal took a practical form: 'Mummy, what are they going to do now?' Giovanni glanced back to her. 'Shall we abandon them on this beautiful island, Rosa? Perhaps they will not mind it.'

Rosa caught on at once and retorted: 'Do you want to abandon your nephew? What will his mother say to you?'

'You are right, of course, signorina,' Giovanni said gravely. 'But Toni's mamma is not so unhappy perhaps?'

'Life will be quieter without him certainly,' Tania responded. 'You'll be able to read in peace, Rosa, and you won't have to watch any more horror films on television.'

'So shall we just forget to return, Rosa?' Giovanni asked. 'They can become Burano fisher-boys. You can decide.'

'And Giorgio's mamma?' she countered.

'His mamma? I suppose she will miss him. They are

59

strange people, women, girls. Men are always a trouble: they make wars; they think only of themselves; they make women unhappy. And women always make excuses for them. Ah well. But you think I should go back for that little monster, I suppose. All right, Rosa. *Andiamo.*'

He swung the boat in a half-circle and made for the island, rounding a corner to their departure point. A small figure could be seen standing disconsolately looking out across the water, while a slightly taller one continued his study of the distant buildings on Torcello with his repossessed telescope. As soon as he saw them, Toni started waving and shouting like a sailor marooned for years on a desert island. Immediately the boat touched land, he bore down on it in fury, retreating in some dismay as Giovanni hoisted himself ashore, and, ignoring the boy, started to tie up the boat. As Toni attempted to slink on board, however, he found his shoulder gripped in a firm hand while a magisterial voice bellowed above his head, 'Giorgio!' Giorgio lowered his telescope, detected the source of the summons and arrived at the double to stand to attention before his superior officer. Giovanni addressed the pair quietly and in precise Italian for a whole minute and each was seen to shrink visibly at the impact of his words. With a gesture, he then ordered them on board where, after a muttered 'I'm sorry' addressed to nobody in particular they stood one on each side of the wheel, looking straight forward. Giovanni in his turn made his apologies to Tania in a quiet, grave voice.

'I am sorry, signora, to be always the policeman, but these two young men must learn to consider the needs of other people and to obey instructions. Otherwise they will give big problems later.'

Tempted to utter the normal 'But he is so young', Tania remained silent: her son was already well aware of what he was doing. A sudden smile that suggested shared responsibility transformed Giovanni's face and she was unable to resist returning it while deep blue eyes held hers momentarily. He touched her shoulder lightly before returning to the helm and almost immediately they were again under way.

They moved over the smooth water in a dreamlike hush, broke only by the purr of the engine, Tania trying to expel from her mind vague imaginings and speculations which had no right there, Toni brooding sullenly, Giorgio longing for his confiscated telescope and Iris trying to make sense of her map she had at last again succeeded in unfolding suitably. They rounded Burano and moved eastwards along a channel which led to the considerable island of Sant'Erasmo. Around them and as far as they could see, lay the mudbanks, great and small, relieved here and there by scrubby grass and a few dejected bushes that survived rather than grew. The sun was sinking towards the horizon and by some quirk of the diffusion of light, its orange glow transformed the gloss of the water surface into amethyst and sapphire bands, while unending ruffles of turquoise slipped along either side of the boat. From time to time Giovanni turned towards the open cabin door to give an account of the islands they were moving alongside while Iris traced their route across pale blue paper.

According to the map, they were now in the narrow Canal Sant'Erasmo. A short way ahead they could see a dazzlingly-white cruise liner, with possibly the last of this season's sea-borne visitors crowding the rails, on its way to the open sea. The motor-boat turned into the broad access canal soon enough after the liner's passing to be rocked by vigorous rolls of disturbed water left in its wake. With the boat now set on course along the Lido shore and with no other craft in the offing, Giovanni touched the silent Toni, still standing motionless beside him. 'Do you want to help me to steer the boat?' he asked.

Toni hesitated: any form of cooperation might diminish the effectiveness of his protest withdrawal. Then, after a look of triumph mingled with contempt directed at his mother, he stepped in front of the boat's captain and added his two small hands to those on the wheel. A moment later, by removing first one and then the other of his own hands, Giovanni was able to inform the new seaman: 'You're in charge of the boat now, Captain Vescovo.'

His authority was short-lived; they were approaching the

61

channels frequented by the water-buses and Giovanni again took full control, murmuring to his junior officer: 'Another time, Captain. If you can persuade Mamma, you can take charge of the ship again, perhaps for a longer time.' He glanced back at his two adult passengers and started to identify and describe the islands straddled across the water, dwelling particularly on San Lazzaro with its monastery for Armenian monks, its richly-endowed library, printing presses for many languages and alphabets and its beautiful trees and gardens. 'We must visit there together some day,' he concluded.

They were still following the Lido shore, close-packed with newish blocks of flats, each separated from its neighbours by a few square metres of garden, in welcome contrast to huddled Venetian stone and brick warrens. A short distance from San Lazzaro they approached a smaller untended island.

'*Ecco!*' Giovanni announced, 'Lazzaretto Vecchio where our hosts will not be fishermen or makers of lace or glass or monks or even grave-diggers: only dogs and—' catching the eye of a newly-awakened Rosa—'of course, cats. Like many of the islands we have seen, they are abandoned by people who have the duty to care for them. And here is my friend Massimo who cares for them now. I telephoned him from Burano. He will show you.'

Massimo was in fact a small man, who greeted cheerfully the signore with the bambini as Giovanni helped them ashore. He led them first into a high bare building, which Giovanni identified as the oldest isolation hospital in the world, refuge for plague victims from Venice and infected travellers five centuries ago. Beyond they could hear yapping, barking, baying as the colony of abandoned dogs added their greetings. Wire-netting enclosed and separated multifarious groups: of every age, size, breed and mixture of breed, those waifs and strays of Venice and its surroundings turned loose to starve in the streets and fortunate enough to have been rescued and at least given food, medical treatment and basic shelter.

Toni wandered along the lines of enclosures, eyeing the

groups of distraught would-be family friends in some bewilderment. A chill dampness was rising from the rough grass and daylight was fading rapidly: he seemed tired and dispirited at his surroundings, even his immature mind sensing the unhappiness of the unwanted pet. He shook his head dejectedly when Giovanni asked, 'Do you see a dog you like, young Toni?' Giorgio had by now departed for a wider exploration of the island: there was an air about him of geographer or research biologist: at any moment he would surely produce camera and notebook, if not, if these circumstances, his telescope.

Tania who was standing between two lines of enclosures looking desolately around at the black, tan, liver, gold and white figures, forepaws clinging to the wire, voices insistently imploring affection, had shaken her head at Giovanni's question. 'I'm sorry,' she said despondently. 'It's the usual problem. Who will care for the poor thing when we go to Finland?'

Giovanni, who had been feeding an eager dachshund with a biscuit he had extracted from a pocket, turned sharply. 'You will return to Finland?' he inquired abruptly.

'Only to spend Christmas there. My father has been ill.'

'And your family goes with you?'

'Oh yes. The grandparents must see the children. And Stefano, my husband, loves Finland, especially at Christmas.'

'But he is Italian, your husband? Surely Toni is an Italian boy?'

'Italian and also Finnish. He is my son too.'

Giovanni smiled deprecatingly in response to her rebuke. He looked across at Toni who had now selected for his admiring attention a solitary and particularly ugly boxer glowering at him from the end enclosure, and said reflectively:

'Until now I have seen only a rather difficult and temperamental Toni, a characteristic Italian male. But when he smiles, I see the real Toni, a charming young man, your son and a Finn.'

Faintly irritated by the smooth diplomacy of his response,

Tania turned away to look round the enclosures. 'But where's Rosa?' she asked.

Iris had joined Toni, though without in any way sharing his admiration for the unwelcoming boxer. 'She's gone off to look at the cats,' she called over. 'Here she is.'

Rosa appeared round a corner clutching a glowing furry ball. She half-stumbled over a hummock of grass as she rushed towards her mother. 'Mummy, Mummy, Mummy,' she burst out, 'this is Goldie. He likes me very much.' The plump ginger kitten, supremely contented after a large meal, had settled comfortably in her arms and was purring enthusiastically. Toni and Iris strolled over to investigate the newcomer and Rosa sought her brother's support. 'This is Goldie,' she informed him. 'Isn't he lovely!'

In reality much attracted by the kitten, Toni had to find some cause for complaint. 'Goldie's a silly name,' he opined. 'He's Ginger—no, he's, he's—I've got it: he's Marmalade Joe.'

Concerned only with ownership, the kitten could have remained Puss so far as Rosa was concerned. She pressed the now resisting ball of fur towards her mother, and with her eyes filling with tears implored again, 'Mummy, please, Mummy, can't we keep him? He hasn't got a home.'

'But, Rosa, what's going to happen to him when we go to Finland? And we'd have to ask Daddy first anyhow.'

Unexpectedly Toni gave his support to his sister, the boxer having rejected his advances by baring his teeth, snarling ominously and finally charging at the netting. He ruffled the kitten's fur gently. 'Cats are better than dogs. He'll catch the mice, won't you, Marmalade Joe.' The sudden extension of a claw-ringed paw was countered with a gentle tap.

'But we haven't got any mice,' Tania protested. 'Perhaps after Christmas, when we get back.'

Giovanni extended his hands to Rosa. 'Can I have him?' he asked. Rosa surrendered him a little reluctantly and the kitten climbed up Giovanni's coat sleeve to stand on his shoulder, rubbing his head against a new subject for cajolery.

'I have a suggestion,' Giovanni went on. 'I live alone on Pellestrina in house that has a small garden behind it. The little cat can live with me till after Christmas and can return to me if you travel again. Or to the lady in the next house if I am not there. She has already two very nice cats.'

Delighted children's cries greeted his suggestion. He turned to Tania for her approval. She hesitated briefly, calculating possible implications and responsibilities, distracted by Rosa's 'Please, please, Mummy,' and finally temporized, 'We'll ask Daddy first and if he says yes, we'll come back another day.'

Giovanni had removed a squirming kitten from his shoulder and was holding him in mid-air, gazing serenely into blue eyes. 'I'm going to have this kitten,' he said, 'that is, if Massimo will let me. If Father agrees, you can borrow him from me when you are in your home here and I take him back when you go away. You will come with me, Goldie, Marmalade Joe, and you will be a good policeman's cat.'

He slipped the kitten into a pocket, holding it there securely and turned to grin at Tania, touching her elbow in a gesture of complicity. 'I think that Rosa and perhaps Toni will want to visit Goldie sometimes in his new home. I can come with my boat to take them and if you are not too busy, you will come with them. And soon it is dark so we must leave now and I must first take Goldie to my house and you will come with us to see if it is satisfactory, no?'

The sun was already supported on slate-blue water while Giovanni, having shouted for the absent explorer, successfully negotiated with Massimo, who gratefully pocketed a contribution towards the maintenance of work in hand: hospitality and care for a new type of Venetian in need. As Giorgio appeared and they made their way back to the boat, the sun slipped finally below the horizon and they were aware of a slight thickening of the air. Once on board and before starting the engine, Giovanni handed the kitten to Rosa, with instructions to hold him tightly. They continued along the shore between Malamocco and Poveglia towards the deep water separating the Lido and Pellestrina. Half way across Giovanni and his first mate Giorgio became aware of a clamminess that softened and then obscured the lights of San Pietro ahead, as, like smoke drifting from a forest fire, the fog closed in on them. A moment later, the distant baying of a ship's horn told of approach or withdrawal. Giovanni slowed slightly but was near enough to Pellestrina to feel confident of his direction. The preliminary cloud of fog drifted past, allowing him time to locate the narrow shore channel and increase speed, at some risk, as visibility ahead was still limited and short-lived. Guided by lamps close on the wall above him, he followed the channel, moored successfully and assisted his passengers ashore, leading them straight to a nearby ochre-painted house, one of a group of four that in normal conditions would look out over the lagoon.

Inside they removed coats and were shown into a large room extending the length of the house, which even at first glimpse suggested unusual comfort. The room was pleasantly warm and their host switched on lamps, saw that they were seated, offered cigarettes and aperitifs, both politely refused, and excused himself. 'Always when I come home,' he explained, 'I must first control if are telephone messages from my post in Chioggia.' He returned to the hall, closing the door behind him: a semblance of a metallic voice was just audible, followed a short time after by Giovanni's own voice, speaking quietly and incisively.

Inside the sitting-room there was silence, Rosa stroking the kitten, Toni yawning, while adult eyes wandered round the room taking in every astonishing detail. Apart from a table whose slender elegantly-carved legs suggested eighteenth-century workmanship contrasting with a well-stocked cocktail bar in one corner, the basic furniture was unremarkable. But the two richly-embroidered rugs almost covering the polished wood floor were from China, the magnificent chandelier and sundry ornaments had been created in Murano, the cut-glass vase filled with huge bronze chrysanthemums must surely have come from Czechoslovakia. Pictures in elaborate gilt frames had the appearance of originals by Venetian artists while leather-bound books lent distinction to built-in shelves. A large cream television

66

with video equipment and a music centre might have appealed to carabiniere taste, but other items—the oval convex gilt-framed mirror, the curiously-shaped fin-de-siècle divan half-hidden by the table—how were these supposed to adapt themselves to a small fisherman's cottage occupied by a dedicated policeman?

Tania and Iris caught each other's eyes questioningly but remained silent: in these startling surroundings, with a world of swirling fog and invisible water just beyond the ivory curtains glowing in the soft light shed by a silk-shaded standard-lamp, Iris, who seemed to detect even a faint sweet perfume, felt that fantasy was not out of place. Did that quietly-ticking onyx-mounted clock which had just chimed six conceal a hidden microphone? Was the now-silent Giovanni, the remote enigmatic stranger who had insisted on bringing them to his exotic home, now listening quietly behind the door? Could there . . .?

Her speculations were interrupted by the reappearance of their subject, obviously under stress. 'Now I must excuse myself, ladies,' he greeted them. 'There has been a recorded telephone message for me. I must depart for Chioggia *subito* —immediately. If I tell you why, please do not repeat, though journalists perhaps know it already. This afternoon the carabinieri have arrested two people, man and woman, who are probably terrorists. They were living, hiding in a room in Chioggia. I have had much to do with terrorists and I must interrogate, perhaps identify them. I have wanted to invite you to dinner but now is impossible. I have already telephoned for a taxi to take you to Lido: it comes soon. I think the ferry from San Pietro still functions in spite of the fog. I go with my own car to the boat stop for Chioggia: is a boat in fifteen minutes though possibly is late tonight. Please is that OK?'

'Does Goldie come back with us, then?' Rosa asked.

'Goldie?' Giovanni caught sight of the ginger ball. 'Oh, the kitten. I do not know how long I am away but I give her to my neighbour who has cats.' He picked up Goldie before Rosa could protest, disappeared through the front door and could be heard knocking at the next house. The conversation that followed was drowned by the arrival of the taxi. Tania and Iris were already putting on their coats while tracksuited Toni and Rosa and sweater-enveloped Giorgio pushed past them to the taxi.

'How about Giorgio?' Tania asked a returning Giovanni.

'Giorgio, yes,' he replied. 'I arrange that the taxi takes you all the way. Giorgio takes the *motonave* to Venice at Santa Elisabetta and I telephone now to his parents to meet him at San Zaccharia.'

The taxi-driver greeted him as an old friend and was given instructions and money. While the five short-stay visitors were arranging themselves, shutting doors and winding down a window to say goodbye, Giovanni waited motionless, and it was to Tania that his final words were directed.

'*Arrivederci*,' he said softly, when all was ready. 'That is in English "till we see again each other". I hope that is very soon.' He stood erect and unsmiling, his eyes passing each of them to rest finally with a brief smile on Tania as the taxi moved off and he turned back to re-enter his Kubla Khan cottage.

The fog had indeed retreated to some degree and there was some delay but no difficulty in crossing to the Lido. Tania and the children were deposited outside their home while the taxi continued on its way to the centre. From an interminable smoky tunnel, dimly-lit at intervals by hazy street-lights and irradiated by the occasional glare of approaching car headlights, Iris and her young companion emerged into an encapsulated zone of brightly-lit shops, women weighed down by bulky plastic bags, men arguing against counters in neon-illuminated bars, abandoned buses gathering strength for the next trip and cars venturing on to a large roundabout where traffic from the right claimed precedence. With Iris's telephone number in his pocket in case of emergencies, Giorgio attached himself to a surging mass of local inhabitants intent on a Saturday evening in Venice whatever the weather. Beyond the waiting-pavilion windows, and to the far side of a wide platform, the mist-shrouded side of a *motonave* was just visible. Already it appeared considerably lower in the water than it should have been though the crowd was still moving forward confidently.

'He will be OK,' assured the taxi-driver in basic English, as he veered to avoid a NO ENTRY before returning to a street edged with grey nothingness and the clang of fog-bells. A turn to the right and Iris was home.

Tired though they were, Tania insisted on giving the children large cups of hot milky cocoa, their favourite cream-cheese and shrimp open sandwiches and chocolate cake. Toni's silent listlessness she put down to exhaustion and it was only after he had been put to bed that Rosa, herself now ready for bed, came up to her mother in the kitchen and said:

'Mummy, Toni says he hates you.'

'Oh, Rosa, you know he doesn't mean it. He's always saying that.'

'But, Mummy, this time he says he's going to remember what you said for the rest of his life. He told me while we were in the boat during the fog. He's very cross indeed with you.'

'But what did I say?'

'When we went on the boat together and left him behind, you said life would be quieter without him. And then when Giovanni was cross with Toni and Giorgio, he told Toni what you'd said. Only from what he said, you'd said you'd be much happier without him.'

Tania managed to sort this out, though with some impatience. Surely a policeman was trained to give accurate reports and to have some knowledge of human if not child psychology. Possibly he had misunderstood or had hoped to produce the maximum effect without taking into account the possible consequences.

'I'll talk to Toni tomorrow,' she promised. 'And you could tell him what I really said.'

'He doesn't believe me,' Rosa said sadly. 'He wanted to phone Grandma when we got home but I said she wasn't in Venice.'

And that was one consolation at least. Tania followed her

daughter to her bedroom, tucked her up in the lower bunk and glanced at her son above. He was restless even in deep sleep, muttering incomprehensibly, his two clenched fists moving on the pillow.

She returned to the kitchen to prepare herself coffee and sandwiches to relax with in the sitting-room. From below came the noise of the thumpings and wails of a tormented pop group which forced a retreat from sitting-room comfort to hard-chaired kitchen peace. Her mind insisted on returning to the day's events and particularly to Giovanni: surely a wise and compassionate man who would give comfort and protection in time of need: a friend one could trust, with reserves of strength and at the same time gentleness. And there were hidden depths to him that would reveal themselves gradually as friendship itself deepened. Perhaps he had sensed in her a kindred spirit: he had certainly shown a great interest in further meetings, naturally to include Iris and the children. He could be a good influence on Toni, the kind of father, no, uncle, he needed. Tania drew herself up abruptly and went to turn on the television in a now bearable sitting-room, switching through twenty-four-odd channels absent-mindedly, without finding one that appealed. She turned it off.

Stefano wouldn't be home much before midnight and there seemed nothing, not even a mediocre book she had started reading, records, embroidery, that would hold her attention. She was aware of an intense feeling of depression, futility, restlessness, obviously the product of tiredness, though the day had been far from strenuous. Bed was the only solution and she was too soundly asleep even to hear Stefano's midnight return from La Fenice.

During the night, Stefano woke up coughing and obviously with a high temperature. He moved around the flat restlessly, propping himself upright on the sofa and promptly bending over to cough, begging Tania to make tea as his throat was so dry while his face was flushed and drenched with perspiration. His temperature continued to rise and the cough worsened until Tania finally persuaded a doctor to come. He diagnosed acute bronchitis with immediate hospital treatment essential if pneumonia was to be avoided. An ambulance was summoned and Stefano departed for the large hospital fronting the Adriatic.

It was not until Monday that Tania could locate and inform Camillo so that Angelo could be alerted. All comforts, including a private room and the advice of the most distinguished Venetian consultant, were promptly organized though Angelo would naturally have no time to visit his son and he had no idea of the present whereabouts of Stefano's mother. Tania visited her husband daily and could gradually see an improvement. All recollection of a need to ask permission for the adoption of a marmalade-gold new member of the family had gone from her mind, though occasionally in the grey humidity and fog that almost daily shrouded the lagoon, she recalled nostalgically a day of sunshine and warm sympathetic companionship.

Iris meanwhile had resumed her normal placid existence despite the weather. Soon after nine on Monday morning, the importunate waiter of Burano telephoned to say he would like the first of his English lessons as soon as possible. Most of Iris's school teaching occupied afternoons and evenings, concerned as it was with older students, so punctually at ten o'clock the following morning, the fog having let up for the day, she opened her flat door to an earnest young man who, besides a large exercise book and two old school grammars, was burdened with two enormous (English-Italian and Italian-English) dictionaries. He had moored his boat along the canal outside: was this allowed, he wanted to know. Never having had a boat to moor, Iris supposed it would be all right.

The lesson, which involved the use of a cassette, dealt with common English situations with Iris explaining grammar and vocabulary and advising on her pupil's pronunciation and responses. At the end she lent him the cassette to practise with and he handed over the exact fee in cash, 'Better cash than cheque, perhaps, signora,' he said meaningfully. Sandro, the only name he vouchsafed, then departed, disappearing outside over the grass verge down

71

to the canal below, the first time a visitor had gone off in that particular direction.

An hour later, very much to her surprise, Giovanni telephoned. He inquired first about her health and her homeward journey the previous Saturday. He then hoped the Signora Vescovo and Toni and Rosa were well. Iris, who had already shared her friend's problems over the telephone the previous evening, reported Stefano's admission to hospital, a matter that caused him considerable concern. He then asked if she could spare him a few minutes of her time: he would very much welcome her assistance. He was on the Lido already and could call at her house probably within ten minutes if she would give him her address.

Iris gave her permission and address while wondering slightly about what assistance, other than that of a suspect, a carabiniere might require. It was in fact little more than five minutes later when Giovanni drew up outside in car and full uniform and approached the house, identical paper-covered packages in each hand. On entering, he followed her to her sitting-room and with a slight bow presented her with one of the packages, which with the paper removed proved to be a bowl of azaleas. 'With my deepest respects, signora,' he said. 'May I ask you perhaps to offer these others to your friend, Signora Vescovo?' He placed the package on the table and at Iris's request sat down, refusing the cup of coffee or glass of wine she offered him.

'I was very concerned to hear your news of Signor Vescovo,' he started. 'This must be the reason she was not at home when I have telephoned. I would like to be able to give her all the help possible in her difficulties but unfortunately am commanded to take the afternoon aeroplane to Rome. I have only this morning free to prepare myself. I told you, I think, on Saturday of the detention of two terrorists whom I have helped to interrogate. They belong to a group who are active in Rome, it seems, and I must continue my investigations there. Perhaps I am away a few days, a week or possibly longer. Can you please explain this to the Signora Vescovo and perhaps give these to Rosa and her brother.' He produced a folder from which he extracted copies of photographs he had taken in Burano and on the island home for dogs, which he handed to her.

'I fear we do not meet again before the signora and her family depart for Finland, but after Christmas I hope very much that we can travel together once more.'

He drew himself up, saluted, bowed slightly and took Iris's hand. '*Arriverderci*,' he said gently, 'until the New Year.' He turned on his heel and was through the flat door before Iris had time to open it herself, locating immediately the release button for front door and gate with an efficiency rare among her first-time visitors.

'Attractive, no doubt about that,' Iris meditated, as she tried to remember what she had done with students' essays awaiting correction. 'Pleasant, thoughtful, kind. I wonder why I don't like him.'

CHAPTER 6

DISTANT SHORES

Darkened by fog and frequent heavy rain-clouds, lashed by occasional gales, November lurched along its gloomy and unsteady course into December when the northerly Bore extended its path from Trieste to include Venice, clearing the skies for chill sunshine. Stefano had been discharged from hospital a week after admittance, having avoided graver complications and almost recovered from bronchitis. He rested at home for a week, gathering strength and breath for his flute-playing and was able to rejoin the orchestra later in November.

The azaleas had been delivered by Iris shortly before Stefano's return and in explaining their presence to her husband, Tania referred to the meeting in Burano with an older but pleasant carabiniere whose nephew attended the same school as the children. He had kindly brought them back and for the children's benefit had included a visit to the animal sanctuary where Rosa, having fallen in love with a ginger kitten, had wanted to bring it home. Tania had naturally insisted on consulting Stefano and to soften Rosa's, and also Toni's disappointment, the carabiniere had volunteered to house the kitten until a decision could be made. He lived on Pellestrina though he was now on a police case in Rome and had delivered two bowls of azaleas to Iris, one of them for Tania, before he had left. Told in this way, the story seemed to lack probability but Stefano accepted it calmly enough, and Tania added:

'Iris says he's asked us all to visit him and inspect the kitten when he returns.'

Tania had chosen skilfully her moment for confession after the evening meal, when Stefano was relaxed comfortably in an armchair and Toni and Rosa were both listening intently. Rosa climbed on to her father's lap and stroked his cheek, as skilled as any kitten in getting what she wanted.

'Please, Daddy,' she begged, 'can he come and live with us, when we're back from Finland, of course. We've called him Goldie.'

Toni seized and shook his father's arm. 'Please, Daddy, I want him too, but he's not Goldie. He's Marmalade Joe.'

In common with most sensitive or subtle people, Stefano himself had a weakness for cats, but for the moment he temporized. 'If he's going to cause arguments even before he arrives, the answer's no. But maybe we'll go and see him after Christmas. He'll have to be Goldie, though, at any rate when we call him in at night. Imagine yelling Marmalade Joe twenty times into the night air!'

Early in December, Chiara materialized again in Venice and telephoned on an evening when she knew Stefano would be at home to invite them to the palazzo for Christmas. Stefano explained politely that they had arranged to visit Tania's sick father in Finland, a statement which she countered heatedly with a reference to Stefano's devoted mother who had done so much for him, though with less emotional display than he had feared. She was invited to Malamocco for dinner before their departure, but having

74

already learned that Rosa was developing a slight cold, regretted that her many engagements would make this impossible. Having informed herself of the date of their departure but without accounting for her own long absence, she rang off promptly, calling again a moment later to inform him that she would dispatch the children's Christmas presents by special messenger and wished to express her Christmas greetings. Camillo arrived the following day with a number of gaudily-wrapped packages to be opened on Christmas Day.

They had booked their flight to Finland for the earliest date Stefano was free and soon after seven that morning embarked on the water-taxi which on request calls at the Lido on its way across the lagoon to the airport at Tessera. An ageing moon was nearing the horizon, casting a silver cone of light across black water, decay and decrepitude still invisible in darkness, though the eastern sky was brushed with the first premonition of daybreak. Supremely contented at the prospect of enjoying again the tranquillity of her own country, its lake waters now protected by gleaming ice, with the first snowflakes delighting scarlet-coated blue-eyed children, Tania could ignore the hidden menace of this polluted inland sea that was now quietly eating away so many of the islands it had itself created.

They had arranged to travel by plane to Frankfurt where they could change into a Helsinki connection and had about half an hour's wait ahead. The two still sleepy children had little interest in an exploration of the somewhat limited resources of the airport building—they had seen it all before anyhow—so after checking in, the family huddled together on four of the available seats while they awaited the departure summons. With only a few minutes to go, Tania noticed a carabiniere in full uniform who was examining the arrivals board intently with his back to them. Something about his height and build reminded her of Giovanni even before he turned and with a look of astonishment, hurried across to them, bearing somewhat incongruously a large bouquet of red roses.

Both children yelled simultaneously, 'It's Giovanni,' Toni

adding, possibly with mixed feelings: 'Are you coming to Finland with us?'

'Would you like me to, Toni?' Giovanni asked, before removing his hat, standing erect, bowing to Tania and saying, 'I am delighted to meet you again, Signora Vescovo, and your delightful family. *Ciao*, Rosa and Toni. Your kitten is well but wants to see you both again.' He turned in Stefano's direction and bowed again, extending his arm. 'Lieutenant Giovanni Fedele,' he introduced himself. 'You are, I believe, the signora's husband.'

Stefano shook the hand offered and invited the Lieutenant to join them. As soon as he had lowered himself on to a chair, his hat perched on his knees, Tania asked,

'Are you also flying somewhere this morning?'

'No, I am happy to say. I have been too much away from my job. Now I am meeting my sister who comes from Milan. So you are leaving for Finland now. By way of Frankfurt, I suppose. There are only few minutes before you will be called to your plane, I think.'

From his right a small voice pleaded, 'Please, Giovanni, is Goldie really well and happy? Will you give him a specially nice dinner on Christmas Day?'

Giovanni smiled at her and took her hand. 'Your Goldie and Toni's Marmalade Joe is a very fine active cat though he is not always very obedient.' He turned to raise an eyebrow mockingly in Toni's direction. 'However, he eats much and plays much with my neighbour's cats. He will have chicken and freshly-cooked fish for his Christmas dinner. And he waits eagerly for your return to Italy.'

A loudspeaker announcement summoned all Frankfurt passengers to the departure exit and the small group rose to collect cases and bags. Giovanni hesitated as they turned to say goodbye and on a sudden impulse pushed the roses into Tania's hand. 'These were for my sister,' he explained. 'But I cannot allow a Finnish lady to leave Italy without a present for Christmas.'

Unsurprised at this traditionally Italian gesture, Stefano shook hands with his fellow-countryman, who wished him a good journey, turning to give Toni's hand a manly shake and to kiss Rosa's forehead. He turned to Tania last, as the others were moving away, looking deep into her eyes and taking her hand. 'Life has separated us until now,' he said quietly, 'but I have often thought of you and my thoughts go with you now. *Arriverderci* for the present, my dear, until the New Year brings us together again.'

Tania's flushed cheeks passed unnoticed as the assembled passengers made their way in the direction of the plane.

Disillusionment only too often waits on joyful expectation and the Helsinki where a much-delayed plane from Frankfurt landed late in the evening was scourged with the lash of a brutal wind, the frozen earth bare of snow and nobody was at the airport to meet the exhausted family. A loudspeaker announcement directed Tania to the information desk where she was handed the transcript of a telephone call: her detective brother Arvo had been called out on an urgent case so was unable to meet them as planned but her sister-in-law would be waiting at the air terminal in the city centre. They had missed the Imatra train with sleepers booked for them and the children were predictably fractious. In less than two hours, however, they were all sound asleep after a good meal: the children in sleeping-bags on mattresses in Arvo's small flat which had often had to stretch its resources to accommodate unexpected visitors. Early the next morning they were on their way to Imatra from where they were fetched by car to a snow-framed red-washed farmhouse beside a still lake with silver birch branches before it patterning a pale-blue sunlit sky.

Iris was to spend the Christmas and New Year period with her mother and sisters in England, but she and the younger Vescovos all returned early in the New Year. Tania's depression had revived during the return journey and intensified on landing at Tessera. It was, however, briefly dispelled on the daylight taxi-trip across the lagoon. Far to the north the Alpine foothills gleamed snow-white in sunshine so close it seemed they must be just beyond the lagoon shore and so remote as to lack conviction, like ideals in a corrupt world. And then they were at home, with

Stefano in his old place on the sofa with a copy of the *Gazzettino* in front of his nose, while Tania cooked, served, cleared away, unpacked and kept the children reasonably quiet and contented. Toni at least had improved after spending the Christmas week as one of a larger group, Arvo and his wife having joined them for Christmas with their own two boys.

A few evenings later Tania had put the children to bed and was watching a television documentary devoted to holiday areas, when she was disturbed by the measured purr of the telephone. Hoping her caller would be Iris and not Chiara, she turned down the TV volume and gave her number in English. A warm fatherly voice answered playfully. 'Is that the charming signora returned to us from ice-cold Finland?'

'Oh, it's you, Lieutenant Fedele. How nice to hear from you! I hope you had an enjoyable Christmas.' The television screen was still visible from where she was sitting and she could watch a cruise ship arriving in the heart of Stockholm. Seen from Italy, Sweden was almost home.

'I am quite sure you enjoyed Christmas in your own beautiful country, though perhaps you missed *la bella Italia* just a little. Is your father now in better health?'

'He is well enough but can't leave the house, especially now in winter.'

'I am sorry. To be old is often sad. We have to enjoy our lives as much as possible while we are still young. Don't you agree, signora?'

An aeroplane was moving over a world of forests and serpentine lakes. 'I suppose so,' she said abstractedly. 'How is Goldie?'

'In excellent health but he is growing big. Would you and your children like to greet him again in your home? I am free this evening and could bring him now. Tomorrow and afterwards I must work in the afternoons and the evenings so I cannot come then.'

Tania's attention switched from the film to concentrate on his words. After his earlier suggestions about their visiting

78

his home to meet the kitten, his sudden wish to dispose of it was unexpected. Probably though he had had enough of the responsibility.

'It is rather late,' she protested mildly, 'and the children are asleep now. I think they'd like to be around to greet him when he arrives.'

'I understand, Signora Tania.' His voice caressed, almost hypnotized as it lingered over her name. 'But if they are awakened by the kitten tomorrow morning, how excited they will be! And I would be so happy to talk with you again: about your journey and your beautiful Finland.'

The television cameras had now moved to Finland: Rauma with its homely, beautifully-preserved houses and streets: she recalled her first visit there as a schoolgirl. Then into a snow-white forest: everything: undergrowth, paths, compact fir trees blanketed, birches festooned with scintillating fringes, a lone skier gliding vigorously along smooth double tracks. A cold that froze the cheeks, that was honest and clean and unpolluted. She found herself saying:

'If you are free on Saturday morning the children will be here and ready to receive the new member of our family. My husband, I know, very much wants to renew and extend his short acquaintance with you. Would it be possible perhaps for you to drop in and have lunch or at least a drink with us then? We should all like to thank you for your kindness.'

There was a pause of several seconds so that she inquired sharply, 'Are you there, Lieutenant Fedele?'

'Yes, Signora Vescovo. Please excuse me. I was thinking.' Was it her imagination or had his voice really hardened? 'Saturday morning would be very good, though I regret I could not stay as long as lunch. Perhaps about eleven o'clock, if that is good. Please give my greetings to the children from Goldie or maybe Marmalade Joe.' She must have imagined the hardness: his voice was warm with friendship and respect. 'And a very good night to you, Tania my dear. Sleep well.'

The click of a positioned receiver and Tania raced to turn up the volume again slightly. A springtime Lapland, with assembling reindeer herds which tourist brochure photographers but few Finns have ever seen.

An odd coincidence it seemed, that this programme should have coincided with his telephone call but life was really crammed with coincidences if you kept a record. Though the past three months did seem to have produced an unusual crop of oddly-related ones.

Chiara had been publicizing Stefano's musical talents in certain influential quarters. As a result, he had already been asked to perform at a few assemblies and élite parties and had been referred to extravagantly in a local paper as the Italian James Galway. He was practising when Giovanni arrived the following Saturday just before eleven, carrying a wickerwork basket from inside which escaped meows, plaintive, indignant, terrified, suggesting a creature being subjected to hideous torture. Wildly excited, Toni and Rosa waited while Giovanni untied neatly-secured cords and opened an ineffective catch. The tension deepened as Stefano and Tania joined the awed reception committee gazing with bated breath into the semi-darkness at a huddled orange shape lurking within. The shape eventually advanced cautiously, crept out and, adroitly dodging welcoming hands, streaked into the kitchen and under the lowest cupboard. Two small bodies prostrated themselves on the floor but neither twisting cord nor savoury morsel could lure it out. After some five minutes they gave it up and two minutes later, a wary kitten started investigating every inch of skirting-board and carpet edge within reach of himself and out of reach of eager hands.

Giovanni examined with interest Stefano's flute before sitting down and accepting a drink. After a brief inquiry about the Christmas holiday, he returned to the subject of music and especially opera and showed an informed interest in the current programme at La Fenice. Unfortunately he knew nobody who shared his musical tastes and had always felt isolated and a little awkward sitting alone.

'You aren't married, then,' Stefano asked in some surprise.

Giovanni hesitated and then said stiffly, 'Not now, unfortunately. I have to say that my wife, my former wife that is, left me to go to another man: I understand it: with my police duties, and sometimes I was tired and perhaps irritable, she wanted more variety and company. She remarried as soon as a divorce became possible.

'So you live alone and look after yourself?'

'A neighbour cleans for me and cooks when I need a hot meal. And I rent a house from an Italian lady, a widow, who has gone to live for some time in America. Your signora and Miss Iris Lawton have visited there with Goldie—' he glanced round as he spoke but Goldie was now investigating the children's bedroom. 'The furnishing is a little—how shall we say?—a little extravagant, exaggerated perhaps, as you must have noticed, signora. But I no more notice it except that I must always remember to be careful with the glass and the other objects of value.'

There was a pause, while Tania reflected on the 'extravagance' and recalled also a faint unidentifiable perfume, surely not a relic of the presumably wealthy expatriate. Giovanni returned to the subject of opera. 'I should like to see *Rosenkavalier* in the nowadays programme,' he observed, 'but this time I prefer to share the experience. May I have your permission, Signor Vescovo, to ask your wife to share a box, not only with me but also, if this is possible, with Miss Iris Lawton, who I am sure enjoys opera. I naturally should pay the tickets and I should like to ask you to come with us in a quiet supper after.' He smiled gravely at Tania before turning to hear her husband's reaction.

It was Tania, however, who broke the thoughtful silence by reminding him, 'I'm afraid it's impossible, Lieutenant Fedele, on account of the children.'

Giovanni looked in the direction of the children's room from which coos of gratified delight suggested that Goldie had either allowed himself to be caught or was in a position to be admired. 'I had thought to that,' he said. 'Not far from here is a teacher: she works with young children in a school near. Her father is policeman in Venice but her family lives in Mestre so she rents a room here near to her school. I have heard she enjoys to go baby-sitting—for a small payment, naturally. I can ask her if she is free.'

Stefano finally welcomed the suggestion, having for a long time felt guilty about Tania's virtual imprisonment in the evening. It had seemed impossible to make any contacts, let alone friendships with local inhabitants: like people everywhere, they had their own families, concerns, problems and interests. He produced a programme from a drawer and a date was agreed on: provisionally, as Iris still had to be consulted and a box might not be available. Rosa emerged from the bedroom clutching in triumph the new family member. 'He wants something to eat, Mummy,' she said.

Giovanni rose, rubbed a hand over the soft fur and bade farewell to his charge. 'You are welcome back at any time, Goldie,' he reminded everyone. 'Often you have made me to laugh.' And having extended his farewells to the other four, he departed.

The evening at La Fenice was enjoyed by at least three members of the audience and a contented quartet made their way afterwards to a quiet and simple trattoria. Throughout the meal Giovanni took pains to pay discreet homage to a knowledgeable and highly-talented artist, seeking enlightenment on the playing of the flute, on the state of opera in Italy and the United Kingdom, and on music in general. The conversation moved to Finland which each of his companions could inform him on and if his eyes seemed to linger slightly longer and more intensely on Tania's face, this was surely due to the fact that she could describe the Finland of a past age, of her childhood. His boat was moored conveniently near: the moon eclipsed the glittering worlds beyond it and as they moved past the brooding, darkened Salute, the shadowy Palace of the Doges, San Giorgio and its attendant campanile, Giovanni at the wheel sang through the repertoire of the hired gondola entertainer, suggesting at one and the same time, mockery and tenderness, passion and melancholy. As they were passing the island of San Servolo, he looked back through the open door and asked Iris:

'Have you the intention to go to the Carnival, Miss Iris?'

Iris, who hated crowds, noise and the mass entertainment provided in the Piazza on the 'big' nights, explained her lack of interest.

'That is because you have no companion who knows where to go.' Giovanni was gazing at the lamplit edge of the Lido ahead but his voice was raised so that not only Iris could hear him. 'I know many parts of Venice that are never crowded: a quiet promenade along a canal that reflects the lamps above in a world of—' he hesitated—'of ghosts, yes: a lady and gentleman of the Settecento in velvet and silk, a Cossack with a Spanish gipsy, an Arab with a Japanese lady, Harlequin and Columbine. All unknown and mysterious in their beautiful masks. And somebody sings and somebody plays guitar. Miss Iris, may I take you to the Carnival?'

Iris's first impressions of an unusually cultured and sincere police officer had been jolted already by the visit to his exotic home and, possibly unfairly, his vocal performance and Latin-lover rhetoric had had the opposite effect from what he'd intended.

He's playing a scene, she thought, and he'd hate me to accept. She answered him hesitantly, as if only half believing in her amazing good fortune, moving as she did so to the doorway.

'You're describing a Carnival I've never seen. It sounds wonderful. Can you really spare the time?'

Surprised and the merest trifle suspicious, Giovanni sought in vain a means of retreat. 'The final night of the Carnival and the weekend before, that you would not like. Last year was so much people the police had to close Venice: cars from Mestre had to go back. But perhaps the Thursday before, if only I am free, I could . . . I would be delighted if you accept to come with me. May I telephone you about this, Miss Iris? The Signora Tania will want to go with her husband, of course.'

They had already turned in the direction of San Nicolò and were approaching the canal dividing the street Iris lived in, so little more was said. For the rest of the journey to Malamocco, Giovanni seemed abstracted, singing snatches of melody to himself as he stared ahead.

The teacher of young children, hair a blonde frizz, eyes peering through mascara, was intent on a TV programme turned to maximum volume when Stefano and Tania crept in. A fog of cigarette smoke obscured the room and Stefano's prized Drambuie had been discovered and more than dipped into. She sprang up from the sofa, demanded twice the fee that Tania knew to be normal and, having hunched herself into a shaggy synthetic fur coat, departed hurriedly.

'Anybody would think she had a date,' Stefano muttered, as he recapped the Drambuie and Tania opened a window.

To Iris's relief it poured with rain on the night of her own date so she gave little thought to preparing an excuse. The phone rang shortly after six.

'Do I speak to Miss Lawton?' an easily recognizable voice inquired.

'You do indeed, Lieutenant Fedele. What a shame the weather's so awful!'

'For the Carnival in Venice, I am sorry, yes. But here in Pellestrina is a very nice restaurant where people come to eat when the weather is not good at Carnival time. They wear masks and beautiful dresses inside the restaurant as they cannot wear them in the streets. I will be very happy to bring you here in my boat, Miss Iris.'

'Oh, what a pity, Lieutenant Fedele! A friend telephoned a short time ago to ask if I could babysit for her: their usual standby has 'flu. And because of the rain, you see, I said I'd go.'

Giovanni expressed regrets but also resignation. 'But there are other occasions and possibilities,' he consoled her.

Iris agreed politely, reflecting as she did so that in a world of deceit and intrigue, one additional whitest of lies need not trouble her sensitive conscience unduly.

For Sandro, the new year brought disaster. His brother-in-law's boat having given some anxiety, it had been taken to an expert for inspection and he travelled to his next lesson with Iris via Venice, with the idea of doing some shopping there on his way back. On his return he had settled comfortably in the non-smoking section of a *motonave* and was about to open an English reader Iris had given him, when a large hand was laid on his shoulder and a remembered voice greeted him in his native Sicilian.

'Well, Sandro, what are you doing in these parts? A long way from home, eh?'

Under the pressure of that hand Sandro froze like a trapped animal before the self-defence reflex he had learned to rely on in the past came to his aid.

'Oh, it's you, Mr Vescovo,' he responded. Even to himself the feigned geniality rang false and he came to a stop, his mind empty of ideas about what to say next.

'Where are you living now?' his interrogater proceeded.

'Er . . . in Padova. I've just been visiting a friend.'

'But you haven't got a job there, it seems.'

'Yes, I have. I'm a waiter. Tuesday's my free day.'

Angelo considered for a moment. The boat was only just under way so they still had some ten minutes. There was an empty bench on the far side.

'Shall we sit over there?' he suggested. 'We've got a lot to talk about.'

'I'm quite comfortable here,' Sandro assured him.

'You're not being very sensible, are you, Sandro,' the big man reminded him. 'And I'm only trying to do you a good turn. I could do you a bad one, a very bad one, as you well know. Come over here.'

Sandro followed him helplessly to the empty seat. 'So nobody's caught up with you yet?' Angelo commented when they were seated.

'Only you,' Sandro muttered.

'You know I wouldn't harm you, Sandro. Not personally, that is. Though I realize there are some that might. You or your wife: you weren't wearing that ring when we last met. If they knew where you were, that is. After all, nothing you told the police could have touched me. But those that were touched: their friends don't like traitors, as you well know.'

'They killed my brother.'

'Your brother killed himself. Nobody else injected him.'

'They got him into it as a kid. Persuading him he could

85

take it or leave it. So that once he was hooked they could use him.'

'They used you too. You were one of their most intelligent operators.'

'Not on narcotics. I never touched them. It was when they'd killed my brother . . . I was with him all through the last few weeks. That's what did it. Some of them got a tenth of what they deserved.'

'And some of the rest are still on the lookout for you, don't forget. Or your wife. Women aren't exempt nowadays. Have you got any kids, Sandro?'

'We'll go abroad.'

'A waste of time and you know it. Now I know where you are, Padova, Venice: it won't be hard to find out, and then it'll be easy enough to keep tabs on you wherever you move off to.'

'What have I got to do?'

'That's more sensible. I've got a good job for you, well-paid. Just giving some assistance to my secretary, who objects to fetching and carrying for me. And making yourself useful generally.'

'Not . . .?'

'A few packages, that's all. You won't know what's in them.'

'So my brother's to die again and again and this time I'm to be his murderer myself.'

'Don't be melodramatic. They're their own murderers, the half-wits. You'd have no responsibility. Except for what might happen to your wife, of course. Once your friends knew where you are, it could be either of you, though not both, I think. One of you would have to be left alive to feel what it's like. By the way, where do I find you? You'll have a residence card on you, of course.'

'I've left it at home.'

'That's against the law, isn't it. Oh well, I can make my own inquiries. Who's your Lido friend. A girl?'

'Your police stooges can give you my address but they can't tell you that.'

'Probably a girl. Maybe Sicilian. Young, pretty. We've a

86

number of contacts on the Lido who might be able to tell us something. Just useful information. I've organized a big Congress there for the spring, you know, so I'll be backwards and forwards. I'll probably need your help with it, so you'll be able to drop in on her from time to time. I've got a suite in the Danieli at the moment while my wife's got some restoration in hand at the palazzo—a lot of banging—tends to be disturbing. Come along now and meet my secretary Camillo. You can give him your address for checking and I'll put you in the picture a bit more. I might even give you some lunch.'

A large hand below his shoulder again guiding him to the side of the boat and the platform beyond. Sandro thrust the unnoticed English reader deep into his pocket. He wouldn't after all be needing it again.

It was the same evening that Sandro called Iris from a public callbox near his home. He had told his wife and her family only that he had run into an old acquaintance who'd fixed him up with a good job for the winter season, at a time when an additional waiter was hardly needed.

As soon as he heard Iris's voice, he started to speak, using at first some of the carefully-practised expressions he had collected.

'Sandro speaking, Miss Lawton. I'm sorry I won't be able to come to my lesson tomorrow and never again.'

It was easy enough to hear his misery. 'Oh, I'm sorry too,' she said. 'Why not, Sandro? Is there something wrong?'

'All is wrong. Is terrible.' Grammar was being overwhelmed by anxiety. ''Ave met a man, very bad man from Sicily. 'E knows bad things about me, past things, so am dangerous—no, in danger. So I must do what 'e says, though is 'orrible.'

'But, Sandro, can't you go to the police? People can't just force you to do things that are wrong.'

'Bah!' Sandro made an unseen gesture of impatience. 'In Italy is impossible. Am gone to the police too much already. Is impossible, Miss Lawton, to explain. But please excuse me. I liked your lessons. And please say nothing to nobody. Is better.'

He rang off abruptly, almost in tears, and Iris replaced the receiver slowly, with the uncomfortable realization that fear and horror can be contagious, even at a safe distance.

Sandro turned towards home, found it impossible to face the people there and then started off on a brisk walk, glancing back furtively at intervals to check that he was not being followed. An old discarded habit, he realized, was reasserting itself, together with a sick uneasiness impossible to shed.

CHAPTER 7

LOOMING CATASTROPHE

Winter dragged on with alternating fog, rain, sleet and frosty sunlight accompanied by piercing northerly winds, which lasted a day or two before skies and distances were again obscured. Then, on a grey morning at the end of March, while Tania was on her twice-daily journey to Venice, Giovanni telephoned, Stefano taking the call. He apologized for not having made contact earlier as he had had to undertake a lot of extra duties and went on to inquire about the various members of the family, including the kitten (now around six months old and an accomplished entertainer, manipulator and individualist). He then referred to two short films of the lagoon he had acquired, which he had hoped to invite them all to his home to see. Unfortunately a leak in a water tank had flooded his cottage while he had been at work and it would take several weeks to dry it out and do the necessary redecoration. Thereupon Stefano took it upon himself to invite Giovanni to dinner on an evening convenient to all of them: he would consult Tania on her return.

He mentioned the invitation to Tania later in the day and was slightly surprised at her reluctant, 'Yes, I suppose he could come. The children would probably enjoy it.'

'And won't you? You especially in fact, as you meet so

very few people. I thought you'd be delighted. He seems a thoroughly nice fellow.'

'Yes, I suppose so.'

'What have you got against him? He probably feels lonely living all by himself like that.'

'I haven't got anything against him. What evenings could you manage?'

'Given notice, I could arrange a substitute. Ring him up and ask him when he's free.'

'It's you who invited him so you should do the confirming. It's all the same to me.' Tania could not have explained her own uneasiness: she hadn't the slightest belief in premonitions or forebodings, and was unable to justify her sense of hidden menace in this quiet-spoken and unassuming chance acquaintance. A natural Nordic distrust of possible deviousness in the over-civilized southerner, she surmised, which was warning her against making any kind of advance.

Stefano suggested dates, one of which was decided upon, and on a blustery April evening Giovanni arrived in his boat carrying two plastic bags, one bearing the name of a Chioggia toyshop and containing two dolls: a black-haired Sardinian girl for Rosa and a splendid carabiniere in full-dress uniform for Toni. The other unadorned plastic bag held chicken and liver scraps with two ping-pong balls for Goldie, who had taken himself off somewhere an hour before. The films, for which he had brought a projector, showed sunlit islands in deep-blue water with colour-washed fisherman's houses, churches and campanili, newly-painted fishing-boats in placid canals, lace and glass and embroidered blouses and a long golden Adriatic beach. Somehow the chimneys and oil tanks and abandoned crumbling islands had been missed, together with the fogs, mudbanks and turgid waters.

Throughout the evening Giovanni showed himself a model guest, making a great fuss of Goldie when he eventually turned up for a meal and taking several photographs of the children playing with the kitten, with a promise to provide copies later: this was a different camera from the one he had had on Burano. He complimented Tania on her cooking and entertained the children with fascinating accounts of local incidents and places, including the horror story of the Cason dei Sette Morti, the House of the Seven Dead Men, existing once on an island in a remote area of the lagoon waters. These small lodges are still used as temporary accommodation by fishermen working at some distance from their homes and in this particular case six men and a boy cook had been involved. Having dragged a corpse out of the water, the men had teased the lad by pretending it was a man asleep and had told him to wake up the sleeper and invite him in to a meal. The boy managed this all too successfully as the corpse had tramped in to join the company. And when the boy had brought in the meal, he had found not one but seven corpses huddled round the table awaiting their supper. Oddly it was Rosa who asked placidly, 'Is the house still there today?' while Toni sat rigid and wide-eyed as if, in company with the boy, he was staring in horror at seven hideous corpses, stark and sightless, crouched round a rough wooden table while the open door creaked and scraped the threshold in the rising wind and the waves beat against the walls of the dark, ice-cold house. Giovanni's voice lowered to a sinister whisper. 'Would you like me to take you there one day, Toni?' while Tania, seeing the boy's face, broke in quickly, 'No, Toni. That would be impossible. I read somewhere that the island is almost completely under water now. And it's only a story that people tell to frighten one another. It couldn't have happened.' Toni glanced at her mistrustfully and continued to brood, and when she frowned across at Giovanni he merely smiled and raised one eyebrow in mocking collusion. It was at that moment she realized how much she disliked him.

From this point on, the evening proved an ordeal for her, with Giovanni, possibly knowingly, a source of uneasy irritation. Often when she was speaking, she was aware that he was watching her fixedly, willing her to look at him. She always resisted, but whenever she was forced to turn in his direction he would flash a warm smile at her, his eyes holding hers as if there were a secret understanding between them. Stefano's presence at the side of the table facing him made no difference and Tania sensed her husband's uneasiness and bewilderment. She could well be exaggerating a form of Italian social courtesy, the guest expressing his sincere admiration of his hostess and, implicitly thereby, of his host. But surely not even a good-looking Italian would persist in suggesting this degree of intimacy, even connivance, in front of a shy and sensitive husband and regardless of her own obvious embarrassment. Increasingly she felt out of her depth and longed for Giovanni's departure.

He on the contrary seemed determined to prolong his stay. Coffee and brandy were provided for the adults when they moved to comfortable chairs and Giovanni begged for the children to be allowed to remain a little longer. With a rare opportunity for intellectual discussion within his own home, Stefano pursued an analysis of the previous year's Biennale while Giovanni plied him with questions and comments with what appeared to Tania the deliberate intention of prolonging his stay. Tania had by now withdrawn from the conversation, hoping to convey a not-too-obvious impression of tiredness, while the children, thrilled at first with this unusual chance of a delayed bedtime in adult company, began to fidget and yawn, providing Tania with a longed-for opportunity.

'Please don't let me interrupt you,' she broke in at last, 'but I'm afraid I must get the children to bed now. They've got school tomorrow morning.'

For once Toni made no demur. Giovanni looked at his watch in surprise and sprang to his feet.

'I had no idea,' he exclaimed. 'I have been so much enjoying myself that time has stopped passing. I am a thousand times sorry, Signora Tania. The children must indeed go to their beds and I must myself depart.'

His words were humble but in some way they managed to suggest reproach, that a more competent hostess should have chosen a less unsuitable moment to interrupt an absorbing conversation. Momentarily she felt herself the simple-minded Northern country-girl ignorant of the social conventions of the cultured and sophisticated Mediterranean world. And in the same moment all her various impressions of this quiet-spoken, fatherly policeman cohered instantaneously to form the image of an actual opponent whose subtlety and vast experience of the world would make any kind of resistance futile. The vivid but absurd image dissolved immediately as sensitive but unsubtle Stefano expressed his open disapproval.

'It won't do them any harm to miss an hour's sleep. They're no longer infants. And it's all part of their education listening to adult discussion.'

'Tania is right,' Giovanni observed gently (or was it forgivingly?), 'you can see that Rosa and Toni have difficulty to keep awake. And I must also leave my home early tomorrow morning for my work.'

He came up to Tania, bowed, took her hand to kiss and continued to grasp it while he expressed his thanks, concluding, 'This is an evening that I have enjoyed more than any other in my life. We will meet again very soon, I hope.'

He kissed each of the children lightly on the cheek, shook hands with Stefano and after a last glance of shared understanding directed at Tania, accompanied his host to the door.

After a token resistance, Toni followed his mother to the bathroom while Rosa carried glasses and dessert plates to the kitchen. Stefano returned from the hall, called to Tania in the bathroom to hurry up and disappeared into the bedroom to undress.

An hour later, with the children sound asleep and the kitchen in order, the breakfast things already in place on the table, Tania could at last follow him.

Over an unusually late Easter the weather remained sullen and grey with long periods of heavy rain. On Easter Saturday, Stefano left by air for Rome, his mother having made use of various acquaintances there to arrange a few musical recitals for him, one in a small but prestigious concert hall and two others in the drawing-rooms of highly-placed patrons of music. According to her, it was time for her son's already considerable reputation in Venice to be extended to the nation's capital. He was to return home the following Friday.

Tania and Iris had planned several excursions during what they had hoped would be a springlike school holiday, including trips to Torcello and Murano and further afield to Padova and Verona, but cold and rain restricted them to chilly homes where the children fretted, Toni in particular becoming increasingly obstreperous. Tania herself felt depressed and too lethargic to make the effort to don waterproofs and go sightseeing in Venice where, along with their school classes, the children had already seen most things likely to interest them at their age. At the same time she felt guilty about missed opportunities.

On Tuesday there was a TV forecast of better things to come and although chilly, Wednesday was at least dry, with mild sunshine from time to time. Early in the morning Rosa discovered in the postbox in the hall below a bright pink envelope addressed to herself. She brought it upstairs and extracted from it a folded birthday card adorned with the picture of a simpering white kitten with blue eyes and blue ribbon round the neck. As her ninth birthday had been celebrated a month previously, she eyed it with some bewilderment, opened it to read the barely legible message within, and then handed it over to her mother.

Chiara had wasted no words:

Dear Rosa,
Next Thursday I visit the shops in Venice to buy for myself dresses. It likes me to buy also for you a present of birthday. You are not now in the school, I no, but I meet you there outside at the four. We have tea in the palazzo and then go to the dress shops til seven-thirty. Then I bring you to your home.

Auguri,
Grandmother Chiara.

Tania was less appreciative than she might have been of this peremptory gesture, largely because experience had shown that Chiara never acted generously out of pure altru-

93

ism. The suggestion might merely be a well-aimed expression of contempt for her daughter-in-law's choice of
clothes for the descendants of doges: equally it could well
conceal some more damaging intent. She unwillingly stood
the coy kitten on the sideboard (where it was soon knocked
down on one of his perambulations by the normally careful
Goldie and remained flat on its face) and went to the
telephone to make one obviously essential inquiry.

She was answered first by Beata, followed by her mistress,
who assured her haughtily that 'next Thursday' could only
possibly be the following day. Tania expressed her gratitude
and acceptance on condition that the weather was reasonable.

'I 'ave it from the 'ighest authorities,' she was informed,
'that the sun will shine.' A click gave notice of a replaced
receiver.

Chiara's authorities must have been of a celestial order
as the last cloud vanished within the next half-hour to reveal
a brilliant sun. It was now too late to organize an excursion
but at least they could go to the Lido centre during the
afternoon for a walk along the beach in the direction of Iris's
home. Just as they were leaving, Iris telephoned to invite
them to tea.

It was Iris's tabby, bird-watching from the balcony, who
greeted them first as they made their way from outer gate
to main door. Iris was waiting at her own door where she
greeted them in her turn, before making tea and serving
chocolate ice-creams for the children to consume in the
kitchen. Tea and cake were carried to the sitting-room where
she and Tania could enjoy temporary peace.

'Giovanni telephoned about half an hour ago,' she informed
her visitor. 'He said that now the weather is improving he can
at last invite all five of us for a trip in his boat to Torcello, Murano
and wherever else we'd like to go. He'd apparently been trying
to get in touch with his good friends the Vescovos without success but obviously you're invited too.'

'He must have been unusually unlucky as I've been in
most of the time. Did he mention what time he wanted to
leave?'

'Ten or eleven in the morning with an invitation to lunch in a restaurant on Torcello. He must be a rather highly-paid policeman to be able to afford lunch for six people there,' Iris reflected, 'though his home does rather seem to bear that out.'

'There'd be only four of us anyhow. Stefano's not back from Rome till Friday and for some odd reason Chiara wants to take Rosa shopping for a dress in Venice, for a birthday present of all things.'

'Will she be away for the whole day?'

'No. She's to meet Chiara in Venice at four so she'll be leaving home before three. That puts Torcello out of the question. Anyhow they've both been there already with the school and weren't very impressed.'

'You're not keen on going, are you?'

'No.'

'Because you don't like him or like him too much?'

'I distrust him in the same way as I do Chiara. How about you?'

Iris considered for a moment. 'Vain, certainly, and over-clever. That day in Burano I really liked him: apart from a few small things, he really seemed sincere. He obviously fell for you, but then he's not the only one.' As one who treasured her independence, Iris spoke without envy. 'And then there was his home and that didn't fit. There's a kind of sleek and self-satisfied egoism about him. Is that what you mean?'

'No, though he did explain his home when he visited us once. There's genuine evil in him, I'm sure. Not just ordinary human ruthlessness but something sinister and inhuman. I'm afraid of him.'

'So you don't want to come?'

'Not really. Am I a coward, over-imaginative?'

'I'll be there. And Toni surely. And carabinieri don't usually go around murdering or molesting daughters-in-law of the Venetian aristocracy.'

'I suppose not. Though it would be something more subtle than murder. Perhaps I saw a Dracula film too early in life. I have the idea he knows I'm afraid of him and revels in it.

But Toni would enjoy being in the boat. Could we make it a shorter trip after three, when Rosa will have left for Venice? Perhaps just Murano where she's been already with her school.'

Giovanni had supplied Iris with his unlisted number and the arrangements were soon made. With tea and ice-cream out of the way, they went for a walk in the late afternoon sunshine towards San Nicolò and the northern end of the island, blocked off by a small airport and a military zone, pausing on the way back to gaze through the gate of a mysterious old Jewish cemetery. A huge orange sun suspended above the horizon confronted them on their return journey, dyeing the smooth lagoon surface with a broad band of gold. Company and sunshine had done much to relieve Tania's tag-end-of-winter depression and she found herself actually looking forward to the following day's outing.

Giovanni was already waiting when Tania and Toni arrived at the pick-up point punctual to the hour. He greeted them pleasantly and helped them aboard without trace of flirtation in his manner. Tania started reproaching herself for misinterpreting the normal conventions observed by a polite Italian guest. Here was only a sincere and kindly acquaintance, lonely probably, and forced to live in uncongenial surroundings, so delighted to be welcomed to the home of a friendly family.

Despite the cloudless sky, the air was chilly so that Tania installed herself in the cabin while Toni shared the captain's duties, even for short intervals taking over the wheel. Iris was waiting for them on the narrow path bordering the canal and they moved into and across the lagoon to pass through the gap separating Venice and La Certosa on the direct route for Murano.

Despite the sunshine, the Murano streets lacked somehow the charm of those of Burano and they spent most of the time in the Glass Museum and then in one of the glassworks, watching the heating and moulding processes. Giovanni had resumed his role of guide and instructor: informed, polite and helpful but slightly remote, almost as though this

96

were a first meeting. They paused for a coffee with an ice-cream for Toni and while Giovanni was ordering at the counter, Tania commented quietly to Iris,

'I suppose this is genuine and I've been misinterpreting him, but I can't seem to get rid of the habit. He seems so honest and genuine and my every instinct says he's not.'

'Machiavellian, do you think? Maybe Mrs Radcliffe, or *The Castle of Otranto* and those other eighteenth-century Gothic horrors? No, you won't know them: they're unlikely to have been translated into Finnish.'

Iris had a pupil coming at six so they deposited her outside her house at a quarter to and set out for Malamocco. It had suddenly become much colder and more humid and Giovanni sent a shivering Toni into the cabin and closed the door as the boat turned into the lagoon.

Toni looked sullen and dejected, probably, Tania thought, because of his dismissal as crew member, so she chatted to him pleasantly, trying to cheer him up and failed to notice her surroundings. She looked around her only as they were passing Malamocco village already beyond her home and went out to Giovanni to ask what was happening.

'I am sorry,' he said, 'I could not leave the wheel to tell you. I intended to take with me the photographs I made in your home but I forgot them in my home in Pellestrina. Now we can go quickly to get them. It will take only twenty minutes, I promise.'

Now that she was in the open air, Tania noticed a change in the atmosphere which immediately recalled a previous experience. The sun, which was now sinking on their right, was being obscured, though not by clouds, and they seemed to be approaching a wall of grey dampness. Giovanni was looking worried as he urged the boat ahead at maximum speed, his eyes moving intently ahead and from side to side as he examined his surroundings. They were almost at the point of Alberoni when, almost punctual with the earlier occasion, as if it were a daily occurrence, the fog swirled round them. He switched the forward light on without slowing down, guessing at Tania's uneasy surprise.

'I have seen no boat or obstruction for half a kilometre, perhaps more. Soon perhaps the fog disperses: that happens often. But here is the most dangerous part. There are enormous vessels, oil tankers and freight ships that come through the Porto di Malamocco between Lido and Pellestrina and there are motor-boats like this and passenger motonavi connecting the islands though I noticed one waiting at Alberoni so no need to worry about that.'

'The bigger boats have sirens, surely.'

'And what do we do when we hear the sirens, eh? Fly into the air,' was his scornful comment on that.

Toni had joined them and was clutching his mother's hand, terrified of a danger that he realized could not be controlled. For a time the fog drifted away as Giovanni had predicted. Pellestrina lay not far ahead and they could make out the mussel grounds offshore with multiple rows of corded stakes emerging from the water and a few fishermen's lodges scattered among them raised on stakes above the high tide level.

'You see our problem if the fog comes down again,' Giovanni explained. 'And to make things more difficult, it lacks three hours to the high tide so there are still mudbanks on or just below the surface where we can run aground. We must reach the deep channel along the shore quickly and remain in it.'

A fishing-boat was coming towards them, keeping to the same channel as they were following as they approached Pellestrina. Giovanni slowed down and moved the wheel to give the boat a wide enough berth and it was at the moment that they were at the farthest point from the direct course that the fog closed in again, clammy and suffocating. He punched the wheel with his fist, swearing quietly and savagely as he did so and bringing the boat almost to a standstill.

'Now we are off course,' he muttered. 'I can only hope that I have luck. Otherwise . . . Go back to the cabin now: you can do no good here. Can you swim?'

'Yes. Both of us.'

'Perhaps you will have to. I must try to find a place to

moor the boat. If only we can avoid the mussel beds. But go inside.'

Shivering and terrified, Toni had already returned to the cabin where he crouched on a seat, staring out of the fog-enveloped window. He ignored his mother when she came in, pushing her away as she tried to comfort him, as usual making her responsible for all disasters. Tania sometimes wondered what part in this Chiara might have played, with a well-placed 'That was your mother's fault' or 'I suppose your mother did nothing about it' as she drew from him accounts of imagined unfairness or indifference. Perhaps not: she had made little effort to see much of him recently. Tania herself felt curiously resigned about what might lie ahead: having mistrusted the excursion from the start, the unpleasantness seemed to be coming from a quite different direction from the one she had vaguely anticipated and a Finnish stoicism in face of the menace of natural forces induced a feeling of patient acceptance of dangers in store.

The boat appeared to be drifting on a rising tide moving inwards from the Adriatic with an occasional forward spurt whenever the fog thinned sufficiently for Giovanni to see a few metres ahead. She wondered whether he might be attempting to steer by the sound of the clanging fog-bells and comforted herself that he must surely have had previous experience of similar situations. From behind, a resonant bass siren warned of a ship moving up the strait they had now left, or were they so lost that they were still in it? The powerful depth of sound suggested a monster oil-tanker, apparently as lost and helpless as they were but in reality well aware of the exact position of itself and every other sizeable craft within range. The sound died away in the distance and in the now pitch darkness, only the bells continued to toll.

After what seemed eternity, there was a jerk as the boat bumped against something. Giovanni's head appeared through the cabin door to ask for a torch that was in one of the lockers. It was a large and powerful one, as Tania discovered as she handed it over and he switched it on. Giovanni moved back to clutch a post or stake of some kind and he swung the torch around to examine the structure above. Satisfied, he located the mooring-rope and made the boat fast to the sturdy object against which it was resting.

'We have found a fishermen's house,' he said. 'At least we are safe here. I go up to explore. Please hold the torch so I can see.'

As Tania directed the torch forward and above, she could glimpse a solid structure on a level with her head, supported on close-packed stakes embedded in the lagoon floor. Giovanni clambered up on to the structure, reached back for the torch and moved forward a little way. He gave a grunt of satisfaction.

'Is a *peocera*,' he informed her, 'a house they use when they collect the mussels. Nobody is here now but perhaps I can manage the lock on the door.' Aware of an ominously silent Toni in the cabin behind her, Tania waited impatiently, conscious of the fog invading nose and throat. Above, there were furtive sounds of scraped metal followed by the creaking of a door and receding steps on wood, the light of the torch now invisible.

A minute later Giovanni was back in the boat. 'Is good,' he reported. 'We can remain here. The house is in good condition and we can eat and sleep there.' There was an odd exultant air of confidence about him, due possibly to his relief but in some way disconcerting to Tania.

In her case relief had recalled responsibilities. 'We can't stay,' she insisted, though with little conviction. 'We've got to get back as soon as possible. What will Rosa do when she gets home and I'm not there?'

'You said this afternoon that her grandmother will bring her home. If you are not there she stays. Do you want that we risk our lives to return? I think this fog will not disperse tonight. First I control again what is in the house and then I help you and Toni to get up there. There is a terrace in front of it. Is not far now the tide is higher.'

She could do nothing but agree and as Giovanni climbed up again, she returned to the cabin to inform Toni, only to discover him crouched on the floor in the far corner moaning and shuddering.

'It's all right, Toni,' she comforted him, kneeling on the floor beside him where he kicked and pushed at her so fiercely that she moved away a little but remained sitting on the floor. 'We've found a fishermen's house where we can spend the night safe and warm out of the fog. We can have something to eat and we can sleep there. There's nothing to be afraid of now.'

The boy remained petrified, but when Tania attempted to take his hand he leapt to his feet, clutched his head and jumped convulsively up and down screaming, 'It's full of dead men. Round the table. With the other boy there. I won't go! I won't go!'

Giovanni had returned and moved towards him from behind her. 'Toni,' he said in a headmasterly voice, 'stop being a baby. You know well that that was only a story and not even very small children would believe it.' With a sudden switch to Venetian, he continued reproaches and persuasions, even trying to pick up the boy who clung limpet-firm to one of the seats. Tania intervened.

'You can't force him. You can see he's terrified, as well he might be after what we've been through. You go up and I'll stay with him.'

Giovanni hesitated an instant in silent calculation. 'Signora,' he said, the policeman uppermost in a moment of emergency, 'I make a suggestion. I must remain here with my boat. As soon as the fog will dissipate, I am ready to leave and I wake you up.' He addressed Toni briefly in Italian and the boy nodded in apparent relief. 'He indicates that he is willing to stay here with me and he wants that you sleep in the house. I help you now on to the terrace before the house and you find some food: I think there will be some tins and perhaps some biscuits in the cupboards. Have you matches? A cigarette-lighter?'

'No.'

'Neither I. And there is only gas for lighting and cooking: do not fall over the container just inside the door. Take my torch with you and find some tins and biscuits to pass to me. I think there will be bottles of beer and also of water for drinking. And of course something to open the tins. Are you afraid of rats?'

'I was brought up on a farm.'

'Good. I don't think there are rats and they would not hurt you. I saw some blankets in another cupboard. Please let us have two of them.'

The boat was now riding higher in the water and with help from Giovanni, she was able to scramble on to the terrace, where he handed the torch up to her. It was a small area where the men would work stripping the ropes of the molluscs who had made their homes there, and just in front of her an open door gave access to a wooden house, sheltered by a low pointed roof. Moving the torch from left to right, she crossed the terrace and entered the house, carefully avoiding the heavy gas bombola left just beyond the threshold. Unidentifiable objects probably connected with fishing and the men's activities occupied corners: there was a cooking stove, shelves and cupboards and two constructions for bunk beds. With some slight misgivings about the duration of the torch battery, she explored cupboards and discovered, as Giovanni had predicted, a few tins of meat and tuna, bottled beer and also water, a couple of packets of hard biscuits and a box of processed cheese. Various packets of spaghetti and other pasta would be of no use in present circumstances but she thought that a bottle of grappa might be appreciated. Hardly a banquet, but sustenance enough for a starving man and boy. Rough blankets were piled in a cupboard and she pulled out three of them, including one for her own use. Giovanni received these contributions, which included a tin-opener, with little comment, though he refused the grappa. He trusted she would sleep well.

She had expected to find isolation in this fog-shrouded, water-borne box an eerie experience, but oddly she felt at peace here as in a quiet safe refuge in the midst of a storm and it was to enhance this feeling of complete security that she dragged the gas bombola against the door, unlikely though it was that intrusion would occur. Even her anxiety about Rosa—whom even Chiara would surely not abandon

—and the inevitable stormy reception she must expect from her mother-in-law, seemed superfluous. She had too little appetite to bother about opening tins and champing on biscuits. Shivering in the chill dampness, she stretched out on the lumpy mattress that covered a lower bunk and drew the blanket round herself, not over-clean but this didn't seem to matter, and was soon snugly warm in a rather scratchy cocoon. Convinced that she would be unable to sleep, she reflected dreamily on her own inert attitude towards Chiara's bullying. Just to keep the peace on Stefano's account. Stefano must break free. A vague reflection on how Toni might be coping dissolved in deep, untroubled sleep.

She woke up suddenly, alarmed by a loud thumping on the door. A pale light seeped through the window and she lay still for a few seconds, trying to orient herself. Suddenly aware, she scrambled up, moved the gas cylinder slightly and opened the door. Giovanni was silhouetted against a sky silvered by a waning moon and the first frail touch of dawn, while she was aware of waves splashing against the supports of the *peocera*.

'It is five o'clock,' Giovanni told her, 'and now the wind blows and there is no more fog. We depart at once.'

'A moment,' Tania requested. She went back into the room to fold and replace the blanket while Giovanni followed her in with the two he had borrowed. Empty tins and bottles would be floating in the lagoon, she suspected.

'Can't we leave a message and payment for the fishermen?' she suggested. 'They'll be wondering who's been here.'

'It's OK,' she was assured. 'I know the fishermen from here and I will explain and pay. We are not the first who have used this place without asking permission.'

The boat deck was deserted as Giovanni helped her down to a lower level than she had climbed up from and she found Toni still asleep in a chilly cabin. He half-awakened as Giovanni started the engine but was soon again deep in dreams, though he stirred restlessly and murmured angrily in his sleep. Tania's mood of serene determination was fast evaporating as she looked out over the paling sky and the restless water. She had the strange impression of having abandoned a comfortless refuge of courage and serenity for bleak incarceration in her own well-tended home in the company of those she loved. And the image of a contemptuous and ruthless Chiara was blending oddly in her mind with an identical one of a devious and ruthless Giovanni, though the latter had surely been dispelled by his behaviour on this calamitous excursion.

The landing-stage and access road at Alberoni were deserted in what was still gleaming moonlight rather than pallid early morning. She roused Toni as they passed Malamocco village but he was still half-asleep when Giovanni helped him off the boat. The policeman looked tired and sombre as they disembarked, casting off immediately as they walked towards the flat, in a window of which a light was ominously burning.

Having opened the main door, Tania climbed the two flights of stairs to her flat, with Toni, now fully awake but aggressively silent, plodding behind her. She opened the flat door and crossed the hall into the sitting-room, where mother-in-law and husband watched her entrance in stony silence.

On her return journey she had visualized and tried to plan her explanations but whatever ideas she had formulated were instantly upset by her startled reaction to her husband's presence. 'You are back then already?' she burst out in astonishment.

In the circumstances it was the stupidest remark she could have made, providing Chiara with ammunition for a perfect opening salvo. 'I am not surprised you 'ave a shock to see 'im 'ere,' she gloated. 'You 'ave thought you 'ave an extra night to abandon your children and now you find your abominable be'aviour is uncovered.'

Chiara apparently misinterpreted Tania's expression of bewilderment as she pursued the attack, blatantly elaborating on the themes of adultery and child neglect and concluding: 'And I ask myself sincerely: is this only the last of many such occasions?'

Stefano, who had been sitting motionless and silent, observing his wife with fixed intensity, cast at this point a doubtful glance at his mother.

'I intend to say, when your 'usband is working for you at the theatre and your children are in their beds, what lovers do you welcome in your own 'ome or even go to call upon?'

A wave of fury launched Tania into passionate speech. 'That is the most appalling accusation I've ever heard,' she almost shouted. 'It is utterly libellous and both you and Stefano know it.' She turned to her husband to ask: 'Well, Stefano, is that what you believe?'

Bleakly he confined himself to the immediate question: 'Where have you been all night?'

'Quite alone in a fishermen's *peocera* on the lagoon, and in a thick fog, if you want to know. Hardly a love-nest or a resort of assignation.'

Stefano frowned, awaiting further explanation. Chiara limited herself to a hissed 'Absurd. And my grandson?'

Furiously Tania set about relating her story, using the details of her experience as sharply-pointed missiles directed at Chiara rather than as components of the facts she was presenting. From an account of Giovanni's suggestion to Iris about the excursion, the visit to Murano and Giovanni's decision to fetch the photographs, she proceeded to describe their wanderings in the fog and eventual refuge for the night. As she spoke, her eyes rested on her husband's face. There was a brief silence at the end before she added: 'Ask Toni if you don't believe me.'

Toni had crept across to his grandmother during his mother's explanation and now was on her lap, nestling against her with his arms round her neck and his head looking back over her shoulder. Stefano walked across to his mother, standing behind her and looking into his son's face as he said quietly, 'Well, Toni? Did you understand what Mummy was saying?'

Loosening his arms, Toni slipped off Chiara's lap and walked across the room to stand with his back to the sideboard in the position of a child called upon to entertain visitors to his home with the recitation of a poem.

'She is telling lies,' he declared, looking straight at Chiara. Tania stared at him aghast, unable to speak.

'Go on, Toni,' his father ordered quietly. 'Tell us what happened.'

Toni embarked on his recitation, his eyes riveted on his grandmother. 'The part with Iris was true,' he began. 'When we left Iris, Giovanni took us straight to his house on Pellestrina and Mummy knew we were going there. It was a little foggy when we got out of the boat but Giovanni said it wouldn't be much and we could be home before Rosa was back. When we were inside, he and Mummy had some wine to drink and he gave me some Coca-Cola. Then he said he wanted to show Mummy something upstairs and I watched a nice film. After some time Giovanni came back and said it was too foggy to go home. Mummy came down and we had a nice supper she cooked for us while Giovanni told me stories about his job. But when I asked what about Rosa, Mummy was very cross. She said it was nothing to do with me and she slapped my face and it hurt. Then she put a cushion and a blanket on the sofa and made me lie down and told me to go to sleep, and they went upstairs again.

'Giovanni woke me up this morning very early and said we could go home now because there wasn't any more fog. He said that Mummy would say we'd been lost in the fog so that Daddy wouldn't be cross and I was to agree with her. But I won't, dear Granny Chiara, because it's wicked to tell lies, isn't it? Please dear Granny Chiara, take me home with you. Mummy is so nasty to me when Daddy isn't here. She beats me and sometimes she gives me only porridge for my dinner and shouts at me when I don't want to eat it. She loves Rosa but she hates me. She's said she'll drown me in the lagoon if I tell Daddy about . . . some of the things I hear in the evening. Please, Granny Chiara, take me away. I'm so afraid.' He broke into sobs and rushed back into Chiara's embrace.

Two pairs of eyes were turned on Tania, who stared only at her husband. 'Do you believe that?' she asked.

'What reason could he have for lying?' The skin round Stefano's eyes seemed to have tautened and Tania glimpsed

106

him momentarily as he would look in old age.

'That is what I would like to know.' Tania spoke slowly, her barely-controlled rage separating word from word. She turned to face Chiara to ask with the same clipped precision: 'What part are you playing in this comedy, I wonder.'

Chiara said nothing, merely moving her eyes to regard her son as if instructing him to pursue the interrogation.

'Are you trying to make us believe that a child of Toni's age would be able to make all that up?' he asked.

'Someone made it up, clearly. There isn't a word of truth in it.'

Again Stefano moved over to Toni. 'Stand up,' he ordered the boy. Toni waited for his grandmother's unspoken permission before rising to face his father. 'Now look me straight in the eyes,' Stefano continued. 'If I find you are lying, I shall never speak to you again. Do you understand me?'

Toni nodded.

'Were you telling the truth just then? Nothing will happen to you if you admit you weren't.'

Toni's eyes looked into his father's. 'It was all true, Daddy. Every word was true.'

'Enough,' Chiara broke in, getting up from her chair. 'We cannot continue to 'arass the child. One thing is sure: 'e cannot remain with such a devil and she is no fit wife for you, Stefano. 'E will come 'ome with me immediately and I will ask the magistrate for . . . I forget, I was told this . . . yes, custody, legal custody of the child as 'is mother is not fit. Do you come with me, Stefano?'

Stefano hesitated, with his eyes on Tania. With a red-hot fury she had never realized she possessed, like a spark-ignited fire consuming a drought-stricken forest of her own country, she turned on him.

'Get out! Get out!' she heard herself saying, her voice still low, as if screaming would have detracted from her intensity of rage. 'You believe that little liar, as you've known him to be all his life rather than me who has never once lied to you. It was you who reproached me for distrusting Signor Carabiniere Giovanni Fedele—Fedele, Mr Faithful— comic, isn't it. But why, why should he have done this?

What's he getting out of it? As for you, my dear devoted husband, get out and never, never in your whole life come back again.'

Aware of a lingering hesitation in her son, Chiara acted swiftly. She handed Stefano his coat and pushed him out of the door as she would have done when he was Toni's age. After a lingering glance of triumph in Tania's direction, she picked up her own coat in passing without stopping to put it on, probably for the first time in her life. With the coat over one arm, she clutched Toni's hand and swept through the door, closing it firmly behind her.

Reaction overcame Tania immediately they had disappeared and she sank back into her chair, her head swimming but with an almost agreeable sense of battle engaged coursing through her. A moment later she was sitting upright again, the light of combat in her eyes. Stubborn, they called the Finns, did they? She'd show them what stubbornness was. And with the realism of generations of farmers and foresters, she got up and went straight into the kitchen. You can't fight hungry, she said to herself: I've had nothing since lunch-time yesterday: that's why my head's swimming. In the middle of cutting a thick slice of bread, she remembered for the first time her other child. Where was Rosa? With breadknife still in her hand, she peeped round the door of the children's room. There were two sleepers breathing deeply and placidly on the lower bunk: a little girl with light-brown hair and a kitten with marmalade-gold fur. With a sign of thankfulness Tania buttered the bread, added some cheese and bit into it while she started to prepare strong coffee.

She ate slowly and hungrily, planning first what she would tell Rosa so as not to upset her more than necessary. With that decided, she turned her mind to the other matter. However powerful her supporting battalions of ancestors, authorities, celestial or otherwise, people of wealth and influence, Chiara was going to restore her son. Alone and without allies of any kind or even friends, what could she, Tania Laurila of distant Finland, do? She had one friend, as powerless but as practical and determined as herself: Iris

Lawton. And she had a brother, the most brilliant detective in his country.

She abandoned her coffee to put through a long-distance call. Arvo had not left home yet and it was he who answered. As concisely as she could and with the benefit of her native tongue she outlined what had happened. In conformity with police detective training and long practice, Arvo gave the matter rapid and precise consideration.

'I can't do anything for several days,' he said. 'There's an important murder trial going on just now and I'm the main police witness. It won't matter a lot, though. Things can be left for a short time to sort themselves out so that we know where we are better. I'll be with you in a few days: I'll let you know exactly when later. You might be better off spending a few days with Iris, just in case the matter gets into the papers and you're pestered with journalists. Keep your chin up: they won't get away with it. But what the hell's got into Stefano? He must be crazy.'

Arvo had given sound advice about leaving the flat for a time, though she wasn't anxious to bother Iris. However, Rosa must on no account be questioned by inquisitive reporters: she wouldn't put it past them to pester a child. Iris should be up by now and she dialled her number.

An hour later a woman with a nine-year-old girl, two suitcases and a much-protesting ginger cat in a basket were fitting themselves into a car which was then driven by another woman in the direction of San Nicolò.

CHAPTER 8

STORMY SEAS

The first of May, day of rest and celebration for the workers and for a planned musical bicycle parade on the Lido, reverted to the miseries of the bleak earlier weeks of spring. Thunderstorms and torrential rain devastated Northern Italy, howling winds tearing at the few timid leaves that had dared to appear on the lime trees that should by now have been shading the sunken canal outside Iris's home. In fact the view from her front windows suggested that the canal had taken over the whole roadway, drowning the snails that spent the winter camping on the underseal of her car, while a steady downpour sluiced away a pattern of cat pawprints decorating the roof. She would clearly have to wait another year to discover the nature of a musical bicycle.

The delegates attending the Congress of Travel Writers and Publishers who were arriving in water-taxis at their hotel clad in the lightweight coats, suits and dresses appropriate to an Italian spring, looked bewildered, forlorn and decidedly chilly. Their hotel rooms had every facility for their comfort except heating, which had been forbidden by order of the city government in all multi-occupied buildings for the past few days. Complaints poured in from all and sundry, above all the new arrivals from tropical areas, until representations to the appropriate authorities could be made (a slow business on a public holiday) and a special reprieve granted. As physical conditions warmed, tempers cooled perceptibly.

The delegates were a motley crowd. Ages ranged from the mid-twenties to the occasional slightly decrepit but still active eighty-year-old, though the mainstream seemed to be enjoying a prosperous middle age. The majority were of European origin, with earnest Germans, intense French, jovial or withdrawn Scandinavians, blasé British predominating, but there was also a sprinkling of North Americans and Australians, several Japanese, Indians and Pakistanis, an expatriate Pole, a Nigerian and two Egyptian archæologists. No Italians were yet among them but those who might be coming had probably delayed their journeys till later in the day or, having already savoured the beauties of their national showpiece, looked further afield for their professional jaunts.

A welcome party, with cocktails, was arranged for that evening when most of the delegates had settled in. They were directed to a large lounge which was surrounded by tables bearing books and publishers' catalogues in many languages, charts, illustrations and other forms of publicity material. The walls were half covered by pictures, photographs, maps and book-lists beside posters of Venice and the lagoon. Each delegate was checked in on a list and handed a Congress programme in which the flowery Italian account of past achievement and future intentions, together with a detailed rota of events, was considerably more intelligible than were its translations (English, French and German) to speakers of those languages. Essentially it was a summarized and mere functional version of the brochure. In addition identity discs were distributed, blue-rimmed for the publishing fraternity and red-rimmed for the authors, with individual names already inscribed.

It soon became clear that authors were decidedly in the majority: only about half of these, however, had wished or been able to list on their application forms their already-published works though almost all the others had referred to 'work in progress'. The seventy or so directors of publishing houses, some of them accompanied by severe-looking young women editors, seemed to find protection in their own kind when they were not engaged in examining books and catalogues on display or making themselves acquainted with those authors whose features they recognized from photographs on book-jackets or reviews.

The reception was honoured by an assistant deputy Minister of Culture from Rome, several regional notabilities and members of the Venice City Council and various local literary celebrities, novelists and poets rather than travel writers. Angelo himself, red rose and blue violet nosegay in his buttonhole, was much in evidence, accompanied by Chiara in black and pearls and with a tiny silver tiara in her hair, exuding all the patronage and condescension that was to be expected from a descendant of doges. Reporters and photographers, who had been carefully primed as to their targets, dodged expertly round the rotundities of directors, avoiding cigars brandished in expostulation and with less difficulty steered past the tauter and more muscular frames of sun-tanned and bearded writers.

By this time most of the delegates had arrived, and they

111

now included handsome gentlemen in turbans or fezes, many of them with luxuriant moustaches and flashing dark eyes, three ladies in saris of varying shades of green, a heavily-veiled lady accompanying a dark gentleman in immaculate evening dress, and a considerable number of more formidable females, mostly middle-aged, accompanied in some cases by scholarly, bluff or self-effacing gentlemen, presumably their husbands. There was an air of disappointment about some of the solitary publishers as they cast their eyes around for the exotic, alluring or merely prepossessing among the ladies present, the few examples there were clearly having other commitments.

In the early stages of the reception there had been a considerable intermingling—so far as this was practicable in the crush—but gradually a coagulation process got under way, adherence to groups largely determined by professional and linguistic considerations, with in the latter case two choices available: English for those limited to their native tongue, together with others who had been forced to acquire it, and French, claimed by its speakers (almost exclusively natives of France) as the only tongue fit for civilized conversation. Angelo moved from one delegate to another, jovial and affable to all, but pausing for a few more significant words with certain of them identified from their name discs.

At one point in the evening, catching sight of a newcomer, he apologized and broke away from his companions to hurry across the room to greet him, turning to those in his neighbourhood to announce the arrival of his son, one of the leading publishers in the USA. The introduction was hardly necessary, as apart from being younger, very slightly smaller and considerably less dynamic, the son would never have to contest any dispute over parentage. Chiara swept forward and embraced him dramatically, though a close observer might have remarked a slight coolness in her reception. Angelo also glanced back at him once or twice with some misgiving before moving off again in benevolent confraternity.

Most of the delegates retired reasonably early, having travelled far that day and happy to postpone the hazards and delights of a visit to the Casino to another evening. During the night the storms died down though it remained chilly, a disappointment to all but the hardiest (those accustomed to immersion in frozen seas and mountain torrents) who had resolved on an early-morning swim in the grey Mediterranean.

The first session of the day got under way punctually at nine-thirty and the assembled delegates paid alert attention (by means of simultaneous translation into French, German and Italian) to an informative lecture from a business-like Japanese director of Far Eastern tourism who spoke perfect American English. He made intelligent use of an extensive illustrated map of the Far East which included his own country, Hong Kong, Taiwan and a large chunk of the Republic of China, indicating and describing features of unusual interest to the discriminating travel writer, showed slides and short films and distributed brochures and lists (with translations into five languages) of names and addresses of helpful organizations. In conclusion he dealt with a few well-conceived questions.

Not all the speakers who followed were equally effective: one rambled, another pontificated, a third mumbled almost unintelligibly and several made good use of an ideal opportunity for political or economic propaganda. Pietro Vescovo's lecture, on North and Central America, consisted almost entirely of linking passages between glossy film products of the tourist industry. During the afternoon, lectures gave place to group discussion and question sessions, each group chaired with varying levels of competence by professed experts and attended by delegates with interests in specific areas. Between sessions bars were naturally well patronized and it became increasingly apparent that many of the writers were finding they had common interests. Groups muttering vociferously occupied corners of the lounges and areas of the bars and dark looks were occasionally cast in the direction of any publishing directors in the vicinity. There were of course the exceptions: writers who seemed to find publishers, especially those of their own nationality, quite irresistible and the latter were sometimes

113

in the rare and favourable position of having to refuse a superfluity of brandies, whiskies and expensive liqueurs that had been offered in return for earnest conversation.

Angelo radiated patronage, benevolence, unction and self-satisfaction: slapping back or shoulder, gazing intensely into the eyes of the most formidable of ladies, even occasionally kissing a hand respectfully. Now and again he would summon the attention of one, possibly a pair or trio of directors, by a gesture of hand or eyes and they would retire to a corner or to another room for a quickly-spoken discussion which he himself dominated. Occasionally a certain Sandro Greco, one of Angelo's assistants, would make notes on these discussions, memorizing the appearance of those present as if for future reference.

The final morning was to be occupied by delegates' questions in full assembly while the afternoon would be taken up by a variety of excursions: to Venice, Murano and Torcello or Brenta villas. Angelo himself was to chair the morning session, flanked on each side by the various speakers who had already addressed the audience.

The questions during the first half of this session were innocuous enough, most of them based on the many printed information sheets that had been issued, and they were soon disposed of. After an hour or so there was a break for coffee though a considerable number of writers took their coffee and brioches with them to congregate out on the terrace which separated hotel and beach. Earnest conversation was soon under way, giving the impression of an army campaign discussed not only by the officers but also by a fair part of the force to be involved and indeed there was something of a gleam of battle in several eyes as they returned to the now familiar arena.

Proceedings were embarked upon by a distinguished and lion-like Swede, in near-perfect English.

'Perhaps I may put a question which, while not directly related to our programme, is of sufficient interest to many of us to warrant general attention,' he boomed. Without pausing for possible interdiction, he continued, 'Most of us in our time have had or probably should have had recourse

114

to legal advice. We now have here an ideal opportunity to seek the advice of our highly-qualified publishing colleagues, not only about seeming infringements of contract but also about the perhaps insensitive—though some might even term it blatant—disregard of the opinions of those of us who, if I may so phrase it, provide the grist without which the printing mills would have no cause to function.'

Somewhat at sea, Angelo inquired from the chair: 'Perhaps you could explain a little more precisely and—er—plainly your meaning, Mr—I excuse myself . . .' He turned to Camillo, who, after a hasty glance at a list, instructed him, 'Herr Lindblom.'

Herr Lindblom's main concern appeared to be delay in the annual payment of his royalties, up to three months on occasion, and this from a Swedish publisher indeed. And for a man who lived by his writing . . . Several scattered voices referred to four, five, six and a half, even eight months' delay—one unfortunate lady had had nothing for the past year in spite of repeated protests. Other iniquities in re-imbursement were quoted from all sides until a courteous request for order was momentarily obeyed.

Herr Lindblom resumed his seat expectantly but any attempt at an answer was effectively foiled by an alternative to his own question from an Indian writer.

'I ask why,' he demanded in incisive but melodious English, 'I and others, I am sure, must wait three year and more and even then no book appears, only galleys, appalling, illegible galleys getting all the time more appalling.'

Without bothering to raise himself and thus contest his colleague's right to speak, a bearded Australian in the front row of the balcony let out a derisive snort, following that up with a booming, 'You don't know how lucky you are, brother. It was my whole manuscript they lost, two whole copies of it. A bit tatty they were, perhaps—they'd been around quite a bit. Maybe the office cleaner mistook them for scrap. They, the firm that is, offered me 500 dollars—Australian—in compensation. I told them what they could do with it. They went bust three months later. Sorry, brother. Hope I didn't put you off.'

115

But having had his say, the Indian had sat down and at the Australian's apology, two would-be questioners rose simultaneously, an elderly German of scholarly appearance giving place reluctantly to a powerful Danish lady, who demanded in ringing Germanic tones:

'And covers. Who designs the covers? I find that my book *Fact and Fantasy among the Eskimos* is given a cover picture of a Trans-Siberian train emerging from a tunnel. It is perhaps too much to expect the illustrator to open the book, but he might at least read the words of the title.'

'You were lucky,' an unidentified nasal voice intoned from near the back. 'They bound my book wrongly: wrong title, wrong name, wrong picture: the lot. Booksellers found that out on delivery.'

The elderly scholar had claimed his turn, lamenting in thin piping German, 'It's all those printer's errors. I correct them in galleys, hours and hours I correct them and new ones, far worse, multiply in page proofs. I no longer dare to open one of my own books when I find it in a shop.'

A dispassionate observer might at this stage have begun to harbour some possibly unworthy suspicions. Writers, even those hardened by the rigours of crossing Tibetan passes, sledging before wolves over Siberian steppes or evading cannibals on remote tropical islands, are a temperamental lot: one would have expected passionate harangues, sharp exchanges and in general the unco-ordinated dissonance of a large orchestra attempting to render an ultramodern musical score. Despite its briskness this opening was all too carefully controlled, organized, programmed even. Each speaker made his (or her) point, acridly indeed, but concisely and without hesitation. Though there were one or two momentary clashes, all but one of those who had risen to speak subsided at once, uneasily, as if enthusiasm had overtaken instruction. Indeed there was a strong suggestion of policemen or soldiers each making a personal report in conformity with established regulations.

A comfortable-looking Swiss lady, with the appearance of a mother of six, scorned her native German to declare solemnly in English: 'The printers' errors, yes: they are bad and like weeds, impossible to destroy: eradicate a hundred in the first proofs and still two hundred appear in the second. And it is we—us who are blamed for doing them: by editors, readers, critics. But the corrections of our grammar! No, not English grammar: mine is terrible as you hear. But in German. I who write in German since I am graduate in German at university and who create novels, criticism, studies of anthropology—I, with years of experience, must have my grammar corrected and remade by schoolgirls who have written not at all and who do not ask me and do not change when I complain. And I can do nothing!' In helpless resignation the lady gave place to the next witness.

A tall lean Englishman with the voice of a colonel straight in from the parade-ground reported in his own tongue, 'It's the facts they fool about with, out of crass idiocy or deliberate perversion. White's tarred and black's whitewashed. The terrorist planting the bomb's the new plaster saint and the police or the army that get shot at arresting him before it goes off are the Fascist thugs. Commentators, journalists, historians: they're all the same. Cranks or perverts, the lot of them.' The Englishman jack-knifed smartly back on to his chair.

He was followed immediately by a passionate gentleman with a truly magnificent beard but no easily identifiable nationality who sprang up as if a poisonous snake had been inserted beneath him, yelling, 'I write the truth, the whole truth and nothing but the truth about my country, and none of them, not one of them—' his arm swept from left to right in the direction of the serried publishers—'dares to put it in a book for the world to read.'

The woman at his side tugged at his sleeve and he sat down abruptly, to be followed by a long sequence of the wronged and aggrieved. By this point in the proceedings, the system, whether programmed or not, was rapidly disintegrating, as, moved by smouldering passions and resentments, the oppressed seized the only chance they were ever likely to get of revealing their sufferings to the world. Feverishly they leapt up, often three or more at a time, gesticulating, bellowing or screaming in chorus in an at-

117

tempt to achieve audibility, subsiding in triumph or frustration. And while the publishing fraternity had started by surveying the early childish criticisms of their benevolent despotism with amused condescension, there was more than a suggestion of irritation, even alarm, as the temperature rose rapidly.

Together with his flanking team of experts and guides, Angelo had been watching with delighted interest, a Nero engrossed in a mass gladiatorial combat in the Colosseum. But as the opposing forces shouted their way into outright battle, he realized that his publishing colleagues, rivals though they might be, were in a decided minority, and lacking both the stamina and pent-up frustrations of their opponents, were liable to emerge from the fray with at least cuts, bruises and broken spectacles; they might even—horror of horrors—need the attention of an outside medical specialist. All this would probably serve them right but what really mattered was that, innocent as he was, it was he who would have to face the music eventually. He stood up, roared unavailingly, thumped the table, even seemed to be considering mounting it before he wisely reconsidered. As a desperate last resort his hand plunged into a pocket, fumbled and brought out a gun. He brandished it uncertainly and wildly, to the intense alarm of those near him, one of whom was seen to disappear under the table, and then as his gesture passed unnoticed in the body of the hall, where shouting was already being succeeded by encounter, he fired it upward, the bullet smashing a small light bulb and ricocheting to some place unknown.

The explosion was a formidable one and an instant silence ensued, bodies and limbs frozen for a whole second in aggressive postures (time enough for at least a couple of flashbulbs to record them for posterity), before arms were lowered and all heads turned towards him. Two more frozen seconds went by.

'And now kindly sit down.' Angelo's voice was only just above the level of audibility. And after a frantic scurry to places, everybody did so.

And it was then that somebody noticed that besides the

Press, a television camera had been positioned to overlook the edge of the balcony and its operator was still at work. There was a horrified 'Wow, fellows, they've been filming,' and every head turned in startled confirmation.

Still holding the gun, Angelo directed his attention to the unfortunate cameraman, who appeared to be considering instant flight. 'I should like to see that film as soon as it is ready,' the latter was informed in Italian, 'and before it is used. You understand?'

The young man understood perfectly and hastily withdrew his equipment. The delegates, now turned towards the front, sat with lowered heads.

Angelo laid the gun carefully on the table, in the midst of brochures and other papers. He appeared slightly ashamed of his behaviour, a kindly, fatherly man who had been forced into extreme measures by an impossibly unruly family. His eyes moved compassionately over his audience as he admonished them gravely.

'Signori, signore: for we are now in Italy and I must speak to you in my own tongue, which will be translated for your benefit. We have met here together as students, as learners and at the same time as instructors and teachers, to hear more about the world we record and describe, as instruction for those who have not our opportunities and good fortune.

'Whether as writers we gather and assemble information or whether as publishers we make it available to readers, we are allies in a common cause and as allies we must surely work in harmony together.

'But harmony in human communities is rarely if ever achieved by equality whereby each single contentious voice can disturb harmonious relationships with its fretful cries. I have listened sympathetically to the complaints of the writers among you. As you all know, I am myself a publisher and I acknowledge the truth and justice of all your words. I am full of regret and compassion for you as are all my colleagues here. But you know well, as I know well, you are helpless in this matter. And why, my dear writing friends? Because you lack power, unity, resources. You are the sellers: of talent, of ideas, of dedicated industry, the beggars

119

at our overloaded tables. We are the buyers, the selectors, the invulnerable, whom you may tempt but never harm, while we can wreck with impunity you, your careers and above all your precious creations.

'Have you considered how vulnerable you are? The law, your contracts, your public protect you, do they? How? What sanctions can they impose?

'So your contract guarantees publication within one year, two years maybe. And after two and a half years you are still waiting? So you go to a lawyer and naturally, for reasons of his own, he advises you have grounds to claim compensation; he suggests taking the matter to court. You pay out a very great deal of money and wait a very long time. And your publisher makes excuses, heart-rending excuses and you continue to wait. You correct mistakes, and other mistakes appear: covers lie, your words and ideas are distorted and you have only one resort: to prove conclusively that your reputation has been destroyed and to claim some trifle of money to make up for it. Bah! Such a comfort to the dedicated writer whom the critics have mocked.

'So you give up writing? Others will crowd to take your place. So the impossible is achieved: a trade union of all writers organizes a strike: not another book is produced. And we publishers rejoice. Now the public will have to be satisfied with reprints of the bestsellers of the past, often considerably more entertaining than the mediocrities of today, and of sufficient age to involve no copyright or other outgoings. Writers of the world unite: you have nothing to lose but your royalties!

'But you do receive your royalties eventually, don't you, however long they may occasionally be delayed. Otherwise you would not be staying in this palatial hotel and taking part, a very active part it seems, in this conference. And also, I trust, taking part in one of the numerous excursions you will see have been organized for this afternoon and in tonight's magnificent banquet with the splendid firework display over the sea to follow it.

'And to soothe any hurts and ruffled feelings, I shall arrange for a very special cocktail, one I have myself named

"Serenissima", to be served forthwith before we go to lunch. Thank you, ladies and gentlemen, for your most enthusiastic cooperation.'

Angelo sat down and began to shuffle through his papers but was interrupted by a line of publishers queueing to shake his hand. The other delegates were beginning to disperse amid heated arguments and it was in the midst of the general noise and disruption that Angelo became aware of a presence at his shoulder, only too familiar to him in that position.

'Can't you see I'm engaged? What is it?' he muttered in Italian.

Camillo stuttered slightly in his agitation. 'It is the signora, your wife. She is waiting in your office. She says she must speak with you at once. It is very urgent.'

Angelo hesitated, checked his watch, smiled warmly and gripped another hand thrust towards him and instructed Camillo, 'Tell her I'll be along as soon as I've finished here.'

'The signora says if you do not come immediately, she will herself come here. And there is your son who is waiting for you in the hotel reception. He also seems very agitated.'

Agitato—the word that describes a stormy sea. The jostling of departing bodies, the rise and fall of still indignant voices, the boom of publishers continuing to express appreciation and the waving of their hands: enough to make anyone seasick. Angelo took a grip on himself.

'He can't be in reception: he's here. And he looks anything but agitated.' Indeed it was the greenish pallor and an obvious queasiness rather than nervous excitement that were most apparent when Angelo glanced sideways to where his son still sat immobile, hardly aware of his surroundings.

'No, signore. Your other son. Signor Stefano.'

'Oh, him. Tell him he can wait.'

'He said it was very urgent.'

'Everything's urgent today. Get rid of these people for me.'

A job in which Camillo had considerable experience. Angelo consulted his watch, showed amazement, scattered apologies, escaped.

Chiara was sitting rigidly upright on a hard chair in his office, clutching a lace-edged handkerchief. Eyes red and puffy, she had been genuinely weeping, a rare experience for her.

'The boy's gone,' she burst out. 'He's disappeared.'

Angelo sat down heavily under the burden of life's niggling demands. 'What boy?' he asked.

'My grandson, of course. What other boy is there?'

'Where's he gone to?'

Exasperation was now competing with Chiara's grief. 'That's what you've got to find out. I told Beata I would be having lunch here today and left her to look after him. She telephoned some five minutes ago to say he'd disappeared: she'd searched the palazzo but there was no trace of him.'

'She'd been alone with him in the palazzo?'

'Stefano was with him so she'd slipped out to buy some milk: or that's what she says. When she came back, neither of them was there.'

'Then they must have gone out for a walk together.'

'I don't think so. He'd have changed Toni's shoes first. He'd never have taken him out in his house slippers.'

Angelo remembered something. 'Well, Stefano's here now. We can ask him.' But surely Camillo would have told him if Toni had been in the hotel too.

He touched a button on his desk, waited ten seconds and then opened the door. Sandro was outside.

'What are you doing there?' Angelo demanded. 'Where's Camillo?'

'I think he is having lunch, signore. I have a message for you from your son Stefano.'

'That's all right, Sandro.' Stefano was approaching along the corridor. 'I've got to speak to you urgently,' he said to Angelo.

'About your son, I suppose. What have you done with him? His grandmother's out of her mind about him.'

By now Stefano was in the room, regarding Chiara with a face of stone. 'Where is he?' he bit out.

Chiara rose to her feet in alarm. 'With you, surely. He's not in the palazzo.'

'He's not with me. I left him half an hour ago in the playroom. He promised to wait till I came back.'

Missing completely the implication of his words, Chiara turned to her husband with a wail of despair. 'You must get in touch with the police. Immediately,' she ordered. 'He's been kidnapped: by terrorists, by the Mafia. That woman . . . Phone them at once or I will.'

'Just a moment. We're not phoning anybody. This isn't the time for publicity. It won't be the Mafia: that's out. Terrorists? Perhaps, but I doubt it. It's not their usual method and so far as I've been informed there aren't any in Venice now.'

'It's her then, that foreign bitch.'

'If you mean my wife,' Stefano interposed, 'she couldn't have got into the house. Beata wouldn't have opened the door and I didn't.'

'You still stand up for her after all she's done to you.' Chiara reached for the telephone receiver, lifted it and asked, 'What's the telephone number of the Venice carabinieri? They'll have to arrest her and bring him back.'

Deliberately, Angelo took the receiver away from her. There was a frantic struggle but he held it firmly in place. 'Sit down,' he commanded, and when she ignored him, pushed her back forcefully into the chair where she crouched gasping and repeating viciously, 'Murderer. Murderer. Mafia murderer. She's your mistress too, isn't she? You arranged it for her, didn't you?'

Angelo eyed her in silent contempt. 'We can be sure of another matter,' he said coldly. 'That child is going back to his mother if and when he decides to reappear again. I'm not taking responsibility for him in any circumstances. Do you realize, woman, the scandal and publicity that will be involved? I forbid you to try to gain custody and I would controvert personally any such application.'

Stefano had watched the performance with loathing. She had stopped gasping and muttering to listen and now she turned desperately to her one trusted support.

'Stefano,' she pleaded. 'Stefano, my darling little Stefano, help your unhappy mother.'

123

He regarded her with an ice-cold rigidity of mouth and eyes. 'You're my mother, all right, an evil witch who's done everything possible to wreck my life.'

Enormous disbelieving eyes examined Stefano's face. 'What are you saying to me, Stefano? What lies have you heard?' But the eyes expressed too a horrified realization.

'What lies have I heard?' he echoed. 'What lies have you told me? Much worse, infinitely worse, unforgivable: what lies have you taught my son to tell me?'

Accusation, indignation, reproach: all stifled, frozen with mute horror. Stefano waited in silence while there was a slight air of impatience about Angelo, as if he had known, or at least suspected, already what was about to emerge. Unable to bear the menacing silence any longer, Chiara croaked feebly: 'What are you talking about?'

It was the question Stefano had been waiting for. 'You've managed to keep us apart rather well so far, haven't you? You thought I was at the theatre this morning, didn't you? It just happened that I wasn't and my son and I had time for a quiet chat. You haven't been paying him so much attention now you think he's yours for keeps. And you've been finding out that you've taken on something you don't know what to do with: not the weak dependent helpless little boy that I was: maybe something of his grandfather in him instead. His company, his chatter, his tantrums were a nuisance, weren't they? You never considered his feelings, that he needs affection and care as well as possessions, that he might miss his mother and his sister, that he could be utterly unhappy with you. That's why I found him not only alone but crying his heart out when I came back to the palazzo this morning.

'And that's why he came out with the truth about what happened on the lagoon that night, the same story as his mother had told us. He'd been promised a lot of nice things if he only repeated that other story: presents and clothes and holidays and freedom to do as he liked. But they don't matter any more: he just wants his mother. So now we know everything.'

Chiara made a last attempt. 'They were together all that

night just as Giovanni . . . Toni described.'

'So it was Fedele who coached him. And it was all a lie. Excuse me, Father,' Stefano added, picking up the receiver. 'I must speak to Tania at once.'

A second contest over the possession of the receiver ensued, with Angelo again the winner, holding it firmly in its place.

'Leave it alone,' he ordered. 'She can wait half a day and the boy can't have come to any harm. Do you realize there are at least a dozen journalists in this building at this moment? They'd have a picnic, wouldn't they? "Congress Director's grandson kidnapped. Where is Toni Vescovo?" And then he turns up but all this messy business leaks into the tabloids in the process. He's just out enjoying himself in the town. He's probably back already for his dinner.'

As Stefano burst into a retort, he was conscious of an ever-increasing tension in the woman beside him. 'So you're ready to risk him wandering around lost and scared, falling into a canal, getting kidnapped if it hasn't happened already, just for the sake of your precious unsavoury reputation. You, the child's grandfather—'

Chiara's voice lashed in. 'Grandfather, grandfather. He's no grandfather and he's got no grandson, and if his only one son continues in the way he's going now, he never will have. No legitimate one, anyhow. So your Toni, our Toni, can hardly take after him much, can he? And he's not your father either. And well he knows it, or if he doesn't, he's a bigger fool than I've ever taken him for. Why do you think he's always despised you? And hasn't dared to do anything about it? For the sake of his snow-white reputation. The Mafia bully-boss who trembles at the least breath of scandal. Look at him, the hypocrite, the phoney, the puffed-up windbag.'

The silent rigidity that froze each of the assembled actors extended over a full ten seconds: Chiara a triumphant Goneril or Regan taunting a now powerless tyrant father, chin, nose and eyebrows elevated in icy contempt; Angelo glaring defiantly at her, fists clenching and unclenching before he shrugged his shoulders and turned his own con-

125

tempt on the son he had never fathered; and Stefano open-mouthed, fixing stony eyes on both of them. It was Stefano who broke the silence, his eyes now riveted on Angelo's face.

'So that was why,' he enunciated, each word separate and precise, 'that was why you always despised me, degraded me as an imbecile. You knew well enough that I wasn't your son but you didn't dare challenge your main source of income—and prestige: she might too readily have walked out on you—together with her money and her prestige. So you took it out on a helpless child: you used a child to torment his mother because you hadn't the guts to face up to her yourself.' He paused fractionally as he looked from one to the other before continuing even more incisively, 'You'll see. Yes, you'll see. Maybe the imbecile child could prove to have more guts than his tormentor ever had.'

Summoning every last shred of dignity, like a Roman senator charged with bribery, Angelo gave a downward twitch to his jacket as the senator might have given his toga an upward one over his shoulder, then turned and stalked silently out of the room, closing the door firmly behind him. He must then have scurried like a rabbit along the corridor, for when Stefano opened the door, he had vanished. Without a word to his mother, he also left the room and made his way in the direction of the hotel exit. Chiara remained for some time in her chair, head and shoulders sagging in defeat rather than despair, a Calpurnia overtaken by a more than usually vivid nightmare of the impending fate hovering over her over-ambitious husband, though in wide-awake reality confronting the wreck of her own earlier dreams and machinations.

In fact Angelo had hurried to his bedroom on the floor above to put through a hurried call to the palazzo, before making his way to the restaurant where he arrived to find his colleagues in the final stages of the meal. After apologizing briefly, he proceeded to do his best to catch up with those at his table and soon recovered his habitual geniality on such occasions, only a slight air of abstraction remaining. As he lingered over a cognac, Pietro came up and whispered

126

a few words in his ear. He looked brisker and more competent than he had earlier and agreed readily to his father's suggestion, 'Make it three o'clock.'

Back in his office, Angelo rang for his secretary, but it was again Sandro who appeared at the door. 'Where's Camillo?' Angelo asked.

'He's been called away, signore. It is an urgent matter: I don't know what. He will return as soon as possible.'

'He'd better. However, as you're here now, I've got a list here for you with eight names of delegates on it. Between now and their departure they are expecting to make various arrangements with you. You will find your own way of approaching each of them privately, of learning the requirements, means and other details from those marked with a cross, and terms, methods of supply and like matters from those unmarked. Those underlined I'd like to see personally for, say, a quarter of an hour each. Try to fix suitable times for them between three-thirty and five-thirty. Do you understand?'

'Yes, signore.' Sandro's face was sullen, his whole attitude one of revulsion and suppressed fury ignored by his master, who scribbled out and handed him a cheque.

'Enough there to set you up in your foreign hideout, eh? You're a lucky man, Sandro, until you get any ideas about using it that way. Tell Camillo to report here as soon as he gets back.'

Sandro retired and Angelo picked up the receiver yet again. He dialled the switchboard and asked for the carabinieri post in Chioggia.

'Angelo Vescovo,' he announced himself when the call came through. 'I'd like to speak to Lieutenant Giovanni Fedele if he's in.'

Giovanni was available though his voice was almost inaudible when he replied:

'Lieutenant Fedele here. Good afternoon, Signore Vescovo.' Nervousness but no surprise. Chiara would have been in touch with him.

'Ah yes. There is a matter in which I shall need your expert and discreet assistance, Lieutenant.'

'I am at your service, signore.' The voice had strengthened, gathered confidence.

'You were recently, I understand, concerned in a certain unfortunate occurrence involving my daughter-in-law and her son.' (Never again my grandson, Angelo brooded, had been brooding for the past hour, with all his suspicions now confirmed.)

'I regret that is the case, signore.'

'We've had bad news, I'm afraid. The child, who was as you may know domiciled with his grandmother, has disappeared.'

'That is terrible, signore. I trust that no criminal activity has been involved.'

'We don't know. His mother may have removed him of course, though that seems unlikely. At this moment a highly important Congress here in this hotel, with participants from all over the world, has reached its final day. It would be extremely inconvenient if any news of his disappearance were to be made public, at least during the next twenty-four hours. I am not so confident of the complete cooperation of the Venice police in this matter: that is why I approach you, who may have the requisite authority to impress upon those concerned in the search of the need for absolute secrecy: there must be no publicity of any kind.'

'You want the boy found, signore?'

Was this crass stupidity or a capacity for depravity equal even to his own? Angelo snapped back:

'Of course I do. What do you think? He's my only grandson.' So it wasn't so difficult in the name of duplicity. He would soon get used to it again. 'And by the way, Lieutenant Fedele, there is another serious matter we must discuss tomorrow. The boy has changed his story considerably and has suggested your responsibility for what appears to have been at least obvious slander, if we can put this interpretation on his words. But you know what children are: personally I am sure you would not have jeopardized your present position and indeed your whole career by implicating yourself in blatant calumny. First the boy must be found and I make you, Lieutenant, responsible for his

128

security and welfare. Only then can we investigate the other matter. Do you understand?'

'I will do everything within my power, signore.' Giovanni's voice was still bland and confident but his unseen face was haggard and grey.

A few minutes before three: time for a glance at the local paper, which, slightly to his disappointment, made no reference to yesterday's conference proceedings. But of course there were conferences throughout the spring and summer. On a sudden thought he asked to be put through to Stefano's home in Malamocco but, as he expected, got no reply. For a few minutes Angelo's thoughts were with Tania. He had met her only a few times and, unexpectedly, for a man of his tastes, he had admired her. Beautiful certainly and unaware of it: the blonde beauty that appeals to the Latin but would be common enough in her own country to pass unremarked. Reserved, though certainly not shallow: unapproachable, at any rate for him or anyone like him: that rarity in his experience: an attractive woman worthy of respect. Compared with Chiara . . .

A knock at the door and Pietro inserted himself, so much everybody's carricature of an American that he obviously couldn't be one. He slumped down at his father's curt order, smiling ingratiatingly. This then was the proud bearer of his name that he had set up in the States twelve years before to blaze the family tradition across the New World.

'You wanted to see me,' Angelo reminded him, as he sat there passively, content to wait for his father to make the opening move.

'Yes, Papa. I'm afraid it's rather a long story.' Pietro's Italian had lost some of its former fluency, or was the hesitant, slurred speech due to other causes? However, once his story got under way, the words tumbled out quickly enough though with many repetitions and in no properly organized sequence. It was indeed a long and involved account of problems and difficulties, erratic exchange rates, inefficiency of suppliers, unforeseen inflation, unfair competition, governmental interference: in short, the disastrous situation in which, unless a very considerable amount of cash was speedily injected into the no longer prosperous and indeed only just solvent Bishop Euro-American Publishing Incorporated, a collapse was inevitable. Pietro's confidence, also on the verge of collapse, would carry him no further and his story tailed away to an almost inarticulate conclusion: 'So that's how it is, Papa, and it isn't my fault, not really, if you see what I mean.' He crouched back in his chair, deflated, despairing, a miasma of failure, stupidity, self-pity hovering all around him.

Angelo, leaning back, his eyes on the stuccoed ceiling, asked: 'And what has all that got to do with me?'

Pietro regarded him blankly. 'I thought . . .' Not being able to find words to express what he'd thought, he came to a lingering halt.

'You thought I'd bail you out again, I suppose. And you were wrong. Isn't there an English phrase: "pouring money down the drain"? And another like it: "throwing good money after bad"? The Americans, or maybe the British, know about these things too.'

'So it's bankruptcy,' Pietro mumbled. 'But you'll be involved too.'

'Bankruptcy, yes. My involvement, no. I've been pulling out, as you should have realized. I've seen it coming for some time. I've had reports of what you've been up to that I hardly believed. Now I see they were understated. I don't often misjudge people, but maybe because you are my son I expected at least something from you. Not that you'd deliberately chuck yourself on the trashheap.'

'What do you mean?'

Angelo leaned forward to glare at him, both powerful hands flat on the table. 'You know very well what I mean. You were a distributor, not a customer. Do you think I've ever been fool enough to touch it myself?'

'You've never lived in New York.'

'I've lived in Rome. Shouldn't I know the temptations?'

'No, you don't. It wasn't the smart thing when you were young. Nowadays it's the same as smoking was in your days: you're a social flop, an outsider, if you're not hooked, or more or less. If you want to get places, you've got to conform. It's a duty.'

'Whatever your duties, or your hobbies, I'm not interested. You're no use to me so you're welcome to go ahead and destroy yourself. And it's no use asking your mother: she's got no use for failures. As a distributor you might still have some purpose; on second thoughts, no. You'll have got careless and that'll mean risk for some part of the organization: it might even come back to me. You've got your return ticket, I hope? Well, I don't think we've got anything more to discuss and I've a lot to do. Give my greetings to your family when you get back.'

He reached for his large businessman's diary lying just within his reach on the left side of the desktop, unaware or careless of the expression of disgust and horror on his son's face, changing as he looked across at the side of his father's head to one of calculation: a mirror-image of what Angelo might have noticed on the rare occasions when he surveyed himself critically in the glass. Without a word, Pietro turned and went out of the room.

Left alone, Angelo consulted his diary for a number, dialled and waited for some time, drumming the fingers of his left hand on the table impatiently. He was about to replace the receiver when a surly voice identified itself as Cesare.

'You've taken your time to answer,' Angelo growled. 'Listen. I'm withdrawing yesterday's instructions for the surveillance of the Gentiles. Forget what you were told to do.'

An aggrieved voice stuttered indignant protests which Angelo cut short with a 'Then you got what you deserved. I told you to wait for confirmation before taking any kind of action. Well, you've made an ass of yourself, and you've also forfeited any payment. I don't employ imbeciles.' He slammed down the receiver scowling at a tourist-poster picture facing him of the lagoon by moonlight (including gondolas), and meditating darkly on the shabby treatment life was meting out to him.

A knock at the door aroused him at precisely 3.30 and he

131

moved heavily from desk to door to admit and give a cordial greeting to the first of his appointed visitors.

It had been his wife who had got in touch with Camillo, begging him to come home as soon as possible. Something highly unpleasant had happened to her, though there was nothing to worry about now. Indeed, she appeared exultant rather than downcast.

He left a half-eaten lunch to catch the diretto from near the hotel and was home in little more than half an hour. His aural impression of her state of mind was confirmed: a smug pussy-cat who had stolen and much enjoyed the cream.

'I didn't tell you over the phone,' she said. 'I didn't know who might be listening. Something happened this morning that shook me up a bit at the time.'

She paused to marshal her ideas. 'I was going to the shops along San Lio by my usual route, by way of the Calle della Chiesa and the Fondamanente di Rimedio, alongside the canal. It's a bit roundabout but it's quiet. I was just passing through that rather dark colonnade as you come into the Fondamanente, when I tripped on an uneven paving-stone and sprawled, dropping my handbag as I fell. I'd heard footsteps behind me and thought whoever was coming might want to help me up, though I didn't really need help. You know how it is: you feel such an idiot, like an old woman, being helped to your feet, so I was already on all fours, so to speak, looking back and able to see whoever emerged from under the arches. He was a small dark-faced, dark-haired man like the nastier types you see on TV. There was nobody else in sight either way—it can be a bit lonely along there, but you don't usually think of bag-snatchers in Venice, though I suppose they exist. He'd got his hand in his pocket already and he drew something out: I'll swear it was a knife with a slightly curving blade. He calculated for a second and then took a step towards me with his hand raised—certainly not to help me, and he didn't say anything either. He was only a few metres from me when I reacted automatically, just as we've been learning in class. I think

132

I lunged for his legs and we were just near the edge of the canal and of course he wasn't expecting it. I reacted with the canal in mind, forcing his legs to his right and somehow managed to shove him down the steps there. He went in. There was a lovely niff to the water this morning: the canal hasn't been cleaned out for some time, I think. I didn't stop to see if the poor little thing could swim: I raced back the way I'd come and round to the Questura to report it. Lots of form-filling and the like but they thought it was an ordinary sneak-thief and I'd imagined the knife, though they may look for it—and him—in the water—if he's still there. How nice that would be! I shouldn't think they'd have a lot of trouble tracking him down: he must have been conspicu-ous—if only to people's noses—on his way home.'

Camillo shivered, more upset than he dared show. There had been a few ambiguous remarks during the past few days and this might just have been a more obvious warning. Or maybe somebody just a bit too excitable had been put on to tail his wife, awaiting future more definite instructions. There were sneak-thieves in Venice right enough but this was the first time he'd heard of one with a knife. And his wife had never been one inclined to imagine things.

Something definite would surely have to be done before the next, more subtle and maybe successful attempt was made.

The farewell dinner for Congress delegates was as usual partaken of in the resplendent hotel banqueting-room over-looking the sea under the glittering crystal array of Murano chandeliers. Mellowed by cocktails and carefully selected and recommended wines, all animosities were laid aside for the moment and talk, like the wine, flowed freely and enjoyably. Courses were served to the accompaniment of music from various parts of the world, and finally Stefano appeared, to play lively, romantic, haunting Italian melo-dies on his flute—rather to Angelo's surprise, who should have remembered that, whatever his personal problems, Stefano was a professional who would never let his audience down. The cabaret that accompanied the coffee and cognac,

133

sought to reveal the hidden secrets of the harem, with veiled and very much unveiled houris (straight from a local ballet-school) gliding sinuously, writhing and gyrating, to unseen recorded strains of Middle Eastern music.

The night was chilly but dry and clear and the company moved on to the balconies extending from the banqueting-room or wandered down to the terrace fronting the sea. Angelo made his way to the lower terraces where there was more space to act the part of courteous host, moving from one group of watchers to the next, wishing his guests a regretful farewell. Chiara, an ageing moon-goddess in silver, accompanied him until the first rocket zoomed into the sky. She and her husband then moved aside, making their way to an unoccupied table where they sank down wearily on two chairs. Their earlier hostilities, as so often before, had apparently merged into everyday indifference and they sat together in silence for a few moments, before Chiara mur-mured a few words and moved away towards the door of the hotel as rapidly-multiplying streaks of colour festooned the sky. Over the next ten minutes, sound and scenic effect built up to their appropriate climax on such an occasion, a multi-coloured re-creation of the *Santa Maria*, the ship that had borne Cristoforo Colombo on his discovery of the Great New World, with no travel writer or photographer, alas, to record the voyage for posterity. The set-piece having burnt itself out, a few gaudy and noisy rockets wound up the performance, leaving the audience uncertainly watching the night sky in case more was to follow. Eventually the full lighting came on and waiters started to appear in quest of further orders. There was a considerable exodus in the direction of the Casino, some distance along the Lungomare, though Angelo was not among the hopeful. He was noticed only some five minutes later, shoulders and head hunched on the table, blood oozing from a deep hole at the base of his skull.

CHAPTER 9

FRESH AIR FROM THE NORTH

Arvo travelled on the same flight from Helsinki as the Vescovos had taken earlier, arriving mid-morning on the Lido on the final day of the Congress. Before collecting her present guests, Iris had already washed away from the top and sides of her car the winter's accumulated adornment provided by weather, wind, tree, cat and bird, and had run the engine, a weekly chore she too often forgot, though only once with the result she deserved. She and Tania had collected the new arrival, together with a small suitcase and rucksack, and brought him back to the canal-side flat. Coffee was served as a form of Finnish welcome, Arvo sitting between them, an unmistakable Finn, stocky, with placid squarish face, sand-blond hair and blue eyes that missed little, including the drawn pallor of his sister's face.

They spoke of the journey, family health and happenings, the recent interminable Finnish winter, with temperatures too low on occasion even for skiing. The two women left him to decide when the ball should be set rolling and he blew the whistle for this casually enough.

'Rosa's at school, I expect.'

'Yes. I still usually take her to the boat and meet her but both of them know the way well enough in Venice. She's nine now, you know.'

'And Toni's still with his grandmother?'

'So far as I know.'

'And Stefano's with them?'

Tania shrugged her shoulders. 'He hasn't informed me. I suppose he'll come for his things sooner or later. I noticed he'd been back to collect his flute and evening suit when I visited the flat for a short time yesterday, but nothing else seemed to have been touched. He doesn't know I'm here.'

Iris interposed, 'Shall we sit somewhere more comfortable?' If the grilling was to begin, she thought, hard chairs were best abandoned.

Brother and sister moved to armchairs and when Iris started to gather up crockery, Tania told her to leave it and join them. 'You may remember things I miss,' she said.

She knew that Arvo would expect a sequence of happenings from the beginning and with all relevant detail. Even so, he started off with a diversion.

'I've yet to meet your charming in-laws, so let's have a sketch of Dad and Mum to start with.'

There wasn't much to say about Dad, whom Tania had met on only a few occasions and described as a typical flamboyant business tycoon, a big name in the publishing world with various other financial interests. Apparently he came originally from Sicily.

'Oh?' Arvo commented.

His companions caught the implication but had nothing to add.

'And mother-in-law? You've got rather more to say about her presumably.'

'A good deal more,' daugher-in-law concurred. 'Descendant of the illustrious Venetian commercial aristocracy and a lot richer than most others of her kind today. She owns a palazzo that she can actually afford to keep in good repair and then spends most of her time elsewhere. She's entirely egoistic, spoilt, neurotic, spiteful, amoral and, I should guess, utterly cold.'

'Well, well. She seems the type to give even mother-in-laws a bad name.'

'There isn't a daughter-in-law alive who could even imagine a worse one.'

'And I gather she's not particularly fond of you.'

'I'm that foreign witch who trapped her innocent son and is now brutally ill-using her helpless grandson.'

'And not her granddaughter?'

'Girls have to put up with what they get and be thankful. She having been, one assumes, the exception.'

'How does Stefano fit in with all this? He seems very amiable, hardly a leader of men but quite fond of you.'

'He was the sensitive younger son protected by Mummy against bullying Papa and she still wants to treat him as a Mummy's darling.'

'How does he like that?'

'Not much. But it's a habit that's very difficult to break away from.'

'Yes, that's probably true.' Arvo hesitated a moment, reflecting on his sister's newly-acquired brittleness before suggesting, 'Let's start on the plot now, in chronological order, as far as possible.'

Tania had turned events over in her mind often enough during the past few days, and all sorts of isolated incidents had now grouped themselves together into a semblance of a pattern. She started her account with Chiara's Saturday afternoon appearance at Malamocco as an indication of character and motive. Then there were the arrangements, cancellations, recommendations for the Burano visit.

'Had there been a special children's day organized?' Arvo asked.

'Not for that Saturday. But Giovanni, the carabiniere we'd got acquainted with on the boat, made inquiries and told us it had been the previous Saturday.'

'A carabiniere, indeed. And on Christian name terms! What people you do meet! But one thing at the time. Did you actually hear his inquiry and the answer?'

'No.'

'So he might just have been asking—er—if there was an art gallery on the island?'

Tania and Iris exchanged surprised glances. 'He could have been,' Iris agreed. 'But that's surely presumption of evidence, not evidence?'

'True,' said Arvo, 'but worthy of note. Anything more about the carabiniere?'

Tania described the encounter between Toni and his schoolfellow, the carabiniere's nephew.

'No signed, sealed and witnessed family tree, I suppose?'

'Does that matter?'

'I don't know. In certain circumstances it might. So that provided a means of introduction to our presumably

137

good-looking policeman. Not in full-dress uniform, I suppose.'

'In sweater and slacks,' Iris recalled. 'Good-looking in a middle-aged way: crinkly hair with a touch of silver and dark blue eyes. Tanned complexion.'

'So you both fell madly in love with him at first sight?'

'He seemed—' Tania paused for a word—'as Italians say: *simpatico*. You have to agree with that, at least,' she admitted to Iris.

'And, in an Italian, that should have been a clear enough warning—to both of us,' Iris retorted bitterly.

'He just seemed kind,' said Tania regretfully. She went on to relate Toni's outburst and the offers made, the abandonment and recovery of the two boys, the return journey and the policeman's far from spartan accommodation on Pellestrina. She stopped suddenly, pursed her lips and shook her head. 'No, that's absurd,' she meditated.

'A wisp of a ghost of a suspicion. Who knows?' her brother challenged.

'Just hindsight forcing unlikely bits into an even more unlikely pattern. It's just that when Chiara was with us, she had a telephone call from a man. She said he needed some papers from Angelo and then refused to take the bus to the boat stop but insisted on a taxi. Stefano noticed that it went off in the wrong direction, towards Alberoni and possibly the boat to Pellestrina. And she'd spent a lot of time making her face up for just going home.'

'Another item for the odd button-box.'

As the story went on, coincidences Tania had already wondered over took on a sharper relief: the roses at the airport, the evening telephone-call while Stefano was at La Fenice (that insidious voice jarring against the open Finnish landscapes), Giovanni's concern with Goldie (at that moment curled on her lap in his fourth home at least) and the calculated worming of his way into a position of trust with the family. And she recalled with revulsion those meaningful glances under Stefano's uneasy eye.

'Having realized your virtue was unassailable. You should compliment me on that and other sentences,' gloated Arvo,

138

turning to his former teacher. 'As you hear, I've extended my reading of detective stories to include Edgar Allan Poe and even Dickens.'

'It wasn't a sentence so Grammar needs attention,' retorted Miss Lawton. 'There was the jealousy ingredient too, don't forget. That was obvious even at the time.'

'The invitation to the Carnival? I suppose so, though I really did think he was taking an interest in you. Who knows what might have followed?'

Iris shuddered and Tania completed her story with the unexpected kindnesses of Chiara, the removal of Rosa and the final disastrous excursion with its sequel.

'And Stefano believed it all?'

It was a necessary but painful question and Tania flinched from answering. Iris took over responsibility.

'What else could he do? How could a small boy make up all that and give those details?'

'Unlikely, but small boys can easily be coached,' Arvo suggested. 'It's not the how but the why that I'm wondering about. Though knowing my nephew, it's not so difficult to guess. Wonderful promises. Presents, sweets, ice-cream galore, freedom to do as he liked including staying up to all hours: *la dolce vita* for all eternity. And from what you've said about the Burano visit, dislike for you assiduously cultivated. Not difficult to imagine Chiara working on him whenever she got the chance: "those lovely times we'll have when you come to live with me, my darling. But don't say anything to Mama till I tell you: otherwise she'll stop you coming. Just wait till we tell you what to say."

'And Stefano still under Mama's thumb,' he continued. 'All her warnings about those libertine Scandinavian women proved to be true. Well, what have you done about it?'

'Nothing. You told me not to. At first I was ready to turn up at the palazzo with Stefano's gun though I've no idea where he keeps it. Then quite suddenly I caved in and did nothing but stare at the wall and sob. I felt so helpless. I've got back some of my Finnish spirit now, though. Having you here makes a difference too. But what can I do? Stefano's in charge, the father, and she'll have any number of lawyer acquaintances, with a magistrate or two thrown in, to grant custody, legal or not.'

'There must be a few honest and unprejudiced lawyers around.'

'How do I find them? Sticking a pin in the yellow pages list?'

'Wouldn't your local friends be able to recommend someone?'

'Try making friends with local people, as Iris will agree. Polite *buon giorno* from the neighbours, but otherwise unapproachable.'

'Well, I've got one or two names I've brought with me. Policemen naturally: one I met at a police conference and we exchanged addresses: a friendly person. I'll have to look him up. But where will I stay?'

'How about Malamocco? We can't both impose on Iris: she just hasn't got the room. I could come with you.'

'That's an idea. But you stay on here with Rosa. I'd rather you were out of circulation for a bit. And now, it may be the Venetian humidity, or jet-lag, or the fact that I came to the airport straight off night-duty: my thought processes seem to be running down. I'll soon be making mistakes in my English and be grilled—no, that's my normal job— hauled over the coals by my teacher. Would you have a nice flat couch or even floor where I can just—go—nicely—to —sleep?'

Rosa returned from school in the late afternoon and was delighted to hear that Uncle Arvo was with them, though not to be disturbed. She was enjoying her stay with Iris, though unaware of the reason for it, Tania having told her that Toni and Daddy were staying with Grandpa while he was in Venice for an important Congress and Mummy hadn't been feeling well so Iris had been looking after her. The story was a temporary expedient. Sooner or later the facts would have to be told, although there was always the hope that everything might come out all right in the end and the bitter truth be kept from the small girl.

Arvo slept longer than he had expected and it was not until eight o'clock that Tania served the meal she had prepared, Iris, the world's most indifferent cook, allowing her to take over this responsibility. They lingered chatting, mostly about Finland, until around half past nine.

Rosa was already in bed and as Iris had to drive Arvo to Malamocco, Tania remained with her, handing over the keys to the flat, together with a list of things needed from it. They drove through a twilight world occasionally bombarded by the roar of cohorts of motor-scooters, girls screaming from the pillions. On the right a polished lagoon rocked gentle amber-coloured lantern reflections from bricole while darker shapes pinpointed with lights moved to and from the lamplit shores of the islands that compose Venice.

'Tania's taking it rather well, considering,' Arvo hazarded.

'It was the shock that swept the ground from under her,' Iris reflected, 'like standing for years over a hidden ravine on a bridge that suddenly dissolves. And the utter helplessness that goes with it. She's surfaced again now with the cold fury of injustice and the more she thinks about things, the bitterer it grows. If she were to run into that Chiara or that feeble reed of a Stefano just at this moment and she happened to be carrying a nice sharp Finnish puukko . . . That's exaggerated, of course, but twice I've had to argue my way through to the hard granite of Finnish common sense to keep her from charging across the lagoon and battering at the door of that palazzo. Underneath, of course, there's still the helplessness. What can any of us do against those nasty types lined up against us: grandmother with all her top-brass Venetian acquaintances, devoted father, cruelly betrayed, and that sinister Mafia boss—which I'm sure he is—lurking somewhere in the background, heaven knows in what capacity?'

'A court case for slander, my girl, is the least you'll have to face if that gets to his ears, the more so if it's true. He's one of those you go careful with.'

Iris parked among a scatter of cars outside the block and

141

Arvo extracted his luggage. A slight shock awaited them: a light left burning in the windowless hall. But there was nobody inside.

'So he's still around,' Iris commented.

Arvo decided he could make do with a bunk bed in the children's room and made it up while Iris went looking for the listed items. A few minutes later there was a tap on the flat door. Iris opened it to find a youngish dark-haired woman outside, who looked disconcerted at the appearance of a stranger. She spoke nervously in Italian, which Iris managed to interpret as 'I thought it was Signora Vescovo I could hear.'

'I'm her friend: she's staying in my house,' Iris essayed, in hesitant Italian. 'The signora's brother from Finland is staying here tonight,' she added, as Arvo appeared behind her.

'It's the little boy. He came late this afternoon and there was nobody at home so he knocked at my door. I took him in till his mother came home.'

An intelligent woman, she spoke slowly and simply for this obvious foreigner, 'He is obviously upset. He is crying all the time, asking for his mother.'

Apparently, with the television on continuously in the evening—the sound apparent through the open door below —and probably working herself earlier in the day, the woman hadn't been aware even that the flat had been empty. Iris was about to follow her downstairs when a small figure exploded out of the door and raced up the stairs, screaming 'Mummy, Mummy,' and, on seeing Iris, changed the frantic cry to an accusing, 'Where's my Mummy? I want my Mummy.'

'Your mummy's in my home, Toni,' Iris said gently, but he threw himself against her, merely continuing his desperate appeal.

They thanked the woman, who looked both doubtful and relieved before returning to her home. Toni had caught sight of Uncle Arvo and, quite unsurprised, pleaded heart-breakingly with him for the one person he couldn't see.

142

With little time to look out clothes that Toni might need, Iris guided him down to the car, with Arvo carrying the case she had already half-filled. 'Better for you to hold the fort here,' she suggested. 'We'll get in touch easily enough if we need to.'

She drove back vaguely aware of streamers of light exploding into coloured stars in the direction of the Adriatic. 'Mummy's waiting for you in my home,' she had assured her passenger who now sat silent beside her, his small fists clenched on his knees. He scrambled out as soon as she had parked and rushed to the high metal gate. She followed with the case, unlocked gate, house door and flat door and switched on the hall light. The rest of the flat was in darkness, Rosa breathing tranquilly in her made-up bed. Otherwise, apart from two cats demanding supper, the flat was empty.

Toni had followed her in silence during her brief search. He was obviously tired out and, crushed as he was by the day's experience, made no resistance when Iris sat on a wide comfortable sofa and took him on her lap, too exhausted now even to protest against life's cruelties. He clung to her sobbing helplessly, occasionally murmuring, 'Where's Mummy? Where's she gone?' as he turned his tear-washed face towards hers. 'She'll be here, Toni,' she consoled him again and again. 'It'll be all right.' Gradually the desolate weeping subsided and his eyes closed. She laid him on the sofa with a cushion under his head and covered him with a blanket.

She sat watching him for some time, feeling almost as exhausted herself and at the same time more than a little afraid, uneasy enough to have to resist an impulse to rush to the telephone to seek help from Arvo. Even in her role of spectator, she had been deeply worried, even alarmed at events. The chess-piece figures involved: the malignant black queen, the sinister conspiratorial black knight and, looming even more ominously, the gigantic shadow of the unseen opponent, the huge menacing Sicilian who, for all she knew, was quietly manipulating this melodrama from behind the scenes. Could he have arranged to kidnap—to

143

dispose of, even—this unwanted daughter-in-law, tracking her down by the simple method of having Rosa followed home from school? Absurd, even as a fevered nightmare. Just as absurd that one of his business rivals, a Mafia agent possibly, would shortly be submitting a ransom note for her return. Not even in Italy, least of all in not over-scrupulous but, in her experience, humdrum, superficially law-abiding Venice. Without conscious intention, she curled up on the far end of the sofa, her head on the other cushion, and followed Toni into oblivion.

She surfaced some unknown time later when the light was switched on. Tania was standing there in her light fawn coat. 'You're back then,' Tania managed to get out before breaking off in astonishment as a suddenly-aroused Toni catapulted himself towards her, yelling triumphantly, 'Mummy, Mummy, Mummy'.

Reflex action impelled Iris to her feet and into the kitchen to put the kettle on and warm some milk for Toni. Biscuits to go with the tea and fortunately there were some choc ices in the ice-compartment. She returned some ten minutes later with the cosy-protected teapot and all else needed crammed together on a tray.

Tania with Toni at her side looked brisk and at the same time relaxed. 'That's a good idea,' she said. 'Want an ice-cream, Toni?'

Subdued and still tired out, Toni set to work on the ice-cream as if he hadn't eaten all day, asking for a second as soon as the first had disappeared. 'He'd been left with Beata, he says, but she disappeared and he just let himself out. He'd been shut up indoors the whole time, imagine, and he just wandered around Venice for quite a long while. Then he felt hungry but he couldn't bear the thought of going back to the palazzo so he found his way to the *motonave*, with the season ticket he uses for school, and then got on the Malamocco bus. He says that the main house door downstairs had been left open but of course nobody was in the flat so he sat down to wait until he heard the woman downstairs come home and he trotted down and told her he was shut out: his mummy wasn't at home. She took him in

144

and gave him something to eat when he said he was hungry and let him watch television till she heard you moving above.'

Toni had finished his ice-cream and asked, 'Where's Rosa?'

'Asleep in the other room, where you're going now.'

Too exhausted to ask any more questions, he lay back on the sofa until his mother had made up a bed for him on some cushions in the bedroom and reappeared to undress him and lay him gently on them. She looked in on Iris for a moment to say, 'I think I'll turn in now too if you don't mind,' and at once disappeared.

Just where had Tania been, Iris wondered, as she washed cups and plates. In all the emotional upheaval, had she merely forgotten to mention her mysterious excursion or could she really have something to hide?

Unknowingly following Stefano's example, Arvo reclined on the sofa, his shoes neatly paired on the floor beside him, reflecting on all he had heard. Toni had probably found his own solution to the question of ownership: a rebellious captive, offering his own kind of resistance to all her blandishments would hardly endear himself to his grandmother, who had indeed succeeded in showing she had little enough genuine affection for him. But a viper doesn't necessarily slither away when its first attack is foiled: it can lurk in the undergrowth awaiting an opportunity to inject an even more deadly poison. Somehow he must contrive to meet this Chiara as soon as possible: today he had learned something of the nature of the undergrowth: tomorrow he must start to clear some of it away and get a glimpse of what was hidden within. And first he must somehow make local police contacts.

He got up and wandered across to the bookcase: plenty of English fiction there, though none of the crime species. *Kalevela*, the Finnish national epic, naturally, in impressive leather binding, together with various French and German works. It had been Tania's interest in foreign languages that had taken her to England in the first place and if she hadn't met Stefano, she'd planned to return to a Finnish Interpreters' School.

He was turning over the pages of Henry James's *The Portrait of a Lady* when he heard a key in the lock of the outer door and turned to greet Stefano coming through the hall.

'Hallo,' said the visitor. 'What are you doing here? I saw the light from outside and thought it might be Tania. Do you know where she is?'

'Why do you want to know?' Arvo queried less than cordially, as he replaced the book.

'You've a right to ask, of course. I suppose Iris sent for you. Tania wouldn't have done.'

This wouldn't be contempt for his wife, Arvo reflected. Bitterness rather, or possibly respect. He remained silent.

'And if you're thinking I'm the world's biggest clot, dolt, maniac, quarter-wit, retarded imbecile—' At this point Stefano ran out of epithets and could only glare aggressively.

'Exactly,' Arvo agreed politely.

'Have a drink. Do you like grappa?' Stefano was already rummaging in the sideboard cupboard.

'What else have you got?'

'Drambuie, for special occasions.' Stefano was surveying a recently-opened bottle. 'Shall we get drunk?'

'No, we shan't,' said Arvo. 'But at least we can sit down.'

They retired with filled glasses to the sofa where they sat silent for half a minute. 'Cheers,' said Stefano and drank.

'I've seen Tania,' Arvo said quietly. 'She's staying with Iris.'

'That I should have guessed. With Rosa, of course.'

'And Toni now.'

'Toni? So she did manage to get him away.'

'He got himself away. He turned up here and a neighbour took him in. She handed him over, or rather he handed himself over, while Iris was helping me to settle in.'

'How much did he tell you?'

'Nothing. Except that he wanted his mum. So that's where he went, with Iris.'

A quick intake of breath signifying an overwhelming sense of relief was the only immediate response from his

146

companion. Stefano gazed transfixed at his glass for several minutes, downed its contents at one gulp, set it firmly on the coffee-table and sank back against the cushions.

'He told me the truth about things just this morning. And I went straight off to see my—Angelo and Chiara. They're at a Congress in a hotel here on the Lido.'

'And it was after that I suppose Toni contrived the getaway,' Arvo speculated. 'And that was the first time it had occurred to you that the whole affair might have been a complete fabrication. How well you described yourself just now!'

Stefano picked up his glass, got up and stood facing Arvo defensively across the table. 'No,' he said, 'I believed it when Toni told his story: it sounded all so authentic: it fitted the facts. And it fitted in with several things that had already happened.'

'Even though Tania denied it?'

'She didn't exactly, but I should have recognized the utter contempt she must have been feeling—and the desperation.'

'And you were shocked, I suppose. You'd always thought she was too good for you.'

'That's just why I was so ready to believe. I'd met this Giovanni and been completely taken in by him. He seemed just the kind of man Tania should have married.'

Stefano refilled his own glass after a refusal from Arvo, who grinned and reminded him, 'One glass for a sober, sensible Finn. Two glasses . . .' He shrugged his shoulders and raised his eyebrows. As a one-glass Finn he continued: 'And now what happens? It's up to her, I suppose.'

'What has she said about me?'

'Sorry to inform you, but you got rather passed over in our discussion. I don't somehow imagine she'll fall into your arms with tears of joy.'

'If only she'd slap my face, I'd have some hope.'

'So you find my sister a frozen Nordic goddess?' Stefano started to protest but Arvo ignored him. 'It isn't true, you know, and I think you do know. She's hard-headed and sensible—she's had to be—a bit idealistic for the modern age, the standards of behaviour she applies to herself rather

147

out of fashion and all the better for that. And any man married to her who doesn't know how lucky he is—'

'Time I went to bed,' said Stefano. 'I know well enough what I've probably thrown away.' He finished his second Drambuie and retired to his own room. Arvo worked at *The Portrait of a Lady*, skipping much in the process, and finally clambered up to his own bunk at around one o'clock in the morning. He was awakened later the same morning by Stefano's, 'Coffee's ready.' Just like home, he reflected, except that both voice and language were less musical.

Over breakfast served in the kitchen, Arvo gradually veered the conversation to some of the subjects of the previous evening, but now concentrating mainly on Stefano's impressions of Giovanni and also of Angelo: in the latter case Stefano avoiding for some obscure reason any reference to his disturbing discovery. As soon as they had finished the meal, Stefano cleared the table, washed up and surveyed with satisfaction a reasonably tidy kitchen.

'I'll leave you now,' he said. 'I've got to get this over with.'

'But it's not seven yet,' Arvo discovered to his surprise.

'Tania will be taking the children to the boat on their way to school, at least she'll be taking Rosa if not Toni. Anyhow she'll be up soon after seven and it'll probably take me at least half an hour to get there.'

From the window Arvo watched him move off towards the bus stop and ten minutes later noticed he had departed. An approaching police car, however, came to a stop outside and there was a ring at the door below.

He opened the flat door a minute later to the not unfamiliar sight of a uniformed policeman, dark and slender rather than fair and sturdy, though with an identical expression of impassive solidity.

'Signor Stefano Vescovo?' he was asked.

'Er, no. Arvo Laurila from Finlandia. I'm sorry I don't speak Italian.'

Momentarily impassivity registered uneasiness. The wrong man was bad enough but the wrong language was a matter for real concern.

148

'*Dov'è Signor Vescovo?*'

'I'm sorry. Signor Vescovo not at home. But here is my card.'

The policeman accepted it gingerly, holding it by a corner in his fingertips, as if afraid of leaving prints. He read with increasing uneasiness: Detective-Superintendent Arvo Laurila, State Criminal Police, Helsinki. No great linguistic ability was required to decipher it but he only looked the more nonplussed.

Arvo extracted another paper from his wallet, unfolded and tendered it. 'Do you know this person,' he inquired, indicating the name of the addressee.

'*Sì. È il mio capo.*'

'Ah. Please tell him—' a finger indicated the policeman and then the name on the paper—'that this policeman—' the finger stabbed the name on his own card and then himself—'is at this telephone number.' Arvo added the number of the telephone behind him to his name card. 'Why—' he sketched a question mark in the air—'you—' a pointing finger—'want Signor Stefano Vescovo?'

Carried away by his brilliant comprehension, the carabiniere forgot himself disgracefully. He drew four fingers across the width of his throat: he shot himself in the back of his head with a pointing forefinger. 'Signor Angelo Vescovo,' he growled. Recollecting himself with horror, he drew himself up and saluted, muttered *buon giorno* and turned smartly on his heels.

Closing the door, Arvo calculated that the sooner he telephoned the man's padrone, the more likely might some disastrous misunderstanding be averted.

The door of Iris's flat was opened by Tania, wearing her usual early-morning apron. She regarded Stefano unsympathetically and waited in silence for him to step in. Rosa, eating her breakfast in solitude in the kitchen leading from the hall, caught sight of him and rushed to embrace him, breathing into his ear: 'Oh, Daddy, it's nice to see you again.' Marmalade-smeared fingers left sticky spots on his jacket.

149

'We haven't got much time, Rosa,' Tania's voice warned them both. 'Hurry up with your breakfast. We'll have to leave in five minutes.'

She turned to Stefano. 'We'll talk in the sitting-room,' she said. 'Iris and Toni are still asleep.'

He followed her and sat down obediently when she gestured towards a chair. She herself remained standing, remote and indifferent, some yards away.

'It's no good, Tania,' he said gently. 'You can loathe the sight of me, as you've got a perfect right to do. But the kids, especially Toni, need a father as well as a mother.'

'You of all people have the nerve to say that.'

'What matters now is whether you've got the nerve to accept it, together with myself.'

'So you're quite happy to have a wife who goes round having affairs with any kind of man that offers and takes her children with her as witnesses.'

'I believed that, or half-believed it, for one day only. Then I came to my senses.'

'And having come to your senses, you returned to me immediately.'

'Where to? I was telephoning you five times a day.'

'You could easily have thought of Iris.'

'I thought only of him. Where else could you have gone?'

'So you still didn't trust me.'

'What is trust, Tania? Is it ever absolute, uninfluenced by circumstance? In so many things in life, don't we believe and disbelieve at one and the same time? If you actually think I stopped loving you, that's another thing. I've always been too afraid of losing you to—someone better qualified: that's been the trouble. And then there was the shock of it.'

Poor sensitive Stefano, she was already back to thinking: he also must have suffered. But there was something about her attitude that no longer seemed to apply to the man now facing her.

He went on speaking, soothingly, confidently, as if the past few days had strengthened rather than distressed him. 'You've been badly hurt and you couldn't bear me even to touch you. I don't intend to. We can start again as strangers getting acquainted, if you like. How much does Rosa know?'

'Nothing.'

'So she hasn't been hurt—yet.' They heard the kitchen door open and Rosa appeared. 'Mummy, are you ready?' she asked. 'Will we be going back to Malamocco this evening?'

'I'm not sure,' Tania replied. 'Where's your school-bag? Goodness, look at the time.'

She moved to the outer door without looking back at Stefano, who smiled contentedly at Rosa's parting words as she followed through the door: 'It's nice having Daddy back again, isn't it?'

CHAPTER 10

CHARTING THE REEFS AND CURRENTS

The discovery of a corpse on the terrace caused dismay and confusion among the hotel personnel. The manager was at the time attending a concert in Venice while his assistant manager had the day off. It was the concierge who summoned the local polizia while, unaware of this, the hall porter was using a direct line to summon the carabinieri. Representatives from both forces, who had in fact to travel much the same distance, arrived simultaneously, but, learning of the importance of the murdered man and already at this early stage sensing the degree of ramification this might involve, the polizia surrendered gracefully to the claims of the local carabinieri, who applied for immediate assistance to the Venice command, with its considerably wider expertize, resources and men available.

In his slightly isolated location and in the general dimness outside, Angelo Vescovo had remained unnoticed by the other delegates who had been watching from the terrace, most of them departing immediately after the fireworks in the direction of the Casino in a last attempt to make their fortunes. At this time in the evening, the terrace would have been far from crowded anyhow, especially as the night was now quite chilly, so that by spreading a report that a guest had been taken ill, two of the waiters had been able to clear the section where Vescovo's head still rested on the table, with no sign of life in him. His wife was sought and was finally reported to have left the hotel immediately after the firework display, almost certainly unaware of what had happened to her husband. Neither of the two sons was to be found either: Stefano, who was not registered in the hotel, had probably gone home, and his brother might well have gone off in search of other diversion: nobody had noticed him leave.

Carabinieri experts surrounded the body, a police surgeon examining it and embellishing a rather obvious cause of death with highly technical language, photographers, finger-printers and other specialists busy collecting and recording data. Calculations were made in an attempt to establish the position of the head at the moment of entry of the bullet, though accuracy was impossible if only because the head could have turned or jerked slightly in the act of falling. However, the most plausible suggestion as to the point from which the shot had been fired appeared to be the roof some two storeys above the terrace. Two junior carabinieri sent up there found the roof easy of access through a door and there was a passageway, protected by a waist-high parapet, leading most of the way round the roof edge. They stepped warily to one side in an attempt to preserve any invisible footprints which even if they were proved to exist could have been those of anybody out on the roof to admire the view or carry out repairs. To the naked eye there was no trace of any earlier presence of a human being anywhere near the likely area, though fingerprint experts would soon be set to work here. Experiments with the terrace lighting as it had been at the time of the display suggested that the target would have been distinguishable and could have been hit by a reasonably proficient marksman. Anyone in the hotel could have reached the roof and descended again unob-served, either by an automatic lift or by the main staircase, hardly likely to be much frequented during the firework display. In fact, an outsider even could have been involved.

It was this ample scope for opportunity that alerted the senior officer in charge at that moment to the multifarious problems that the case threatened to present. Available with at least opportunity and who knew what self-justifiable motives, were some four hundred delegates, most of them unknown and respectable foreigners, together with two hundred or so hotel guests, any of whom could have committed the murder. With unlimited time at their disposal, the police might have checked alibis, eliminating those who could vouch for each other's presence all through the firework display, when the shot could have been fired without attracting attention, though even this method of checking would not rule out collusion. And the idea of restraining in the hotel four hundred professional people for the several days that would be needed, while other Congresses got under way and protests poured in from a dozen consulates at least, was quite unthinkable.

Finally, with the cooperation of such clerical staff as could be mustered at this time of night, four officers were set to examine hotel records for names, addresses and other personal details, and all this information was transmitted to the appropriate headquarters in Rome, thence in a few cases to Interpol. With computer assistance it was established that, barring mistaken identities or other possibilities for confusion, some twelve names might be those of persons suspected of involvement in drug-trafficking. These would be questioned by the appropriate department but the others would obviously have to be allowed to depart, though with many misgivings on the part of those in charge. Investigations would concentrate first on those closest to the murdered man.

The night wore on with inquiries being despatched, answers received, reports prepared, presented and correlated. It was at six o'clock in the morning that the officer in charge of the case, a Captain Martello, installed in the office vacated by the man whose death he had to investigate, received a report from the Ballistics section: the bullet which had been extracted from the skull had come from a Berretta .92, a weapon restricted to the carabinieri themselves. A

153

carabiniere's gun is claimed—so far as is practicable— to remain inseparable from its rightful owner. In short, therefore, it would appear that only a carabiniere or a close relative who shared his home could have committed the murder or connived in the crime, most probably a member of a local group. One bullet would be missing from those issued to each holder of a gun and now it was that the far from hidden snag became evident. In the surroundings of Venice alone there were over 2,000 carabinieri and any checking of weapons would take several days.

It was a member of the hotel staff who reported having heard a shot during the final session of the Congress and having been told later that the gun had been fired by the chairman himself, the murdered man. There had been no gun on the body, and though a light bulb in the ceiling of the main conference room was found to have been shattered, a search for the bullet proved unsuccessful. If it had rebounded somewhere on the floor, it might have been ingested by a powerful cleaner that would have been operating in the afternoon under the inattentive care of the member of the cleaning staff: there was a special afternoon litter-collection and by now it could be serving as part of the foundation of a new lagoon island.

Occasional groups of guests at varying levels of sobriety or joviality passed through the automatic outer doors, claimed keys and disappeared into lifts, hardly noticing the one or two police officials standing or moving about but managing to keep a low profile. By 6.30 when one or two hardy souls were beginning to venture towards the sea and a chilly morning dip, Martello was ready to turn his attention from the mechanics to the personal background of the crime. An earlier call to the Vescovo palazzo had been thwarted by the answering tape and a visit by one of his subordinates has been unsuccessful: nobody had answered his ring and the building was in darkness.

The list of hotel guests had included a Vescovo Pietro, citizen of the United States, father Angelo Vescovo, but attempts to make contact with him had run into difficulties. No key had been handed in and a telephone call to his room had failed to rouse him, so the hall porter, after knocking on the room door, finally unlocked it and found him lying on his bed unconscious and breathing with extreme difficulty, obviously under the influence of some narcotic. The hotel resident nurse was aroused and she insisted on having him immediately transferred to hospital for intensive care: whether intentionally or otherwise, he was on the verge of the extinction which had already overtaken his father.

When the hotel assistant manager came on duty he was able to supply details of the name and telephone number of the victim's secretary, Camillo Gentile, who it seemed had preferred his own home to the convenience of a hotel room. He was roused by telephone, news of the disaster was communicated to him and a police boat sent to fetch him from Venice. Martello had decided to install himself in the hotel for the time being and took the opportunity to order coffee and rolls while he was waiting. Similarly fortified, Camillo arrived some twenty-five minutes later, having crossed the lagoon at unfamiliar hair-raising speed. Though slightly unshaven in appearance, he looked immaculately washed, combed and dressed, all achieved in a space of just over ten minutes, and it was indeed the model private secretary who closed the door quietly behind him, greeted the interrogator, took a seat and gazed helpfully across the table, a neat briefcase propped against the side of his chair. Wise in the ways of the business world, Martello wondered how many disreputable secrets were lodged in that meekly attentive head (though probably not at the moment in the briefcase). Its owner was certainly showing no alarm, distress or even curiosity about the tragic news he had been given.

He started his questioning with a summary of the circumstances of the discovery of Vescovo's body and a query as to the secretary's whereabouts at that time. Camillo, it appeared, had been in that very office during the firework display, gathering together and packing for dispatch to the palazzo materials that had been used during the Congress. He had arranged with a hotel employee for the boxes to be stored until they could be collected and had left in the normal boat service shortly before the end of the firework display. Difficult to check, Martello reflected, even if the boat hadn't been crowded; the man responsible for mooring the boat at stops would hardly have paid any attention to this inconspicuous little man.

Questions about the nature and scope of the conference followed and then Camillo was asked to provide detailed information about the activities of the chairman throughout the preceding day.

'I saw Signor Vescovo only briefly earlier in the morning,' Camillo started off. 'He was presiding over a question session in the main conference room while I was left to attend to routine duties such as correspondence, records and receiving visitors.'

'Were there any visitors?'

'Only the Assessore, who had overall charge of arrangements. He came in several times to discuss various matters.'

'When did you first see Signor Vescovo after the morning session?'

'I'm sorry. There was a visitor, though not an unknown one. The signore's wife arrived in the hotel shortly before the session broke up and insisted on seeing her husband immediately.'

'Did she give any reason?'

'No, signore. But she was in considerable distress, in fact she seemed to have been crying. She gave me a message to her husband that if he could not come at once, she would seek him herself.'

'And then?'

'By then the delegates were already dispersing—'

'Just a minute,' Martello interrupted Camillo. 'Do you know anything about a revolver shot said to have been fired during the conference session?'

Camillo looked blank for a moment. 'I remember now that I heard what might have been an explosion, but it wasn't particularly loud. In any case the conference room is effectively soundproofed and it is some distance from this room.'

'Please continue.'

Camillo was starting to describe his encounter with Signor Stefano Vescovo when he was immediately interrupted,

'Is this also a member of the Vescovo family?' he was asked.

'The younger son, signore. But he was not attending the Congress.'

Martello noted down details of Stefano's address, before allowing Camillo to describe the son's request for an immediate interview with his father and his own eventual success in extracting the chairman from his admirers.

'Presumably he conversed with his wife in this office.' Camillo nodded. 'Were you present at their interview, Signore Gentile?'

'No. I think it was a private matter they were discussing.'

'So what did you do then?'

'I had started eating my lunch when I was summoned to hotel reception. My wife was on the telephone to report that she had been attacked while walking through Venice: apparently an attempt at robbery. She was unharmed and had reported the matter to the police but I thought it best to go and see her immediately: my assistant, Signor Sandro Greco, had arrived a short time before and offered to stand in for me if I was needed.'

A matter for further inquiry, this attack, Martello thought, though probably with no bearing on the case. However, he noted down the police post concerned. 'What time did you return?' he asked.

'It was about four o'clock. Signor Vescovo had left a message for me with Reception that as he was consulting with various Congress delegates he would have no further need of my services for the rest of the afternoon, but I was to remain in the hotel in case I should be needed later in the evening. He admitted each of the delegates himself, so I spent several hours supervising arrangements for winding up the business side of the conference and left, I suppose, at about half past nine.'

'Before or after the firework display?'

'Before. I could see the fireworks while I was crossing the lagoon.'

Another matter of interest had come into the conversation: what had it been? Ah yes. 'Your assistant, Sandro Greco,' Martello recalled. 'Will he be here today?'

'I don't think so, signore. He told me he would not be needed during the next few days and would be taking a holiday. Signor Vescovo had intended to leave for Rome.'

'What were his main duties?'

'Partly to assist me, especially during the Congress. I think he carried out specialist duties for Signor Vescovo but he never spoke about them.'

Martello made a note to find out more about Greco later, and then let Camillo go, warning him to be around for the rest of the day as he might be needed again. It was now 6.45 when most working people were already contemplating crawling out of bed, so he summoned a sergeant and gave him Stefano Vescovo's Malamocco address. He was to inform the signore that Captain Martello of the carabinieri of Venice requested his presence at the hotel where the Writers' and Publishers' Congress was being held as the signore's father had had a serious accident.

He now applied to an operator at the hotel switchboard asking if there was any way of discovering whether Signor Vescovo had asked for switchboard assistance in putting through calls the previous afternoon. The very obliging girl got through to a friend on the afternoon shift and learned that the signore had asked to be connected with the carabini-eri post at Chioggia. Unfortunately, when Martello followed Vescovo's example, he was told that the call would probably have been taken by a young recruit who would be off on a training course for the next day or so.

He consoled himself by assuming it might not have been important despite its unexpectedness, and once again tried the palazzo. This time he was answered by a surly voice, probably that of a maid dragged unwillingly from her bed, who informed him that she was on no accoint to disturb the signora before ten o'clock in the morning. Having made it clear that this was to be an exception, Martello waited some five minutes, only to be informed that the signora had clearly taken some kind of sedative, as frequently happened when she'd had a heavy day: all attempts to rouse her had failed as they usually did but she would probably come to at around ten. Martello informed the girl sharply that this was an urgent police matter and that unless the signora woke within an hour, a doctor was to be sent for to revive her. As soon as the signora was conscious, she was to ring Captain Martello of the Venice carabinieri at the number which he refused to give until the maid had pencil and paper in hand. He rang off leaving her slightly though not overmuch impressed, and set to work on preparing a report.

Some ten minutes later a call was put through to the office. A cheerful man's voice said in English, 'Is that Luigi Martello?'

'Martello speaking,' said the gentleman referred to, with guarded suspicion, though the voice seemed vaguely familiar. It continued, 'Arvo Laurila from Finland. Also from the Police Conference in London, England. Don't say you've forgotten me.'

'One of those guys one never forgets.' Martello had an American mother and spoke her language as fluently as his father's Italian. 'Where are you speaking from?'

'Malamocco, not the North Cape. I've just had a visit from a sergeant of yours, a very bright young man.'

'So you're going under a false name, are you? I sent him to Malamocco for a Stefano Vescovo.'

'My brother-in-law, husband of my Finnish sister. He'd gone out just before your man arrived. Can I help you in any way?'

An idea was starting to form in Martello's mind. He'd been very impressed by Detective-Superintendent Laurila, whose ability and enthusiasm had been obvious, and he had heard a good deal about his excellent reputation in Finland. As a foreigner, he could hardly be a full member of the Vescovo clan, but might nevertheless be extremely useful in having or acquiring inside family information. A highly unorthodox procedure in a police force which prided itself on its national and nationalist efficiency, but Martello was essentially a pragmatist. With a plan already forming, he asked, 'If I send my sergeant back as soon as he arrives,

159

could you join me here in the hotel? We could have a lot to talk about.'

Intrigued by recollection of the sergeant's pictorial account of the fate of Angelo Vescovo, Arvo accepted with delight and was soon sitting facing his former acquaintance, after exchanging the normal greetings.

Martello wasted no time. 'I hope you don't think,' he said, 'that all our police work is carried out in surroundings like these.'

'I'd be almost sorry for you if they were,' Arvo commented. 'Has somebody helped himself to some film star's diamonds?' he continued innocently.

'No such luck. Your sister's father-in-law was no film star: on second thoughts he might have done quite well in a Humphrey Bogart role. So you haven't heard he was murdered last night? Your brother-in-law didn't mention it by any chance?'

'Should he have known about it?'

'One of the things I'd be interested to know myself.' Martello went ahead to give details of the murder against its background of the Congress, the near-riot and its termination and the unlocated gun. He referred to the impossibility of forcibly retaining four hundred or more potential suspects and the easy accessibility to all and sundry of the roof from which the shot had almost certainly been fired. There was the mystery of the fatal bullet, fired from a gun that was virtually non-existent without its carabiniere proprietor, explained the reasons for the non-availability of his two most valuable informants, if not actual witnesses, the wife and eldest son of the victim, and hoped that Arvo would be able to assist him in locating the second son. Having summarized Camillo's account of the events of the late morning or early afternoon, the existence of the absent assistant secretary Sandro Greco and the inexplicable telephone call to the carabinieri post at Chioggia, he set to work on the professional informant and ally facing him.

'How well did you know Angelo Vescovo?' he asked.

'A little from my brother-in-law. I never met him.'

160

'That he had a wide variety of interests—and acquaintances?'

'Stefano rarely speaks about him. It was his father who sent him to England in the first place, arranging a job for him in an orchestra. Stefano believes he was ashamed of his son: it was Pietro who had the drive and ambition and got sent to manage Angelo's business in New York.'

'How much do you know about your brother-in-law?'

'He's as different as anyone can be from his father. Unambitious, sensitive, an artist.'

'And the other members of the family: mother and elder brother?'

'Pietro came to my sister's wedding in England some ten years ago. I was there too and so far as I remember him, he appeared much more go-ahead. I've heard about Mother mainly from Tania, my sister. I'll leave you to form your own opinion of Chiara. Personally I've got the impression I'd prefer Father, though I've a suspicion you'll know far more about Angelo, or at any rate what we might call his background, than I do, or than he himself would like to think. Am I allowed to inquire about that?'

Martello paused to consider and weighed his words carefully as he replied.

'In the first place he's the concern of the police in Rome rather than of us in Venice, as it's in Rome that most of his business interests are located. However, with his wife's palazzo here in Venice, he favours us, that's to say our city, with regular visits and could have various highly-profitable sidelines in the port of Venice which we've been investigating, so far without definite confirmation. Now this Congress has brought together delegates from various countries and we're making the most of things to check the information about them in the hotel register against possible records held by the police and other State departments in Rome and in some cases with Interpol. Certain authorities in the capital will be questioning some of them during the next day or two, though thank goodness that won't be my concern. Unfortunately Vescovo has long known most of what there is to know about subterfuge and self-protection, so evidence

161

has been hard to come by, even of relatively minor offences like tax evasion and embezzlement. Here's hoping.'

'Could one of his old associates have caught up with him: a revenge killing by a Mafioso, do you think? Or one of his victims? He could hardly have appealed to the police for protection.'

Martello heaved an enormous sigh. 'How fortunate you are in Finland without all these psychotics. And what have we got? Terrorists of any nationality or colour of fanaticism, gang warfare, nightmare organizations without scruple or humanity, corruption in business or politics that everybody deplores but takes for granted. And don't try to tell me you're catching up on us. But another time for all that. What I'm puzzled about is how to account for Pietro Vescovo's action last night. An addict can easily enough miscalculate, but could something have occurred during the day that finally pushed him over the top? Presumably he did his military service in Italy: he was on the platform at that last session and could have been responsible for the disappearance of the gun. Was it Pietro who fired it that evening? The hospital promised to inform me as soon as he's recovered sufficiently for questioning, if he does recover.'

Martello glanced at his watch and raised his eyebrows a fraction. He regarded Arvo across the table. 'Now, my friend, I think I've put you in the picture,' he said. 'As you'll appreciate, I've now many duties, some of them unpleasant, like forcing my attentions on your sister's mother-in-law who is most unlikely to welcome them. Whether the information about her husband's sudden departure will make them more or less welcome remains to be seen. Meanwhile I think you could be of considerable assistance to me, though you may not like what I'm going to ask you to do.'

'Interrogate my sister and her husband, I suppose.'

'Exactly. I see no reason at the moment for either of them to have been involved. But they'll almost certainly have useful background information which you'll be better able to obtain than I. In return I promise to keep you informed of my own discoveries. I'd welcome the opinion of a highly-qualified expert such as yourself who'd probably regard the

162

case from a different angle. Will you help me?'

Realizing his anomalous position, Arvo hesitated, knowing already that he was suppressing a good deal of information which might well have some bearing on the case and which would almost certainly emerge anyhow in the interview with Chiara. Any mention to Martello of the plot against Tania he might make would have promoted it from a domestic squabble to evidence bearing on the crime and this was the explanation he could give later if or when Martello reproached him for his silence. Presumably the captain had assumed he was on holiday or was visiting Italy on some police business and had been too tactful to ask, or too preoccupied to think much about it. But he realized there was a good deal to be learned, at least from Stefano, who would be far more at ease with his brother-in-law; moreover, he would like to find out more about the Berretta-owning carabiniere from Chioggia, who was as yet unknown to the police and might well remain so when Chiara was questioned.

Martello seemed highly pleased by his positive response when it eventually came, having probably interpreted the delay in answering to unwillingness. He jotted down the telephone numbers of the hotel and also of the carabinieri barracks in Venice, gave them to Arvo and suggested the pooling of discoveries as they became available. He then summoned a sergeant who would transport Arvo to Mala-mocco and wished him good luck.

Left alone, he considered for a short time and then summoned a subordinate, instructing him to inform the hotel manager with maximum courtesy that Captain Martello would welcome a few words with him. The manager appeared almost at once, obviously upset by all the publicity, confusion and clamour of worried or inquisitive hotel guests, journalists swarming all over the place and uniformed policemen giving an unfortunate impression in an exclusive hotel. All this over a most unpleasant incident for which he himself could in no way feel responsibility. Martello soothed him somewhat perfunctorily, thanked him for the facilities the police had been offered and requested his distinguished assistance in various small matters. Having elicited certain details about the hotel itself and the Congress, he referred to the recent ban that had been imposed on the departure of guests, saying that it could probably be lifted after an hour or so, though for various reasons a few of the delegates were already under the supervision of another branch of the police. In the meanwhile, he would very much like to see the platform group of delegates from the previous day: Signor Gentile would be in the hotel and could supply their names. After a further appeal for the speedy withdrawal of the unwelcome intruders, the manager withdrew.

Some ten minutes later an apprehensive group was facing him, five gentlemen of varying ages and nationalities and an extremely capable-looking woman. Martello explained his presence, referred to the tragedy already known to them, and suggested that before their departure it would be most useful to learn from them something about the previous day's discussion. They brightened up at the mention of departure but a slight apprehensiveness returned when Martello wanted first to know about their presence at the firework display. They had all been there and could either vouch for each other the whole time or give names of their companions at the relevant moment who were still available in the hotel, though even this remote contact with the murder made them uneasy. The question session came under review next and Martello was informed of the near-riot and the means taken to quell it.

'So Vescovo had a gun,' said Martello, stating the obvious. 'And presumably it was fired upwards. What did he do with the gun after he had fired it?'

Most of them had been too alarmed even to notice but the Japanese delegate had seen him put it on the table.

'And then what happened?'

'He made a speech,' the obviously American woman delegate responded.

'What kind of a speech?'

A short silence followed while memories were searched. A composite account emerged, made up of statements,

164

qualifications, contradictions, criticisms from everyone present.

'Hardly a speech to appease the dissatisfied members of his audience.'

They all agreed that it had hardly been that.

'It might even have infuriated the more dissatisfied among them.'

None of his companions would go so far as that. Nobody had noticed any further protest, angry mutterings, scowls or clenched fists: the writers had clearly been organized to air their grievances but could hardly have hoped for much satisfaction. Indeed, the ironic peroration had even amused some of the writers and they had dispersed in resigned good humour.

'And your chairman? When did he leave?'

'His secretary came in with a message for him and he left soon after,' a quiet Indian remembered.

'Taking his gun with him?'

Nobody had any idea, each having had his own preoccupations at the moment. There had been various leaflets, booklets and files on the table which, according to the Japanese, Vescovo had started to gather together before he was besieged by enthusiastic publishers and they might have covered and concealed the gun. On the other hand he might have slipped it into his pocket unnoticed during his conversations. After several hours and a change of clothing, Martello had already been informed, it had no longer been in a pocket nor in the dead man's room. And there was a reasonable chance that it had been the murder weapon.

As soon as the group of delegates had departed, Martello listed the names and other relevant details of all members of the Vescovo family and of the secretaries, and ordered a sergeant to add to them the names of all Italians staying in the hotel in order to check which of them held a licence and for what kind of gun. As the bullet had come from a Berretta .92, this information was unlikely to have any significance, though this could not be taken for granted. Almost certainly Vescovo had had a gun licence and Martello was curious to know the type of gun it applied to. He would be interested to learn also which of Vescovo's family and associates was a reasonably proficient marksman. He had already ordered a thorough search of the hotel and its surroundings for a discarded weapon, but with the Adriatic only a few yards away he had little optimism about finding anything.

The sullen maid at the palazzo might have heard of the murder on the radio, so he had already told her to keep the news from the signora until he could break it to her himself. A call around nine o'clock elicited the fact that Chiara had just awakened but was clearly in no condition to see anyone. Martello decided to appear at the palazzo without further notice in about an hour's time; for the present he had plenty to do here checking on the various police activities under way. Later in the morning he would inform himself about Pietro's condition and would try to learn more about Vescovo and his activities from among his most likely business and social acquaintances in Venice. And there was of course that assistant secretary who lived in Burano. Sandro Greco, that was his name, and he had the day off. He must be contacted also in the near future.

CHAPTER 11

SAND, SEASHELLS AND PLASTIC BOTTLES

Arvo had asked to be taken to Malamocco rather than to Iris's home in order to keep her out of any involvement in the case. Stefano had given him a key so he let himself into the empty flat where he set about making coffee. With no bread available, he found some biscuits and made a second breakfast while deciding how best to spend the morning. Just as he was about to pour another cup of coffee, he heard a key in the outer lock and moved into the hall so that, as a guest, he could welcome his hosts into their own home. Stefano came in first, carrying two cases, followed by Tania, with Toni gripping her hand as if afraid he might at any moment be abandoned, and Iris in the rear holding a bag

166

and a large cat basket. Her first care was to release its occupant who set to work assiduously sniffing everywhere as if he had never before even suspected that such a place might exist. Naturally, as the perfect host-guest, Arvo returned to the kitchen to cook (in Finnish terminology) further coffee for the grown-ups and even found a carton of orange juice for Toni. Tania and Iris had followed him.

'No coffee for me,' Tania declared. 'I must do some shopping.'

'Shopping can wait,' her brother ordered. 'You've got a lot to catch up on. We can all relax over coffee and biscuits. Has anyone heard the radio this morning? No? Well, I've got some news for you so you can prepare yourselves for a shock. Toni, if I open a tin of cat food, would you like to give Marmalade Joe some breakfast? He looks starving to me. And you can have the orange juice and the chocolate biscuits there on the table while he's eating it. Just watch him to see if he finishes it all up. The rest of you can make yourselves comfortable in the sitting-room. Coffee will be ready almost at once.'

Having deposited the cases in a bedroom, Stefano had been walking restlessly through the sitting-room and kitchen but at Arvo's reference to news, he had stood motionless staring across at him, until Tania and Iris both obeyed police instructions and urged him to do the same. Arvo joined them after quietly shutting the kitchen door.

'I spoke of a shock, didn't I?' he started. 'And it will be, though I don't think it will cause you much grief. Stefano, your father died yesterday evening. He was murdered on the hotel terrace during the firework display.'

He had expected an instant demand for details but Stefano remained frozen for several seconds while his wife and Iris watched him uneasily. Finally his eyes dwelt on each in turn before resting on Arvo. 'He wasn't my father,' he muttered harshly. 'I was told that yesterday afternoon. By my mother. In his presence, though he might well have known already.'

'Oh?' Arvo raised his eyebrows slightly, considering Stefano's bleak expression. 'In other words, you feel it doesn't concern you.'

167

'It's a relief. He was a thoroughly evil man and the world's a better place without him.'

Arvo wondered how much Stefano actually knew or merely suspected of his father's more evil activities. 'So you're not surprised to learn he was murdered?' he queried.

'Not in the least. He had it coming to him. He's always had it coming to him.'

'And you don't want to know how he died?'

'I suppose you want to tell me. Or, being a policeman, are you taking it for granted I know already?'

'He was shot,' Arvo informed him. 'How much do you know about guns, Stefano?'

'I did my military service, the same as everybody does.'

'And you have a gun now?'

'No. On second thoughts, yes. My mother gave me a package which she said contained a gun for my protection.'

'A Berretta .92?'

'I've no idea: I never opened it. I told her I didn't need it but she insisted. I don't even know what I did with it. Maybe it's in the storeroom downstairs. What's so special about a Berretta?'

'Never mind. It just happened to be the murder weapon.'

'With no fingerprints, presumably. How inconsiderate of the unknown benefactor!'

'Why do you assume we don't know who the murderer was?' Arvo asked. 'Are you deliberately trying to incriminate yourself?'

'I hated him and that's a motive. I was in the hotel yesterday evening, performing at the dinner; that's an opportunity. I didn't return here till well after the fireworks. What more do you want?'

'Well, as a special privilege we'll include you with the other four hundred or so possibilities, a fair number of whom may have shared your dislike. That's the coffee boiling. Someone ought to see to it. I don't know where the party cups and saucers are.'

It was Stefano who forestalled Tania, almost bolting into the kitchen, from where they could hear the clatter of cups and saucers and an exchange of conversation on cats and their ways between father and son. Meanwhile Arvo was explaining to Iris and his sister the main facts he had learned from Martello about the murder, including the present inaccessibility (and its causes) of Chiara and Pietro. He intended to discuss the murder in greater detail when he was alone with Stefano later.

Stefano appeared with the cups and the hot coffee which he poured as competently as if this had been his daily practice for years. Toni joined them and his mother broke the news gently that Grandfather Angelo had died quite suddenly last night. Toni looked worried rather than upset and asked the questions natural to children of his age though, hardly surprisingly, not whether Grandfather was now one of the other *angeli*. He was distracted from them by Arvo's suggestion that they should help Mummy do her shopping and then he would like to see the Lido.

'Can we go on the beach?' Toni suggested.

'An excellent idea,' said Arvo. 'Have you ever walked right along the beach just out of reach of the waves as they come in? All sorts of things can be washed in by the sea.'

'Will there be any letters in bottles from shipwrecked sailors?'

Iris laughed, somewhat sardonically. 'There'll be plenty of bottles and Coca-Cola tins, but no, we can't promise any letters inside. Never mind, Toni. There are lots of lovely shells.'

So an hour or so later, with plastic bags crammed with groceries and greengroceries deposited in the locked car parked near the centre, the five of them slithered and sank across grubby foot-hollowed sand towards an oily-grey sea, too inert to do more than allow lethargic rolls of water to deposit themselves and spread indolently over earth-brown packed sand before withdrawing sluggishly. They brought as gifts an assortment of rejected flotsam: plastic bottles and cans, ice-cream cartons, milk cartons, wine cartons, a medley of bottle tops, strange-shaped chunks of wood, most

169

of these now adorning the beach which was spread with dry seaweed like tangled unbleached hemp just above the high-water line.

The one feature of beauty was the shells, most of them of conventional cockle-shape but in every shade of black, white and gold, reflecting the predominant shades of the local cats. This long sandy playground comes to an end well short of Malamocco, with its defensive wall and rocks, so that Toni rarely saw the beach in the dark days of winter. Now on his first spring visit he suddenly came alive, tearing off his shoes to run into the water, splashing wildly and screaming with delight, until his mother and Iris each took a hand and led him slowly along, stopping to examine the most exotic of the shells to start a collection with. Pausing at intervals for the others to catch up, Arvo and Stefano strode ahead in a southerly direction towards the distant Arabian-nights structure of the familiar hotel.

Having already a reasonably clear idea of the plot to achieve Toni's abduction, Arvo now had the opportunity to hear Stefano's story of the events that had followed. During the past few days, as Stefano explained, he had been more than usually occupied with work at the theatre besides a couple of recitals and he had seen little of his son. Tired out after a return in the small hours, he had got up late the previous day and had found Toni in what had earlier been his own playroom, surrounded by construction kits, picture books, video games and a blaring television, and crying bitterly for his mother.

In the very few moments he'd been free to think clearly about domestic problems, Stefano had become aware of ever-increasing doubts. Whatever the evidence, there were the personalities involved to be considered. He recalled the afternoon of his mother's visit some six months earlier, her neurotic attempts to gain possession of himself and Toni and her disregard, even approval, of Toni's lying. Had Tania throughout all the years of their marriage given the least cause for suspicion? And there was that smooth customer the carabiniere: the veneer of friendliness and sincerity he had accepted now peeling away as he recalled

Tania's distrust and his own uneasiness about Giovanni's open attempts at flirtation.

Picking up his son, who had clung to him desperately as a substitute mother, he had coaxed the true story out of him. So, it emerged, during the night in the fogbound boat Giovanni had made the most of his opportunity. First had come the promises of the wonderful presents and wonderful food he would enjoy at his grandmother's, together with the chance of doing exactly as he liked: all in return for learning a story by heart and repeating it when he got home. No wonder, he recalled, there had been that mistake about a private concert in Rome scheduled for his final evening there and the frantic message from his mother waiting in his hotel early in the day begging him to return home immediately to deal with an unspecified emergency.

The truth out, Stefano had hesitated about what to do next. His instinct had been to take the boy away at once but where could he take him? Tania seemed to have left Malamocco and there were several matters demanding urgent attention, above all a confrontation with his mother and his father too. Hardly an occasion suitable for a child to witness. His unsatisfactory solution had been to give gentle comfort and reassurance, with promises to go and find Mummy and bring her back as soon as he possibly could to take Toni home. Together they set out a kit for a battle-cruiser and started its construction. With Toni's promise to have it ready for Mummy when she came to fetch him, Stefano had left for the Lido and retribution. It was then, unfortunately, that Toni had taken the law into his own hands.

It had been against this background and after a long wait on the terrace that he'd confronted Angelo and his mother and heard of Toni's disappearance. He recalled bitterly the conflict between Angelo and Chiara, the implication of Fedele in the deception and his mother's final revelation about her son's parentage.

Arvo broke in at this point. 'That must have been a shock to you. Or had you suspected it earlier?'

'Hardly a shock, with all that melodrama flying around

171

already. I'd never thought anything about it: why should I have? Angelo had always more or less ignored me: the feeble-minded-idiot mistake—and I'd kept out of his way as much as I could. He'd seemed to me a gigantic, remote figure with Pietro a junior version of father: lots of energy and friends, always ready to try out new ideas that would be to his own advantage and regardless of the consequences, and never scared of things and people as I usually was. I was a typical mother's boy and I realize now that was exactly what my mother had wanted. No, it wasn't a shock: in fact I felt enormously relieved. I'm my own self now. No giant father to live up to. I don't have to exist in his shadow any more.'

'How did he take Toni's disappearance?'

'The only thing he worried about was how best to hush it up. He refused to call the police because of the publicity it would cause during the Congress. Odd in a way. Because he's never lacked foresight and there'd have been plenty of awkward questions coming up later if anything serious like a kidnapping had happened and it hadn't been reported at once. I think he rightly assumed that the boy was hiding or had run away. He made it quite clear then that Chiara would have to send Toni home immediately he appeared not only because of the nuisance he was likely to be but because of the scandal it would cause if the story leaked out. But you can imagine Chiara's reaction to all this. I'm only amazed she didn't go straight off and report the disappearance herself. Probably other fish to fry. I wonder just how she spent the time till the evening dinner. I suppose the police didn't mention to you anything about a report from her.'

'I don't think they know anything.' Arvo was speculating about Angelo's call to Chioggia. Could he have been using a roundabout way to get an investigation going? Fedele would be familiar with the boy and in the circumstances could be trusted to keep quiet about the affair. And how would Fedele have responded? But there was more to be learned from Stefano.

'How did you spend the time between?' he asked. 'Why didn't you contact the police yourself?'

172

They were approaching the Casino now and the hotel was clearly visible, with its domes and pepper-pots: something about it reminded Arvo of an earlier visit to the Basilica in Venice, each an escape into surrealistic fantasy for the stolid Venetian intellect. Easy enough to aim from the roof at someone strategically placed below, he mused. He had already guessed part of Stefano's answer but would be interested to hear how his brother-in-law would express it.

Some kind of argument seemed to be delaying Toni and his escort. Stefano's whole attention appeared to be concentrated on a Jugoslav tourist hovercraft, small but visible, as it made its way towards the long mole round the end of which it would turn towards the lagoon. And it was the distant hovercraft he quietly addressed rather than his companion. 'I telephoned the palazzo from the hotel but the number was engaged at first. When I got through, Beata the maid answered. She said that Toni had turned up. He'd told her he'd been hiding in one of the attics. He was now having a meal and seemed quite happy again. All, of course, what Angelo had just been telling her to say over the phone, and I actually swallowed it. I needed time to think things over, especially what I could say to Tania when we met, so I walked to Malamocco. It took me about an hour and the flat was empty when I got there. There was nothing much to eat so I went out and got a meal in the village. It was while I was there I thought of Iris and tried her number without getting any answer. I suppose it was about the time when she and Tania would have gone off to meet Rosa off the *motonave* but I didn't think of that and just felt helpless. What could I have done with Toni if I'd gone back and claimed him? Of course I should just have cancelled the evening concert. But I'm a coward: I'll always be a coward, I know. I was afraid of Angelo and I was afraid too that if I antagonized him in his present mood, he might decide to hang on to the boy after all, possibly having him removed to Rome, perhaps hiding him somewhere and pretending he'd been kidnapped. And even if we'd got him back eventually, think what Toni would have had to go through in the meantime. All right, after what Angelo had said, that wasn't

173

likely. But I wasn't thinking particularly clearly just then.

'My flute was in the palazzo but I had another in the flat and as there wouldn't have been time to go across to the palazzo and change, I phoned a colleague about my size who lives on the Lido and asked if I could borrow his evening suit. One way and another I only had just enough time to change at his house and get to the hotel in time. I returned to his house to change and have a drink and by then it was too late to do anything about Toni so I got a bus to the flat—and ran into you there.'

'Where had you been during the firework display?'

'I left as it was starting.'

'So you heard nothing about your father's death?'

'You don't think I'd have run away from that, do you?'

'And Pietro? Did you notice him around that evening?'

'Both of us suspects, I suppose. Joint inheritors of the greasy family pickings.' Predictably Stefano was beginning to resent the questioning. 'From the little I've seen of Pietro during his stay, he's in a state where he'd be more likely to turn a gun on himself than his father.'

'Business problems?'

'We didn't discuss them, but I've heard rumours. The previous day he grumbled about not having had any opportunity of a private discussion with Angelo and he was going to insist on having one before he left. He'd intended to go off today. It was obvious to everyone that he'd got much bigger problems than business ones: probably why Angelo was avoiding him. He'd never do anything to save a drowning man, not even waste a lifebelt on him and not even if the man was his own son. He certainly wouldn't have wasted money on bailing Pietro out. I can well imagine what would have taken place in that interview, if it actually took place.'

'Problems connected with narcotics?'

'Obviously. Ostensibly he was a big name in publishing, like his father. And, like his father, almost certainly in collusion with him in fact, he was into narcotics. Oh yes, I know about that—like a lot of other people including the police, I expect, but from the outside without concrete evidence. But there was one big difference between them.

174

Pietro was of the new generation and he'd been spoilt. Angelo had grown up the hard way and learned survival. Pietro had everything, without effort and unpleasant results. He'd got away with playing with fire and enjoyed it. He'd have thought getting high smart, sophisticated, like the kind of people he'd go around with. His wife wrote to say she'd left him you know and taken the children: she was too good for him. Like Tania, I suppose.'

'Would he have thought murder smart?'

'Murder would have been reality, which he'd got used to avoiding.'

Much of this made sense for Arvo. Pietro drowning and screaming for a lifebelt from his once-indulgent parent would now not only have been disregarded but might even have been given a shove under by a disgusted father. He extended the thread of the conversation by asking, 'Would Pietro have had a gun?'

'Almost certainly in the States, from all one hears,' Stefano responded. 'But he would hardly have brought it with him. His appearance might well have attracted attention in Customs and finding an undeclared gun on him, which it would have been to them, wouldn't have appealed much.'

'How about your mother?'

This was obviously a new idea to Stefano. 'Surely you don't think she was involved? And in any case, she'd have had no motive.'

'I only asked if she had a gun, not if she'd used one. We must clear the decks properly, you know.'

'Not that I know of. When I come to think of it, she may have a rifle. She's got a small cottage, hut, whatever you'd call it on one of the more minute lagoon islands where she occasionally organizes shooting parties: they shoot birds for some unknown reason.'

Arvo considered this. In the uncertain light, the shot from the roof would have required a fair proficiency. They were now parallel with the hotel and he examined closely the roped-off area of the terrace with table and chair still in position, before lifting his gaze to the roof immediately above. It was at this point that he recalled a disquieting memory. Years before as youngsters on the family farm in Eastern Finland, he and his sister had often gone shooting hares and other wild creatures who gnawed fruit trees, damaged other crops and even stole chickens. With excellent eyesight Tania had been a far better marksman than himself. If it had been Chiara who'd been murdered . . . But Tania had been left in Iris's home while he and Iris had driven to the flat: she'd been more than a mile from the scene. In any case, where would she have got a gun? Could she have found and brought to Iris's home the gun donated by Chiara? Appropriately shot by her own gun, except obviously that it hadn't been Chiara but Angelo who'd been shot. Mental ramblings that made no sense.

The argument that had delayed their retinue had long ago been resolved and as the two men paused to view the scene of the crime, in common with a fair sprinkling of interested local residents, Toni and his companions almost caught up with them. Arvo waved his hand to the right and the two forerunners trudged over the sand-powder diagonally towards the Lungomare, the Promenade, a little beyond the hotel. 'We could do with a snack,' he suggested, 'but before we all join forces, there are still a few small matters I'd like to clear up.'

'Go ahead,' Stefano agreed. He suddenly appeared more cheerful and fleetingly Arvo wondered whether some danger point had been evaded. However he continued as he'd intended:

'When you were waiting for your parents at the end of the morning, did you go into the Congress room at all?'

'Yes, I did. I thought he might be still in there.'

'Was there anybody there?'

'It was empty. I suppose everybody had cleared off for lunch when my father left.'

'How long did you stay there?'

'A few minutes, actually. I noticed the devices they have for listening to the simultaneous translation: it was the first time I'd come across anything like it. And if that seems odd at a time when I was upset and, I admit, nervous about the interview ahead, it happens, you know. Maybe a subconscious excuse for putting off the evil hour or the distraction that's a form of relief. Why do you ask?'

'Had you heard a shot some fifteen minutes or so before?'

'Not a rehearsal, surely? Or did my father shoot a delegate who argued with him?'

'You might describe it as a rehearsal, I suppose, though nobody died. An outlet for suppressed violence maybe. I'll tell you about it later.' Stefano's sudden flippancy had its own unnatural quality but everything about this case seemed unnatural and overwrought. Now on firm pavement, he looked back at the everyday sanity of a small boy who was having to abandon the fascination of seashore and, almost back to his normal self, was giving full expression to feelings of disgust. Iris said something, on the subject of ice-creams he guessed, and after some hesitation Toni took her hand and plodded into the dusty stretch which separated them.

With only a few minutes left before the reunion, Arvo introduced his final topic. 'There's another person who may well be involved,' he said, 'Giovanni Fedele. I intend to ask him some questions and it's not going to be easy to arrange.'

'Quite impossible, I'd say,' Stefano agreed. 'Though I intend to do the same myself in the very near future.'

'There are ways and means. He obviously speaks some English so that won't be any problem. I understand he's stationed in Chioggia.'

'Yes, he is, it seems. But I've got no idea when he's on duty.'

'He may well be there now. Vescovo apparently made contact with him in Chioggia yesterday afternoon.' Arvo thought for a moment. 'Do you know where we can find a telephone near here? Not in the hotel. I don't want to run into Martello before I've done one or two other jobs.'

'Usually in a tobacconist's but they'll be closed by now. But I know the proprietor of a café not far from here in Via Sandro Gallo who'd let us use his.'

'Right. That'll please Toni at least and probably my sister. I'm going to ask for your help in getting through. We'll find the number in the telephone book, make contact

177

and you'll just ask for Lieutenant Giovanni Fedele. If they ask who wants to speak to him, tell them it's a detective-superintendent working on the Vescovo case in collaboration with Captain Martello of Venice. But don't say that unless you must.'

Stefano agreed, just as they were joined by Iris, Tania and an excited Toni, who produced from a plastic bag a plethora of shells, sombre black and radiant orange, and Arvo suggested painting a box and sticking them on as a cotton-reel box for mother. They wandered lazily along a street in the direction of the lagoon in search of Stefano's café and Toni's ice-cream.

With five unexpected customers to provide for, the café proprietor willingly indicated a telephone and produced a directory. The others discussed orders while Stefano located the number and unexpectedly quickly Arvo found himself in remote contact with this sinister knave of hearts—and of diamonds too in all probability.

The voice was deep and of smoothest velvet. Arvo's request to speak English drew the surprised response, 'Tenente Fedele speaks. Can I assist you?'

'Arvo Laurila speaking. I am here in Italy to represent my sister, Tania Vescovo, whose son has been taken from his home by his grandmother.'

There was a brief silence before the lieutenant replied, 'I have heard of the case, Mr Laurila, but I do not know why you turn to me.'

'You surely had something to do with it?'

'The child told some fantastic story which I have since firmly denied. I can do no more.'

'Had you heard that Toni was missing?'

Again a pause, obviously for thought. 'If that is the case I can only hope that he has been found again.'

The time had come to play a high card with only a surmise to back the move. 'But surely the grandfather, Mr Vescovo, mentioned it to you in his telephone call yesterday afternoon?'

A silence expressed amazement. Then: 'I think you are mistaken. I received no such telephone call.'

'You will be aware that Mr Vescovo himself cannot confirm the matter. But naturally I have been in touch with his secretary.' The whitest of white lies.

'Then his secretary was quite mistaken.' The denial was immediate.

'It was confirmed by the hotel operator who made the connection, so I think not. I should be interested to learn what you have done already to locate the child.'

Arvo half expected the receiver to be slammed down, when he would have been forced to proceed in another direction. So blatant an implication that the lieutenant was lying could have got no other response if this hadn't been the case. But Fedele was evidently curious, probably uneasy. He took refuge in polite generalities.

'Surely a misunderstanding. But perhaps I can assist you in some other way, Mr Laurila.'

'It is I rather who may be able to assist you, Lieutenant. As my sister's representative, I have already spoken with Captain Martello of Venice, who is in charge of the investigations of her father-in-law's murder and have learned several curious things from him. I think we should meet for an exchange of information. As the matter is urgent and I have time, I can arrange to come to Chioggia immediately to discuss with you.'

After a brief show of reluctance on the part of Fedele, an arrangement was made for a meeting on the arrival of the boat from Pellestrina some two hours later. Having learned from the café proprietor the time of the next Pellestrina bus, Arvo lunched off a couple of sandwiches, apologized to his companions for transferring his Finnish official duties to Italy and left to catch the bus.

'I'm going to meet your carabiniere boyfriend,' he informed his sister, 'but we've got far more important things to discuss than you.'

Standing to one side of the landing-stage in Chioggia, Fedele proved easily recognizable in his uniform: a distinguished-looking man, courteous and relaxed though slightly preoccupied, possibly because, as he explained, he was exceptionally

179

busy that afternoon. They made their way to a local café, Fedele acting the part of a thoughtful host indicating to his foreign guest local points of interest on the way.

A glass of wine was purchased for each of them and taken to a table where, apparently still unaware of Toni's reappearance, Fedele expressed deep concern for Tania's desolation. The assumed cause of the desolation not having been mentioned, Arvo chose to interpret this as a reference to a concern about her father-in-law's murder.

'Such an appalling act of violence has been a shock for her, naturally,' he admitted. 'But surely a far greater one for her mother-in-law. I understand you are acquainted with her.'

Fedele's bewilderment was so patent that it expressed itself linguistically in his startled, 'Wherefrom get you that idea?'

'I thought you might be a friend of the family. I return to yesterday's telephone call which among your varied responsibilities you had forgotten earlier. It was, after all, you that Signor Vescovo turned to when his grandson disappeared.'

Fedele eyed him blankly, trying to read his companion's mind to discover how much he actually knew. Finally he admitted, with some approach to the truth, 'Signor Vescovo had heard of me in connection with the unfortunate incident in the fog, when I, the boy and his mother were stranded overnight. There was an important international conference, you understand, and he did not want publicity. The newspapers, radio, television services, they learn from the local police what important things happen. So because I knew the little boy and all that had happened before (you have probably heard about it from your sister), he turned to me in confidence to make discreet inquiries.'

'In spite of the boy's account of what had happened that night?'

'I had denied it. The boy had seen television too much. He was inventing fantasies. I assured him her story was true and he believed me.'

'I'm not speaking about the earlier story he had told. I'm

180

referring to what his grandfather learned later about who had really invented that story and persuaded Toni to tell it.'

The blue eyes had lost their serenity. 'What did you say?' their owner asked incredulously.

'I think you heard and also understand me,' Arvo countered. 'And although I don't know all that was said in that conversation, there are some things I can guess, having some idea of the kind of man Vescovo was and how he might make use of his power.' He paused for his words to sink in and then continued, 'But I promised to give you information. I have learned today that the murder of Angelo Vescovo was carried out with the use of a gun available only to a carabiniere: a Berretta .92. Yes, I am revealing police information. I am a policeman, Lieutenant Fedele, a detective-superintendent of the Finnish State Police, at present working in collaboration with the Venice carabinieri. I have already learned a great deal from Captain Martello and others. At this point I will remind you what as a policeman yourself you well know, that the truth cannot be controverted while lies can only indicate guilt. And I happen to know that your relationship with Chiara Vescovo is considerably closer than mere acquaintanceship and is of at least several months' duration.'

'You appear to accuse me of murdering her husband.'

'Not at present: beyond the fact of the gun, I have little evidence that might point to you.'

'So you waste your time if you look for a murderer here. If the bullet and cartridge are available, you will find they could not have come from my gun. It is here now in my holster. And if Captain Martello this afternoon wishes to have it controlled, he will find I could not have used it last night. And all the bullets I am provided are here.'

'All right. I've already said I am making no accusation. But you cannot deny that you conspired with Signora Vescovo to deprive my sister of her child.'

'That would not be a criminal offence, Superintendent, even if true.'

181

'Don't be too sure, Lieutenant. But there are more important matters. When did you last see Chiara Vescovo?'

Giovanni let out a sigh of exasperation, both arms moving
forward and sideways, the palms uppermost, expressing
apparent despair over the naïve illusions of his small-country
colleague. At the same time he was thinking fast, Arvo
realized.

'You claim to know I have a relationship with the Signora
Vescovo,' he exclaimed. 'I think you are only just come
from Finland. Please to explain how you know something
that I am quite unaware of myself.'

Arvo decided to chance his hand. Despite the fact that
most of his assumptions were based on guesswork, they all
dovetailed so neatly that there must be some underlying
truth, and even if this wasn't the case, no great harm would
have been done.

'Last October Signora Vescovo visited you in Pellestrina
on a Saturday afternoon and later she arranged your meeting
with my sister on the Burano boat. It was she who suggested
your encounter with my sister and her family at the airport
shortly before Christmas and played a considerable part in
planning your recent boat trip and its sequence. Had the fog
not intervened, I suppose there would have been a mysterious
engine failure just as you arrived in Pellestrina with a long
delay while Toni helped you to repair it and my sister waited
in your house. Or you could have got stranded on a mudbank
you'd never realized was there. I repeat my question, or perhaps Martello could better send someone to ask your neighbours. When did you last see Chiara Vescovo?'

Further prevarication being profitless, Giovanni changed
tack to devious cooperation. 'Late yesterday afternoon,' he
admitted. 'After I returned from Chioggia.'

'Thank you. She knew what time you would arrive?'

'Yes.'

'How long did she stay?'

'She returned to the hotel after about an hour. She had
taken her evening clothes to the hotel where she could
change, so I brought her back there in the boat a little after
six o'clock.'

'Did she speak about her grandson?'

'Naturally. She was very agitated and unhappy.'

'And like her husband, I suppose she asked for your help. Why hadn't she informed the police in Venice?'

'She said that her husband had forbidden it to avoid publicity and journalists.'

A light dawned in Arvo's mind. In the circumstances Chiara might well have had little trust in Toni's reactions if he'd been found by the police and asked awkward questions. However, he merely asked Giovanni, 'Was she annoyed with her husband?'

'I think she was only overcome with sorrow because of the loss of her grandson. She could speak of nothing else.'

'Did you tell her about the request her husband had made to you?'

'No, that was a police matter. Now I must return to my duties. Goodbye, Mr Laurila.' Giovanni started to move towards the door.

'One more question, Lieutenant.' Arvo had risen from the table and his raised voice seemed likely to attract unwelcome attention from the men ranged along the bar. He approached the waiting carabiniere and spoke quietly. 'What steps did you actually take to ensure the discreet investigation of Toni Vescovo's disappearance?'

'Not your affair. I have told you all I know,' the carabiniere snapped in the course of a hurried exit.

CHAPTER 12

SKIMMING THE SURFACE

As soon as Arvo had left, Martello ordered coffee and panini and endeavoured to plan the right and proper conduct of a case that promised to become a journalist's dream but a policeman's nightmare. He had seen no morning newspapers but could visualize the Italian-version headlines, from the loftiness of Distinguished Publisher Assassinated through the middlebrow and mixed-up Fatal Epilogue to Literary Banquet right down to the dramatically speculative Death in Venice: Mafia Strikes Again. So far the swarm of buzzing inquisitors had been restricted to beach and promenade, guests only (together with the barely tolerated upholders of law) being permitted within the aerosolled hotel precincts. Martello could only hope that by the time of his own departure the tunnel from hotel to water transport might have escaped attention.

For the time being, he had decided to leave the younger branch of the Vescovos to the strictly unauthorized attentions of his Finnish colleague, other organizations than his own being already in communication with those few delegates worthy of their specialized examination. Most of the publishers and writers were either sleeping after an early-morning return to the hotel, departing hastily or, in one or two cases, prolonging their stay, having got wind of the drama so close to their pens. So it would now be his own reluctant duty to seek contact with sedated wife and stupefied elder son. He had no doubt whatever that the State Finance Authorities would seize with delight the legally-sanctioned opportunity they now had to examine the fiscal background to the crime and he would be happy to let them have that secretary Gentile to help them in their specialist inquiries. And that reminded Martello that there were additional matters he himself wished to discuss with the gentleman in question.

Poor Camillo had had little sleep the previous night and that might well have accounted for his haggard appearance when he sat down as requested, though his pallor might have been intensified by anticipation of what was to come. But the first questions were innocuous enough, albeit on a matter he knew little about.

'I'd like the address of your colleague, Signor Greco, who you say has a free day today. There is no number listed for him in the telephone book.'

Camillo was only too happy to supply details of the

184

Burano address from his notebook: he believed that Sandro lived in his father-in-law's house: hence the absence of his name in the telephone directory. Further questions elicited the suggestion—derived from his surname and dialect—that Sandro hailed from Sicily, though unlike Sicilians in general he was unusually reserved. Partly for this reason, he knew little of Sandro's actual duties beyond the assistance he had given in the general organization of the Congress, providing information for delegates, seeing that all required materials were available and like matters. He had been taken on by Signor Vescovo about three months before and obviously had had some previous business training though so far as Camillo knew, he had done little work in this capacity in his present position.

Sandro Greco, a name that stirred faint echoes in Martello's memory though nothing beyond a feeling of vague familiarity. The impression of having heard it before and in connection with Sicily sharpened as details were added to the name, but Martello's mental computer was reluctant to come up with an answer, possibly because it was becoming clogged with new data.

But mental computer or merely long experience of interrogation was prompting him that Camillo was intent on covering something up. He hesitated for a moment, regarding this unfortunate pawn manœuvred helplessly by masters of the game, and pinpointed the discrepancy. A confidential secretary inevitably conversant with the devious subtleties of an employer such as Vescovo could hardly claim total ignorance of a colleague's 'special duties' and his very evasiveness suggested an awareness at least of their illegality. A certain menace hardened his voice as he resumed:

'What you're saying is absurd, Signor Gentile, and you are thereby implicating yourself in those illicit activities of Signor Vescovo that the police know far more about than you possibly imagine. You will be questioned later about your own duties but if you want to avoid putting yourself in an even more serious position, you will inform me of your suspicions, even if not knowledge, of Sandro Greco's "special duties". I assume they were connected with the distribution of narcotics.'

Far from giving information, Camillo was struck dumb, and stared aghast at his omniscient interrogator.

'Well?' Martello demanded. 'Out with it.'

Camillo fumbled helplessly for words. 'I have nothing to do with it,' he stuttered. 'It's something I don't want to know about. He asked me, that is Signor Vescovo, to take over . . . certain special duties: he would pay me much more. But I refused.'

'When?'

'Towards the end of last year.'

'Before Greco was employed?'

'Yes.'

'But you didn't report this to the police?'

'He threatened violence to myself and my wife if I said anything to anybody.'

'And have you?'

'No, Capitano. I wouldn't have dared. And if you're thinking of what happened to my wife yesterday, there can't be any connection. I've said nothing.'

Martello calculated that while this frightened little man was probably telling the truth about his silence, something that had come to his employer's ears might well have alerted Vescovo's suspicions. Camillo would have been aware of this possibility and of its likely repetition. Could this cautious underling have had the courage to take advantage of the gun left in the conference room, realizing that the evening's firework display would present an ideal opportunity for getting rid of his tormentor? He had in any case intended to ask his next question.

'Before leaving to go to your wife yesterday afternoon, as a Congress secretary you surely returned to the conference room for some reason or other.'

'No, Capitano. I was too anxious about my wife. I left immediately I was informed.'

'And before you were informed? During the period when Signora Vescovo was talking to her husband?'

'I had to collect certain documents, yes.' The words were forced out of him.

'From the speaker's table?'

'Yes.'

'You noticed the gun left there?'

'No, Capitano. It may have been under some piles of brochures that were in some disorder there, but I saw no gun.'

'But you can use a gun?'

'I learnt how to in the army but have probably forgotten now.'

'What time did you return to the hotel?'

'I came back around five o'clock and among other things gathered together papers and brochures. The conference room had been cleaned and put in order though the table seemed not to have been disturbed. I sorted out the various things on it but there was certainly no gun there then.'

'And what time did you finally leave?'

'About eight-thirty. Some time before the fireworks began. I went straight home.'

Having exhausted this line for the time being, Martello returned briefly to an earlier issue.

'Was it before or after Signor Vescovo's request for additional help to you that he engaged Signor Greco?'

'After.'

'Shortly after?'

'Yes.'

There was a lengthy silence, Martello's subconscious computer having suddenly jerked up the required information. Sandro Greco, a minor figure among the Mafia *pentiti*, one of their operatives who had turned on his associates and helped the police. A revenge denouncement, he recalled, something to do with the death of his brother. Not important enough for special police protection, he had clearly got away as far as possible from his native island. Could he have been recognized by Sicilian Vescovo and terrorized into taking on what Gentile had refused to be bribed into doing—if that smooth secretary had indeed been telling the truth? Locating Greco must have urgent priority.

The prolonged pause in his interrogation had unnerved Camillo even more and by now convinced of his immediate arrest as number one suspect, he cowered helpless in his chair, unaware that his most immediate danger lay in a quite other direction.

Apparently inspired by his long deliberation, Martello announced firmly, 'I am applying for a warrant to search the Vescovo palazzo with the object of removing for examination by the Finance Department all forms of documentary evidence that may provide useful information and will include every kind of financial record. As soon as the warrant is received at my headquarters, you will accompany the sergeants responsible for collecting such information and assist them in their search. Needless to say, anything overlooked deliberately or inadvertently will soon be manifest to the inspectors concerned. They are experts at locating concealed documents and in this case they will want to know why full cooperation has not been given. Do you understand?'

Camillo understood only too well and writhed now in his chair. The system of recording the more mysteriously profitable transactions of the local Vescovo undertakings had been brilliantly misleading, the camouflage adequate for all normal inquiry, but exposed to the X-ray vision of the Finance Department . . .?

'Naturally, Capitano,' he quavered, raising himself with difficulty on unresponsive legs.

Having dismissed his shivering lamb to the shearers' cutters in company with two unpitying shepherds who took him first to headquarters, Martello made immediate contact with the Burano number he now had available and was answered by a young feminine voice which informed him that Signor Greco had left home the previous evening.

'Where did he leave for?'

'He told me he had been sent to Rome by his employer to carry out some urgent inquiries there.'

'What time did he leave?'

'About half past seven in the evening.'

'On his way to the airport or the railway station?'

'He didn't say. He went in his new boat which he could have left somewhere for his return.'

'When did he say he'd return?'

'He said he'd telephone when he knew.'

'Are you his wife?'

'Yes, signore.'

'You have heard his employer has been murdered?'

'No, signore. I don't know the name of his employer.' A sudden gasp. 'Not the Signor Vescovo whose death is in today's papers?'

'Yes, signora. I don't want to trouble you unduly but I would like to have some more information about your husband. I shall be sending one of my officers to your address in about half an hour's time.'

'We are very busy now in our café.'

But police matters must have precedence and Martello dispatched the only assistant he had left on his way to pick up what crumbs might have been scattered in Burano about Greco's past history, present whereabouts and actions and future intentions. He himself made a further long-distance approach to the surly maid in the palazzo and learned to his surprise that the signora was awake and extremely anxious to see the capitano.

Allowing her no time to change her mind, Martello alerted a sergeant at headquarters who would be collected by the police boat on its way to the palazzo. He chose a moment when the coast was clear to emerge from the tunnel and was soon on his way across the lagoon to carabinieri headquarters and then the palazzo.

The two investigators gained immediate entrance and were conveyed by lift to what might have been described as a boudoir, in which the bereft widow, adorned in an ankle-length figure-moulding emerald-green robe or dressing-gown, awaited them. Too overcome to rise, she vaguely indicated chairs for her visitors, focused an intense gaze upon them and demanded:

'You have found my grandson after all, then. But where is he?'

The following ten minutes were taken up by incomprehension, explanation, expostulation, further explanation, ramification, reproach, refutation and eventual stalemate. Vast new and unwelcome vistas of the case had been opened up and silently but none the less vigorously Martello cursed that frank and honest Finn who must have been well aware of this particular minefield but had given not the least hint of its existence. It was only after a further interval that he could indicate the original purpose of his visit and he trembled at the prospect of its probable reception.

'It appears, signora, that you have not yet been acquainted with the most recent and regrettable tragedy.'

'My grandson is dead.' A slightly scrawny hand clutched at her throat.

'No, signora.' Martello was very slightly ashamed of the relish with which he added, 'But your husband is.'

'Heart failure, I suppose. I warned him.'

Not even this reaction could surprise Martello after what had preceded it.

'No, signora. He was shot.'

'Suicide?'

'No. Murder.'

'And what do you expect me to do about it? It's your responsibility to ascertain his murderer and bring him to justice.'

The news seemed to have invigorated rather than depressed her. She rose purposefully from her chair to confront them from a slightly higher level and announced, 'So, I have a lot to do. There will be many relatives and friends to inform and the funeral arrangements to be made. Have you told my two sons? Where are they? Why aren't they with their mother in her sorrow?'

'Your elder son is . . . not available. I haven't yet seen your younger son.'

'Really! Please inform him at once and see that he reports to me. And my husband's secretary too if you should meet him. You will realize that in these tragic circumstances I cannot afford to give you more of my time. During the past twenty-four hours I have been bereft of husband and

190

grandson but in my position I have no time for grief. That must come later. Beata will see you out.'

She pressed a bell and was about to open the door to let herself out when, with considerable adroitness, Martello placed himself between her and the gilded panels.

'I regret, signora,' he said, almost with reverence, 'I cannot carry out your wishes without information you alone can provide.'

In frozen amazement she glared at this impertinent public servant before uttering in severed monosyllables, 'Get out of my way.'

With a firm grip on the elegantly-wrought gilt door-handle, Martello slipped sideways a few inches so that he could catch his sergeant's eye. 'Get into touch with the Commandante, would you,' he requested him. 'Tell him I'd like his authority to make an immediate arrest.' He clarified this unlikely request by meaningfully closing and opening the eye beyond the signora's vision and the sergeant got the message and started to dial. At once the lady concerned moved back into the centre of the room where she took up a position with her hands clasped before her regarding him with an air of patient and bewildered injury.

'What do you want to know?' she asked. Simultaneously the receiver was quietly replaced.

'Please sit down, signora. I have no wish to cause you discomfort.' With his subject now below the level of his eyes, he continued, 'I believe you were with your husband at the hotel yesterday afternoon.'

The questioning that followed produced an expurgated description of that stormy occasion. Chiara described her failure to persuade her husband to instigate a police search for her grandson, omitting any reference to Stefano's involvement or Angelo's insistence on sending the boy home on his reappearance. She also referred to her presence at the farewell dinner. She had gone on to the terrace with her husband but had been too upset over her grandson to remain. She had left early in the firework display leaving her husband sitting at a table and after changing her dress had gone straight home, in the hope that her grandson had been found. The palazzo had apparently been empty so she had gone to bed, after taking a sedative to calm her agitation.

'Did your husband own a gun?' she was asked.

'Probably, in fact certainly. I have seen it. It was a Parabellum for which he had a licence.'

Slightly taken aback by this sudden spate of unsolicited detail, Martello continued:

'Have you seen it recently?'

'No, though I understand he carries it around with him sometimes.'

'Have you a gun?'

'No, I have no need of one.'

'Can you use a gun?'

Chiara calculated briefly, assessing risks of further involvement. 'A gun, no,' she said. 'I occasionally hunt and use a friend's rifle. But I am an amateur.'

'Did you visit the conference room at the hotel yesterday?'

'No. I had no reason to.'

'How did you spend the afternoon after you had left your husband?'

'I returned here to wait for my grandson's return.'

'But you attended the dinner in the evening?'

'It was my duty. My personal sufferings have never interfered with my duty to my husband. And now, signore, I have told you everything and I am ill, as you see. I must ask my maid to call my doctor and go to lie down. Please have pity on a wife and grandmother in torment.' She rose, made for the door and was through it before Martello could possibly have reached it even if he had wanted to.

'So much for informing relatives and funeral arrangements,' he commented.

The two men found their way downstairs unaccompanied to the police boat, waiting as in bygone centuries at the water gate on the Grand Canal.

Martello went first to his office in the Venice carabinieri post to check for any information that might have come in there and to deal with other police matters requiring his urgent attention. He had a late lunch and then telephoned the hospital to find out about his chances of an interview with Pietro. It took him some ten minutes to make contact with any of the doctors dealing with the case and he was due for a considerable disappointment. Pietro's condition was worse than had been anticipated: even if his life could be saved, he was likely to remain in a coma for several days.

'What's your diagnosis?'

'You may know already he's a cocaine addict: probably has been for years and would have been in a very unsatisfactory physical condition anyhow. I should guess that some time yesterday evening, he overdosed himself considerably.'

'Would he have done that deliberately, do you think?'

'Difficult to say, but very possibly. Particularly if he'd had any kind of shock or strain.'

'Would he have been capable of aiming a gun before that?'

'The father, you mean? Yes, I heard about that. It would depend on his condition at the time. In a certain state of mind, either one of intense excitement or intense depression, he might well have considered it and been capable of it, at a reasonable distance, of course.'

'And be overcome with remorse afterwards and attempt suicide?'

'Not impossible.'

'When can I see him?'

'Not for days, if you want anything intelligible. Even then he possibly won't remember. Sorry, but you'll have to get evidence, if that's what you're after, elsewhere.'

Martello rang off and dialled again immediately, this time to find out whether any news of Sandro's movements had come in. It had. A Sandro Greco had boarded the plane at Milan for Paris in the early hours of the morning. (Who had lied about the town, Martello wondered: Sandro's wife or Sandro himself in telling her?) He should have arrived in Paris some time before six o'clock. And then where? They could ask Interpol to alert Passport Controls throughout Western Europe but for the time being he had little hope of locating the fugitive from police justice, Mafia revenge or other unknown pursuit. Hardly a day-off jaunt to foreign parts. Superficially Sandro was doing his best to leave the Mafia behind but if he had no knowledge of the murder, why should he have chosen this particular time? A matter whose implications Martello had no time to study just now.

Arvo telephoned him from Chioggia a short time later. 'I've just had a useful chat with Lieutenant Giovanni Fedele here in Chioggia and in your search for the murder weapon I think it might be useful to have a look at his Berretta as soon as this can be arranged. I'll tell you why later when I see you, together with a great deal more that I've learned today.'

'I'll get a message to him,' Martello promised. 'When do I see you?'

'As soon as I can get to you from here. I'll be leaving by the next boat. Where will you be in about two hours' time?'

'Probably on the Lido. In any case I'll arrange for a police car to meet the boat at Alberoni.'

Back in the hotel office, Arvo was offered a beer and a sandwich and with his facts and ideas now sorted out, he started on his tale.

'You haven't asked me yet what I'm doing here in Venice,' he began. 'Hardly as a tourist, though I suppose you could say on a family visit. My sister has been having problems as you may already have discovered. I don't yet know whether these have anything to do with the murder or are just a sub-plot running parallel.'

It was time to fill in the background, which Arvo did as briefly as possible with a summary of Tania's family circumstances and her mother-in-law's determination to break up the marriage, regain her son and take possession of her grandson. 'A repulsive, neurotic woman, she seems to be, though I've yet to meet her,' he described Chiara, with Martello nodding in heartfelt agreement. Arvo described Fedele's attempts to ingratiate himself with Tania, the odd 'coincidences' which must have involved Chiara's connivance, the plot to disgrace Tania and the virtual kidnapping of father and son. He then went on to describe the background to Toni's disappearance and his return home.

'Incidentally it appears that Vescovo isn't Stefano's father,' he concluded.

'Not his father? Not a new complication surely?'

'Maybe. Chiara seems to have lost her temper when her husband refused to report the child's disappearance to the police and somehow or other all was revealed. I got the impression from Stefano that husband wasn't unduly concerned or even surprised.'

'Who is Stefano's father?'

'I'm not sure that even Chiara knows.'

'Certain present-day Venetians don't seem to have much to learn from their eighteenth-century ancestors,' observed Martello, who had been assigned to Venice from his home on the Swiss border. 'So the boy and his father are now back in their own home. I know Stefano's your brother-in-law but I'd like your honest opinion of his reactions to all he'd heard.'

'You mean did he murder the man who wasn't his father? I doubt it. I know he'd good reason for loathing him: he's at no time made any secret of that. But Stefano's the introverted sensitive type. I find it difficult to imagine him firing a gun from that roof and I can't really see an adequate motive.'

'Has he got a gun?'

'Apparently yes, given to him by Chiara for his own protection and according to Stefano never unwrapped. I'll find out more about that this evening. How about the gun left in the conference room?'

'This is my main news for you. I had another word with Camillo this afternoon. He'd come across a gun some time ago in a secret drawer in Vescovo's desk in the palazzo. It's one of those eighteenth-century constructions full of hidden compartments and drawers to hold whatever might have been compromising or best kept from the official eyes at the time. Camillo claims to have little knowledge of guns but he recognized it as a Berretta.'

'As used by your carabinieri?'

'He didn't know the calibre. But if it was, I'd like to know just how Vescovo got hold of it. Only a dead or incapacitated carabiniere would allow his gun to be taken from him.'

Arvo had heard this statement before and he had also heard a good deal about Italy in general and Sicily in particular, where policemen seemed to live more than usually dangerous lives. 'Angelo Vescovo seems to have close connections with Sicily and the Mafia there. I can imagine that a man of his type might have been willing to pay quite a lot for such a souvenir: a gun snatched from a murdered carabiniere. Poetic justice indeed if that was the gun that murdered him.'

'Such things are possible, I suppose.' Martello sounded shocked at the very idea of such criminal misuse of a weapon intended for the maintenance of law and order. 'We've got no proof of its provenance, of course, and if it should be the murder weapon it's probably at the bottom of the Adriatic by now.' He paused before adding, 'We don't go in for murder much here in Venice and those that there are are mostly kept within the family.'

'How do we know this wasn't? Shall we go through our more obvious suspects?'

'Let's start with the nearest,' he continued, 'though hardly the dearest, I suspect. Our friend Chiara. She could use a rifle certainly, a gun possibly, though she's unlikely to own a Berretta .92. But could she have taken the missing one?'

Martello gave the suggestion consideration before saying: 'I suppose she might have gone into the conference room after the encounter with her husband but for what reason? I can't see her foraging among the papers on the table just on the chance of finding something interesting.'

'How about borrowing Fedele's gun? She visited him later that afternoon.'

'Is that so? She told me she went back to the palazzo to wait for her grandson. I see why you suggested the gun inspection. He'll be coming in with it as soon as he's off duty. Come to think of it, she had plenty of opportunity to use it. Her story for that time is that she left her husband

196

sitting at a table on the terrace—probably the place he was found in—changed and went straight home. I've already had some inquiries made in case she was recognized on one of the lagoon boats but no one of the ACTIV personnel has reported noticing her. The boats were probably crowded at that time of night. Perhaps someone in the hotel saw her leave. I'll ask about that myself.'

'You'll need a motive too: even a neurotic like my sister's mother-in-law would need that.'

'True. And we have other suspects. There's Pietro Vescovo, still unconscious in hospital. He might have asked his father to help him out in some financial mess he was in and been refused. He could have seen and picked up the gun from the table and disposed of it afterwards. And who knows, deliberately knocked himself out to avoid questioning.'

'How about Camillo Gentile?' Arvo asked. 'Any motive?'

'Plenty. If what he says is true and it seems likely, Vescovo tried to involve him in narcotics distribution, failed and threatened retribution on his wife if Camillo let out a word about what he'd been told. Yesterday afternoon Signora Gentile was set upon, fortunately unsuccessfully, but how about the next attempt? Easy enough for him to have found the possible murder weapon.'

'We can't complain of a scarcity of suspects,' Arvo commented. 'We've already discussed my brother-in-law. As for my sister, no motive that I can imagine and no gun.'

Martello had to agree. Chiara might well have been a target for Tania but surely she would have had nothing against her father-in-law.

'She might have looked out her husband's gun that he says he had never unpacked,' he suggested. 'But you'll be checking that. The one I'd put my money on is a certain ex-Mafia Sicilian, Sandro Greco.' Martello gave a summary of Vescovo's hold over Sandro, who, besides a possibly relaxed attitude towards murder, would have had a first-class motive and easy access to the missing gun. 'Moreover,' Martello concluded, 'Signor Greco slipped off last night shortly after, to unknown foreign parts, Paris being the first

197

of these. He promised to get in touch with his wife when he got to wherever he was going.'

'Surely he's much too obvious to be the right one, though I'll add my money to yours,' Arvo summed up. 'While it's not really my business, I'd be very interested to hear where you intend to go from here yourself.'

Martello had indeed been formulating a programme during the conversation and was now sorting out the details. 'There's Fedele's gun to check,' he started. 'I'll see him myself when he comes in: I'll have a few other things to say to him as well. He's a disgrace to the service we all take a pride in and . . . Well, you can guess the rest. Unfortunately, what he gets up to in his private life, even corrupting children, is of no official concern.

'Next, inquiries in the hotel about whether anyone noticed the departure of Signora Vescovo yesterday evening or can tell us anything about the movements of the two sons or the two secretaries. The evening reception and porter staff should be on duty in a couple of hours or so. I rather doubt whether Fedele's presence would have been noticed if he turned up out of uniform: one unknown face among five or six hundred.

'I wonder what time Chiara actually got home yesterday evening,' Arvo speculated. 'Who could tell you that?'

'There's a maid in the palazzo who let me in this morning,' Martello recalled. 'A sullen type of girl: I have the impression she might not be over-devoted to her mistress. One of my younger men might get her to talk. Why are you interested?'

'Fedele and Chiara seem to be quite old chums: from what I've heard from Tania, I'd guess that Chiara has given him quite a lot of assistance in furnishing his home. I'd like to know the real reason she left the hotel when she did and where she went. Perhaps she had something interesting to confide in her boyfriend. In that case she may have taken a water-bus to the Lido terminus and got a water-taxi from there—or maybe one from here, though that's less likely if she needed to cover her trail. How about asking around? And if so there'd be the return trip to Venice, though our

198

Casanova Don Giovanni might have obliged here with his own boat.'

Martello made notes while Arvo watched the moving pen and then got to his feet. 'Tania will be expecting me back for an evening meal,' he said. 'As a half-American, do you know the British expression "a busman's holiday"? I wonder what equivalent the Venetians might have. Anyhow it's what I'm quite enjoying at the present time.'

CHAPTER 13

DREDGING A CHANNEL

Iris had been invited to an evening meal with the reunited family. So long as the children were around, nothing was said about the murder. Toni was subdued and on his best behaviour, a state of affairs that was unlikely to last long, though the past year's hostility to his mother had clearly evaporated, probably for good. With family all together again and Uncle Arvo staying with them, Rosa radiated contentment: she chattered exuberantly about anything and everything: school, Goldie, the walk along the beach, how soon they would be able to go swimming. Tania realized she would have to tell the children more about the manner of their grandfather's death before they learned of it in less gentle ways, but had put it off till the following morning. The doorbell was being ignored and Arvo was instructed in a code for use when telephoning which involved dialling a second time. In such ways they hoped to avoid being pestered by thick-skinned reporters.

Tired after the morning's long walk, the children were soon ready for bed and after their room door was closed, Arvo telephoned Martello who was still in his temporary hotel headquarters. He explained the system for getting in touch by phone and asked for news. Martello had made one interesting discovery but had a slight disappointment to report.

'We questioned the water-taxi drivers outside here and at the Lido terminus,' he said. 'One of the latter remembered taking a middle-aged woman to Pellestrina yesterday evening some time after ten o'clock—he can't remember exactly when.'

'There can't have been many middle-aged women taking a water-taxi to Pellestrina at that time of night?'

'We'll have him in for identification if it becomes necessary. There's also a small possibility that some Pellestrinan saw her arrive or leave. She can hardly be unknown there.'

'No indications of how she returned to Venice?'

'No. We inquired in Pellestrina—you'd have to phone for a taxi there—but had no success. Fedele took her in his own boat, I imagine. You were right about the maid. Apparently she had no hesitation about admitting she hadn't got back herself till after midnight, which suggests she hadn't expected her mistress back before then. She'd heard someone moving around about half an hour later and it could only have been the signora returning. Interesting enough, I suppose, but not significant in view of the fact that Fedele's gun had been inspected and cleared and in addition he had all the cartridges he would have been issued with.'

'If only we knew where Vescovo's probable Berretta is now and who put it there.'

'The desk staff who would have been on duty at the time of the murder will be arriving at any minute and we'll be questioning them about comings and goings. I'll let you know what they say.'

Arvo hung up and returned to find the room empty. In the kitchen Stefano, with his hands deep in hot water, was mopping dishes and glasses which Tania was drying. 'Our next investment will be a dishwasher,' he muttered, 'if we're still here. I hope not. I'll be writing around about a job to old contacts in England.'

Arvo understood and approved. He went back to the sitting-room and was just looking for *Portrait of a Lady* when Iris and Goldie joined him after a bedtime-story session with the children. Tania brought in coffee while Stefano produced drinks.

200

It was time for Arvo to describe his interview with Giovanni in Chioggia and to pass on the information he had just had from Martello about Chiara's late homecoming and the gun inspection. This gave him an opportunity to refer to Chiara's forgotten gift. Stefano went down to the flat storeroom in the basement to look for it while Tania poured coffee for herself and Iris, sat down and said to Iris unexpectedly:

'You never asked me where I'd been when I came back so late last night.'

'I'd quite forgotten it,' Iris lied politely.

'I wasn't actually shooting Angelo with Stefano's gun though I might well have turned it on Chiara if I'd had it and run into her. He was an abominable man, of course, who'd caused misery and suffering to who knows how many people, but he was what he was, larger than life and bursting with energy. He grew up in a Mafia world and he'd have taken their morality for granted. He lived the only kind of life he understood. He was cold-blooded and ruthless but he wasn't mean and spiteful. Like Chiara.'

'True, but I suppose you could say Chiara's the result of her upbringing too,' Iris observed. 'Spoilt, selfish, cold and neurotic: on the verge of insanity so far as I can judge without having met her. But yes, you're right. She's mean and vicious in a way that Angelo wasn't. To return to the subject. Where were you last night if you weren't murdering your father-in-law or mother-in-law?'

'The explanation is obvious, known to every suspect. I went for a long walk. I had to. Our discussion with Arvo hadn't had much effect on the tension inside and I had to get exercise, walk as fast and as far as I could without even noticing where I was going. I left Rosa asleep as I shouldn't have done but there was nothing I could do about it. I came back dead tired but I could sleep.'

Stefano returned with a packaged box which everyone watched him unwrap, Iris backing away as she was terrified of guns. As soon as its contents were exposed, Arvo took the box from Stefano and picked up the gun between two forefingers touching only its extremities.

'Not a Berretta,' he pronounced. 'It looks like a Luger, possibly a left-over from the last war. And she seems to have forgotten the ammunition. Definitely not responsible for this murder.'

He put it down on the coffee-table and Tania poured out Stefano's coffee. Iris eyed the gun warily as if it was likely to explode in her face at any second. She looked across at Arvo to ask,

'What's this number on it? Is it what they call a serial number?'

'There's a number on every gun,' she was informed, 'and it'll be entered on your gun licence.'

Some idea was emerging in Iris's mind and she sat silent for a few minutes, unaware of the conversation around her. Arvo noticed her abstraction and asked, 'What's bothering you?'

'I'm just puzzled,' she said slowly, 'trying to sort out all the guns that keep turning up: this one and Angelo's licensed one and Giovanni's and the one that's disappeared. And they'll all have numbers.'

'Naturally. I've got a gun in Finland with a number that's kept in police records.'

Vague intimations were taking shape and linking in Iris's mind. 'It's all the moving about too: I mean Chiara's going backwards and forwards to Pellestrina. By the way, did the water-taxi driver notice what she was wearing?'

'If you're thinking of a long dress, he wouldn't have done. She changed in the hotel.'

'Did she? And where would she do that?'

'You've got something there.' Arvo had suddenly remembered what Giovanni had said about Chiara's leaving her evening things in the hotel. It must have been somewhere convenient for changing and what better place than her husband's bedroom? He suspected that Iris was ahead of him in some way and caught her eye. He looked towards the telephone with raised eyebrows and she nodded. Once again he dialled Martello.

Martello forestalled his questions by saying: 'I'm glad it's you. We've just picked up an interesting piece of infor-

202

mation. One of the delegates, a Greek publisher actually, who's staying on for a short holiday, put in a request to see the officer in charge. He was brought to me, hesitated a bit and hoped he wasn't wasting my time. He'd been talking to one of the conference speakers who'd been on the platform during the final session and who'd mentioned my interest in Vescovo's gun. It seems he'd been the first of the publishers to congratulate Vescovo after his final speech and he'd gone behind the table to shake hands. Most of the delegates reached over the table to do this. As he approached Vescovo, he saw him slip something heavy from between two piles of brochures straight into a side pocket. He had the impression it was the gun but the movement had been so quick that he's not sure. Only the other three speakers on the right of Vescovo could have seen it and they seemed to have other things on their minds just then. I thanked him so warmly for his information that he was quite surprised.'

'So Angelo probably had the lost gun all the time.' Arvo's tone was one of relief. 'But hardly in the pocket of his evening suit, and it wasn't found there of course. So it must have been upstairs in his room.'

'Or somewhere in his office downstairs. I wonder whether he locked his office when he left it.'

'Gentile would have had a key and possibly Sandro Greco also. And they would have admitted family members on request. Much more likely in his private room. But it could still have been used for the murder.'

'This all makes everything even more difficult.' Clearly Martello wasn't sharing Arvo's relief. 'We can't very well involve the hotel staff so who else could have had access to it?'

'I suppose the desk staff would have given the room key to Camillo on request. Certainly to Chiara. And you know, however efficient the hotel, keys are often handed out on request without identifying the guest. Though I should think the desk staff would recognize Chiara easily enough and remember her. How about asking if one of them recalls her asking for a key during the firework display?'

'That's easy enough.'

'Another thing. Was the number of the gun Fedele brought in checked against the issue list?'

'I doubt it. He'd surely not have more than one.'

'With all these guns proliferating, one never knows. I'd like to make a suggestion. Get the number of Fedele's gun from records and then send one or maybe two of your men to his place on Pellestrina. They'll tell him the truth: that no check was made on the number of the gun during the inspection so it will naturally have to be rechecked. He will therefore have to accompany them to Venice. Two men would be advisable as if he's guilty and panics, there could be resistance though from what I've seen of him, I doubt it. He'll expect to be able to talk his way out of every likely situation.'

'So you're suggesting he's got two guns?'

'If he hasn't already got rid of his own, with the idea it probably wouldn't have to be checked for some considerable time, and then he could lie his way out of possible complications. He's an arrogant type and I doubt if he's worried, especially now that they've found nothing on checking the gun he brought in.'

'Assuming there are two guns involved and both are or were in his possession, the fact he brought the wrong one, if he did, must indicate that the shot came from his own gun. The other gun was also fired yesterday but of course there wouldn't have been the correspondence between bullet and barrel.' Martello paused in obvious calculation before expressing his conclusion: 'Yes, I can see how it all fits together now: just a few bits of confirmation. I certainly think Fedele should pay us a second visit, and I'll send two men as you suggest. It's the other interrogation with Signora you-know-who that really frightens me. If all goes well, it's going to be a field day for the popular press, isn't it?'

There was a silence as Arvo returned to the coffee-table, three eavesdroppers having at least gathered ideas from the part of the conversation they had overheard through the open door into the hall, one of them busy piecing the jigsaw together into a recognizable picture. Iris said nothing,

204

however, trying to look Sphinx-like with a small secret smile on her lips but in fact continuing to resemble everybody's spinster aunt with a slight toothache.

'So it was Giovanni who murdered him after all,' Tania exclaimed. 'I'm so glad.'

'Sorry to spoil your sadistic gloating,' Arvo warned her, looking across at his English teacher for her linguistic approval, 'but I think you're wrong.'

'Chiara then. Even better.'

'Really, Tania, you used not to be so bloodthirsty. Don't make a habit of it. I haven't forgotten the unlikely long exhausting walk though somehow I can't picture your breaking into Angelo's bedroom to get hold of the gun. As you've made up your mind, you can present your evidence rationally and in chronological order.'

'Well. She left Angelo on the terrace, went up to the roof, shot him, came down without being seen, left the hotel taking the gun with her and went off to Giovanni's for comfort and support.'

'Possible, indeed, though a few major points are unaccounted for. What can have happened to Angelo's gun left in his room or his office, now Martello's office? And where did Chiara get the gun she used?'

'From Giovanni, of course. During the afternoon when she went to see him.'

'And he said to her, "Be a lamb and murder your husband for me. I haven't got the time."'

'Something like that. I wasn't there at the time.' Brother and sister had rolled back the years to enjoy a teenage sparring match.

Iris joined in, her solid common sense bringing the discussion down to earth again. 'She could have taken the gun without permission,' she observed. 'If she'd already made up her mind to murder Angelo.'

'But why?' Tania asked despairingly. 'Why should she choose that particular moment to murder him just because Toni had disappeared?'

'From all I've heard about her,' Iris suggested, 'she's both extremely neurotic and utterly self-willed. Stefano, you were there when she told Angelo about Toni's disappearance. She taunted him with not being your father but what else happened?'

Stefano had taken little part in the speculations though he had followed them sombrely. In the excitement of the chase, the others had forgotten him and his deep emotional involvement: even Tania, with her understandable craving for vengeance finding expression. He had become conscious for the first time of the revolution in his own feelings: the mother he had adored as a child, and as an adult forced himself into a reluctant loyalty to, was being revealed as the murderer of the father, or rather father-substitute he had always loathed. And now he felt nothing for either of them other than an urge to join in the murder hunt and an undeserved twinge of pity for the oversized bully. He had to admit to himself a deepfelt need for retribution against the depersonalized figure that out of sheer malice and vindictiveness had schemed to deprive her son, her possession, of his wife and daughter and his wife of husband and son. He struggled against his sudden rage and answered calmly enough:

'She tried to phone the police to get their help in finding Toni but he wouldn't let her.'

'That must have infuriated her.'

'It did. Even more when he decreed that Toni would have to be sent home as soon as he turned up.'

'And she'd been scheming for months, possibly years to get hold of him,' Iris reflected, voicing Stefano's own thoughts. 'She'd have been revelling in the thought of Tania's misery and now she'd have to endure her delight and satisfaction. To Chiara, I suppose, it would have been Tania's triumph. Every hope she'd ever had of humbling her by depriving her of husband and child would have been destroyed. How she must have loathed Angelo, that conceited oaf of a Sicilian peasant she'd been fool enough to marry, who was daring to dictate to the Venetian nobility.'

'If she'd telephoned the palazzo she might have heard the same story as Beata told me: that Toni had turned up,' Stefano speculated with forced detachment. 'I doubt whether Beata would have dared to contradict the boss's instructions, not even for her mistress.'

'And in that case,' Iris went on excitedly, 'she could well have been crazy enough to persuade herself that with Angelo out of the way she could manage to keep Toni.'

'She'd have known I'd never allow it.'

'If she'd been normal she'd have realized that but she must have been literally out of her mind with rage and frustration: that state of mind where you're so worked up and obsessed that you've got to do something destructive and violent. I can imagine she's longed to get rid of Angelo for years and this was the spark. And then she could have married darling Giovanni.'

'Fair enough,' Arvo approved placidly, 'you're doing my job very proficiently, Iris and the rest of you, so go on with it. We can assume she came across Fedele's gun during her afternoon visit, and that might well have appeared a sign of divine or rather satanic intervention. What did she do with it?'

It was Tania who broke in immediately. 'She probably had that black velvet bag with her: she could easily have slipped the gun into it, with or without Giovanni noticing. Then she'd have come to the hotel to change.'

'Where?'

'In Angelo's bedroom, surely the best place,' Tania suggested.

'And then?'

'What happened then isn't hard to imagine,' Iris took over. 'It's the roof that's bothering me. Somehow I can't imagine a middle-aged Venetian aristocrat clambering around on a roof during a firework display and firing guns from it. How would the idea come into her head in the first place?'

'Obviously she realized that the ideal time to shoot someone is during a firework display,' Stefano observed. 'And in this case the roof would have been the only place where the murderer could be fairly sure of being invisible.'

'Was she a good shot?' Arvo asked.

'She had a first-class reputation with a rifle.'

'But she claimed she hadn't got or used a gun.'

'How about this one she gave me? You're not going to suggest that she didn't know how to use it. She was fascinated by all kinds of firearms. And just because she'd had experience in hunting, she'd have been capable of locating the ideal place to fire from.' Stefano was speaking with growing certainty and horror. 'She's often been in the hotel and sunbathed on the beach when she might well have looked up at that roof and vaguely considered its possibilities as a shooting-gallery. The door that opens on to the roof is easy to find: it's on one of the upstairs corridors. I've been through it myself and likely enough she has too. There are parapet-protected passages along the side and it makes a wonderful look-out point.'

'But how about her target? How would she have got him into the ideal position to be shot at?' Tania wondered.

'Nobody will ever know that, probably,' Iris observed, 'but we can conjecture fairly realistically. I can imagine that when they left the dining-room to see the firework display she suggested the terrace as a good place to watch from: it wouldn't have been so packed with people as the various balconies and the smaller upper terrace and Angelo might have been only too thankful by then to get away from the crowd. Once they were down there she might have led him to the table where he was found dead: she might even have earlier found a RESERVED notice to put on it. She'd have sat down with him and then almost immediately made some excuse, like powdering her nose, to leave him for a minute or two. People wouldn't have noticed him much: the light from inside, I imagine, might have shown clearly enough his shape there but not so clearly his features. A short spell of anonymity might have been just what he needed then.'

Apart from Stefano, who was brooding over his own reactions rather than the present situation, they were now happily absorbed in constructing their own whodunit. 'I suppose she'd have gone to the desk for the room key,' Tania continued the account, 'and then straight up to the roof to do the deed with the fireworks exploding all around.' For a moment there was silence while everyone round the coffee-table visualized a dark shape leaning over the parapet, aiming carefully at a somnolent figure dimly but adequately visible below in the glow of light from within, while the cool night sky was racked by flashes, flares and the screaming racing streamers of rockets with the salvo of a score of guns shattering the peace of sand and sea.

Arvo brought them back to humdrum reality. 'Martello is going to check on whether she asked for the key,' he said, 'if anyone remembers.'

Tania's confidence had waned in the face of a remembered obstacle. 'She must have been using Giovanni's gun,' she speculated, 'and in that case how does the second gun, Angelo's, come into it?'

'Didn't we hear you say that Angelo had the second gun all the time, Arvo?' Arvo nodded in answer to Iris's question. 'All right,' she continued with increasing conviction. Couldn't we assume from what you said on the telephone that he'd left it in his bedroom, most likely slipped into a drawer. Chiara comes in to change and maybe she's curious or is looking for a paper handkerchief or something. She opens the drawer, sees the gun which looks the same as the one she's used and picks it up to compare. She may be emotionally unbalanced but she can still realize she'll have left fingerprints on it and wiping them off won't help. When the inquiry starts, she'd have been the only person apart from Angelo and a maid, who'd hardly come into it, who'd have visited the room. So she must dispose of it. She slips it into the symbolic and sinister black velvet bag together with the one she's used and has got to return. There's no chance of dropping it into canal or lagoon unobserved so she takes it to Giovanni who'll probably think of something. She has to tell him what she's done—I wonder what his reaction was—and beg him to get rid of it. A wonderful chance of blackmail, when you come to think of it, which he probably did, but rather too dangerous.'

In silence they awaited Arvo's verdict. 'On first hearing it seems to fit,' he pronounced. 'And my far-from-stupid Chioggian colleague might well have anticipated the recovery of the cartridge and the possibility of a gun check.

He'd have taken Chiara back to the palazzo where I can quite well imagine she'd have had need of a sedative while he'd sit tight and wait for developments. And Martello will be taking care of them at this very moment. He must be tired, poor chap: he'll soon have been on duty for around twenty hours. And the salaries we're paid, probably all over the world . . .'

'Sometime I'll have to teach you an English song,' Iris said. 'It's called "The Policeman's Lot is not a Happy One". Would you like me to sing it to you?' An immediate burst of conversation on other matters followed her generous suggestion.

CHAPTER 14

PLUMBING THE DEPTHS

In the event, Martello postponed further action till early the next morning, having first ascertained from Chioggia that Fedele would not be on early duty there. He recognized that after some twenty hours without rest, he was too exhausted to deal competently with the tricky situation that undoubtedly lay ahead. In addition he must arrange the attendance of at least two and possibly three other people, Chiara naturally being one of them, and not improbably already deep in sedated slumber, and Fedele another.

Furthermore he was hoping for information to add to that of the water-taxi man: was it possible that a neighbour in Pellestrina had seen or at least heard Chiara's arrival at the cottage late the previous evening? He suspected that the locals were not unfamiliar with the arrival of lady visitors (at a house which, if Martello had known it, was ideally furnished for their reception); in fact they were probably taken for granted. But presumably Chiara had been a more regular visitor and her obviously more exalted social background might well have provoked comment and even condemnation. At least she was unlikely to have escaped notice.

Like Chiara, however, the good people of Pellestrina would also have retired by now to more merited slumbers, ready to rise soon after five the following day. Another valid reason (or excuse?) for postponement.

Having unexpectedly located Beata in her rightful place in the palazzo, he impressed upon her over the telephone that two representatives of the law would be arriving there by eight o'clock next morning and it was imperative that the signora should be ready to receive them. The risk of Chiara's taking flight was minimal, he decided. He next arranged for a ballistics expert to be available at headquarters at half past seven and finally, after sandwiches and a beer, made his way to his own quarters where he set his alarm clock for five-fifteen and sank into an oblivion at least as profound as Chiara's.

He was back in his hotel office at six and soon after was instructing an officer of equal rank to Fedele with an assistant to bring the lieutenant first to headquarters. The escort was to observe due courtesy but was to request possession of Fedele's gun, the serial number of which the officer was to check unobtrusively from memorized records before pocketing it himself (thereby avoiding an 'accidental' disposal of it into the lagoon en route). They were to report to the ballistics expert who would be awaiting them.

At six-thirty he instructed a carabiniere on duty in Pellestrina to make discreet inquiries among Fedele's neighbours and to inveigle anyone who could assist with identification to the hotel as soon as possible. Finally, shortly after half past seven, he dispatched two sergeants to the palazzo to request the presence of its owner, recommending tact fortified with firmness and wishing them luck.

The neighbour arrived first, was offered coffee for his trouble and requested to wait in an adjoining room. A telephone call which followed shortly after eight from headquarters informed him that Fedele had been brought there and his gun with the correct serial number examined: the five remaining cartridges corresponded with the one extracted from the head of Angelo Vescovo. Martello gave instructions for Fedele to be brought to the hotel without

211

delay. He had already arranged for Chiara to be taken to the room occupied by the Pellestrinan immediately on her arrival and left to wait there. At this stage he was concerned with linking Chiara with Fedele rather than with the murder and as the resultant identification would not be used in court, no full identify parade would be required for the moment.

Five minutes later the Pellestrinan was shown in. He proved to be the elderly father of the obliging cat-minder in the next cottage where he occupied a small bedroom adjoining a similar room in Fedele's house. The intervening wall being far from soundproof, he could hear any noise of above-average volume originating beyond it and between eleven and twelve of the evening in question, he had been treated to the sound of raised voices and what had seemed to be a furious altercation between the lieutenant and a woman in the adjoining room. On hearing steps going down the stairs, he had looked out of the window just as a woman was emerging from the brightly-lit hall: he had seen her face in the light from the hall but as she glanced upward at one point, he had quickly withdrawn from sight so he did not know if the lieutenant had followed her out. But he had no doubt at all that the woman he had just been sitting opposite was the one he had seen leaving the house. He added that he had seen her on various occasions in the past. He had a quiet, gentle face, tanned by wind and sun, which suggested that he still spent much of his time fishing: he made no comment on the information he had given apart from a slight shake of the head as he finished. He was requested to wait a little longer and was taken back to the other room. Martello was then informed that Lieutenant Fedele had arrived and was waiting with his escort in the corner of one of the deserted lounges.

Chiara was shown in by a sergeant, who closed the door quietly behind her, and she remained standing helplessly just inside the door, her eyes focused on the captain standing behind his table, though without apparently seeing him. In a dark grey coat over a black dress, her near-white blonde hair (bleached from the earlier russet-red) uncombed, and no make-up on a face that was haggard and vacant, she suggested something of a body that had floated in and dried out on a deserted shore of the lagoon. Martello indicated a chair that he had already placed to one side not far from the door and invited her to sit down. She moved towards it like an automaton, sat down and eyed him blankly, a very old woman who had lost all contact with reality. Coming round to her, the captain offered her a cigarette, which she ignored for a couple of seconds and then extracted from his case, drawing on it hungrily after he had lit it, as if desperately needing the comfort it might give. She continued to gaze uncomprehendingly into space as the captain expressed his insincere regrets for inconveniencing her.

After a half-minute of resounding silence, the door opened and Giovanni strode in, saluted his superior officer and stood to attention, looking straight ahead. A gasp from the chair, which he had passed without noticing it, drew his attention to its occupant: his eyes widened momentarily in brief alarm but it was with an impassive face that he again regarded Martello, who addressed him curtly:

'You have been brought here, Lieutenant, to account for the fact that the gun you earlier presented for examination was not your own.'

Even as he spoke, Martello was aware of the extreme tension in the man facing him and the tightness of control he was imposing upon himself, a control that he suspected might snap at any moment. However, the voice that answered him after a slight pause retained the confidence and gentleness it had had on the few previous occasions when the two men had met.

'I would prefer, Capitano,' he said, 'to speak to you privately and not in the presence of this lady.'

'Why?' Martello snapped out. 'Is this lady a personal friend of yours?' He had not missed the sudden transformation in Chiara at the arrival of the lieutenant and the even keener effect of what had just been said. She was staring at Giovanni with a strained intensity equal to his own, though it was less rigidly controlled.

Giovanni ignored her. 'I am acquainted with her, yes,

213

and what I have to say might cause her pain.'

The reaction to these considerate words was instantaneous. Chiara sprang from her chair and towards him in a single movement until her face was only a few inches from his own, her eyes glaring into his.

'Just what have you got to say that could cause *me* pain?' she spat out at him.

Giovanni directed a weary man-to-man glance at his superior that expressed as clearly as any words could, 'You see what I mean.'

'Signora,' Martello enunciated in a peremptory tone calculated to paralyse near-hysteria, repeating the admonition even more menacingly when it had no effect. Her eyes slowly turned to meet him. 'If you want to stay and hear what is said, you'll have to sit down and be prepared to listen.'

With a look directed at her likely betrayer that combined hatred and mistrust, Chiara returned reluctantly to her chair.

'You will agree, Lieutenant,' Martello continued, 'that the signora has the right to hear anything that you have to say which may involve herself.'

Ignoring the woman behind him, Giovanni looked directly into Martello's eyes. 'I have to say then,' he began, 'that my reason for presenting the incorrect gun was to protect the signora, for whom I have a deep respect.' He bowed his head as if to confirm his words.

'Continue,' Martello ordered.

'Shortly after my return from duty on the afternoon preceding Signor Vescovo's assassination, I received a visit in my home from the signora.' As police witness, Giovanni was presenting his evidence with admirable precision and conviction. 'She was excessively distressed on account of the disappearance of her grandson, which she blamed primarily on the intervention of her daughter-in-law but almost equally on her own husband. It seems he had refused not only to apply to the police for help in locating the child but also to take any further responsibility for him when found, insisting on his immediate return to his mother. She implored my advice about what she could do in this situation.'

Chiara muttered something that might well have been an expletive though its exact nature was drowned by Giovanni's continued explanation.

'I counselled patience and diplomacy, qualities that the signora seems to have some difficulty in cultivating.' Giovanni paused at this point, apparently realizing that spite was curdling somewhat the detached purity of his exposition. He returned to factual narrative. 'The signora left me soon after six o'clock, with the intention of returning to the hotel to change for the evening programme and it was not until an hour or so later that I discovered that my gun was missing. It could only have been taken by her, probably concealed in the large bag she was carrying.' Rigidly alert now, Chiara seemed to be restraining herself by phenomenal will-power. 'Aware of her state of mind and appalled by the loss of the weapon, I immediately left in my own boat, which I moored in the canal approaching the hotel, where I arrived just at the end of the firework display. I looked in vain for the signora and finally assumed she had already departed so I returned to my boat and was home about forty minutes later, intending to call at the palazzo the following day.

'The signora arrived at my home some ten minutes later when I was already preparing for bed. She has a key to my house and apparently came straight upstairs. When asked about my gun, she produced it, explaining she had taken it on impulse. Knowing nothing of the murder, I saw no reason to check it as I was in no way alarmed, though I made clear my very considerable annoyance at what had happened. Later I took her back to the palazzo in my boat. It was only the following morning and after I had heard of the murder on the radio that I discovered the other gun which she had hidden behind a curtain in the sitting-room before coming upstairs. I—'

He was interrupted by an infuriated tigress who launched herself upon him, scratching, kicking and screaming wildly, 'Liar, liar, you killed him! You know you did! You've wanted him dead all the time: so you could marry me—and my money.' She let him go for a moment, her eyes blazing with hatred, to continue: 'From the start you begged me to divorce him. I'm a loyal and devoted wife: how could I and why should I? As if I'd marry a murderer, an imbecile! Dolt, devil, sadist, brute!'

Again she launched an attack, her fingers directed towards his eyes, while, effortlessly, Giovanni held her at arm's length, screaming and kicking but with hands and nails immobilized.

'I would suggest that handcuffs might be advisable,' he suggested quietly.

Martello had been regarding the scene with combined amazement and acceptance, the former on account of his previous unawareness of Chiara's superb acting abilities, on display throughout the interview but deceiving even himself, the latter because her present behaviour was fulfilling his darkest forebodings, though this time more appropriately directed against the real villain of the piece. He had to admit that while deserving everything he was getting, Fedele seemed far more adept at coping with hysteria than he himself would have been in the circumstances. But the lieutenant was awaiting his response.

'Will they be necessary, signora?' Martello asked, equally quietly.

Chiara shuddered, looked around wildly and apparently emerged from a hideous nightmare. As she went limp under his control, Giovanni released her. Having eyed him in stunned horror, she turned to stare at Martello, and it was him she eventually addressed, all emotion now drained from her voice.

'Now I shall tell you what really happened,' she said.

'Thank you, signora,' he replied noncommittally, praying that nothing would distract her but at the same time speculating about what new persona she would assume.

The silence prolonged itself as she moved about the room: to the window to look out across beach and sea where she had so often sunbathed and swum, to the door as though in the hope of escaping from disaster closing in, back to the table, where unexpectedly stubby fingers smoothed its glossy surface. Finally she raised her eyes to gaze into Martello's, the superb tragic actress confronting her judge and tormentor with unyielding dignity before an enthralled but non-existent audience.

'Here before you stands the man,' she started, quietly and slowly, 'whom I respected, admired, adored. I was prepared to give up everything to win, and to preserve his love. I have been loyal to him when he has been disloyal to me, generous and he has taken all I have offered and given nothing in return. And now he has revealed himself to you for what he is: a craven, a cheat, a liar.

'Yes, I visited him that afternoon, hoping for comfort in my misery. And what comfort did he give? Only to use that misery for his own ends. The only hope for both of us was the removal, the murder of my husband, not by himself, the man trained in violence, but by myself, a weak helpless woman. In that way we should be free for an eventual marriage. Bah! Did he imagine I would accept that? He who had taught my grandson to lie to me and feared the justifiable anger of my husband would destroy him and his miserable career? How could I feel anything but horror at his suggestion, however much I still loved him? Perhaps I no longer loved my husband though I respected him, but I am not and never could be a murderer. I left him, horrified, and there was no gun hidden in my bag.

'I have always disliked fireworks: they are childish and dangerous. So as the display started, I left my husband enjoying a few moments' peace sitting at a table. I too needed to spend a short time alone in quietness and the one place I could find it would be in my husband's room. I asked for the key and let myself in, changed into my outdoor clothes and then sat there for some time quietly thinking. Just as the fireworks ended, there was a knock at the door and believing it was a maid, I opened it. It was Lieutenant Fedele who burst in and told me he had just shot my husband as I had been afraid to do it myself. He took his own gun from his pocket, saying he wanted to clean it in case he should be stopped and searched by the police, who would arrive at any moment. He looked for some tissue, opening several drawers and in one of them he found another gun, which looked very like his own. I watched him, too horrified to speak and he said nothing either, just examined it closely: then he put it into a pocket and his own into the holster he was wearing and hurried out of the room without saying a word. It took me several minutes to recover from the shock and then I knew at once that I must follow him. How I got to his house I hardly remember but he was already upstairs when I let myself in with my key. He was furious when he first saw me and shouted at me but then he calmed down and told me he had killed Angelo only for my sake. He said we mustn't meet for some time and I must say nothing, above all to the police, as I also would be accused of the crime or at least of helping him to carry it out. I promised to say nothing and he took me back to the palazzo. What else could I do?'

She turned at last to face Giovanni, who had made no movement and they stared at each other in a frozen intensity of hatred. It was Giovanni who finally turned away and when he spoke, his voice was as bitter as hers had been as he countered:

'You're lying, you bitch. Every word you say is a lie. I never asked you to murder him: would I have asked a woman to undertake a man's job? I wouldn't have been able to murder your husband: how could I, when it was you who had my gun? I admit I submitted the second gun for inspection, in the knowledge that you had used my own for the killing, and wishing to protect you from the consequences. But why in the name of heaven should I have burdened myself with a second gun after using my own to commit a murder? Tell me that, will you?'

Chiara was ready with an answer and their voices rose, accusations and counter-accusations becoming ever more vitriolic, with Martello all ears for the shreds of truth that might inadvertently slip out. At the height of the fray, however, and despite Martello's instructions to hold all but urgent calls, the telephone provided a sudden interruption. Having listened for a few seconds, Martello said in English, 'Please wait a minute,' and laid the receiver on the table. He strode to the door, opened it and gave orders to the policeman outside. 'Take these two to another room and stay with them,' adding quietly, 'Make a mental note of anything they might say to each other. They'll both have to be detained and charged.' And with what? he added to himself. Silence had descended on the contestants who may have relished a change of battlefield as they followed their new guardian meekly out of the room. Martello took up the receiver again.

'Glad you've rung me, Arvo. You've got only ten minutes before leaving, you say, so I'll be very brief. Things are moving here all right, at high speed in tight closed circles and my head's spinning with them. And if I sound more than somewhat unbalanced, that's why. Would you like a three-minute run-down or were you wanting to contribute something?'

'The run-down, telegraphic if you can, so there's time for your—and maybe my—comments. It's not all sewn up then, I gather?'

'I actually thought it was for a moment. Fedele supplied all the stitches you'd already suggested and I was about to start a thorough test of the finished article when friend Chiara ripped it all wide open again. You know she's a whole education to meet, that woman: you've really missed something: Sophia Loren in one of her primitive roles. The performance was staggering.'

'All in addition to being a murderess?'

'That's Fedele's story.'

'And hers? I suppose he's the villain.'

'How did you guess?'

'And what's your verdict?'

'If only we had time to talk it over together. The one new item they both agree on is that he also was at the hotel.' Martello continued with a précis of the two stories, seeking possible flaws and inconsistencies as he related them for the first of many times.

'A murderer and his or her accessory. So you can hold them both,' was Arvo's comment.

'Yes, but on which individual charge?'

'Hm. Well, you're giving me something to think about on the plane. How about motives?'

'His, according to Chiara, to marry her for her money and avoid retaliatory action from Angelo for his corruption of an innocent child. Not so incredible as it might seem, the latter: most of these Mafia merchants are decidedly strait-laced when it comes to the family. In Chiara's case, a fixation on wiping the floor with her foreign rival for son's and grandson's allegiance thwarted in the moment of triumph by peasant-bred husband: how she must have despised him! She's neurotic to the point of megalomania and cunning as a vixen. With a clever lawyer, her acting talents and, let's not forget, her connections in high places anxious to cover up scandal, she might still get away with it: whatever "it" may prove to be.'

'Our murders tend to be less subtle,' Arvo observed, 'an unpremeditated knife-thrust while under the influence. I'd recommend the psychological approach in this case: play upon his arrogance. I'm sorry I never met Chiara: somewhat uncommon in Finland.'

'You haven't seen much of Venice either. Come back again in the summer.'

'Summer? In Venice? Come and join me in Central Lapland. Plenty of good fishing there—and good weather—if you can survive the mosquitoes. And keep me in the picture, won't you? That's the taxi I can hear. So *arriverderci* to you.'

As soon as he had replaced the receiver, Arvo bolted downstairs to the street, where Stefano was fitting his suitcase and rucksack into the waiting taxi. The children were at school so only Tania and Stefano were going to the airport to see him off, with Iris waving goodbye to him at Santa Elisabetta.

With the slight feeling of deflation that almost inevitably follows a farewell, Iris strolled back alongside a lagoon already sprawled limply in an early heat haze, its muddy greenish water stained by the weed illegally scooped from its floor by Chioggia fishing-nets. Crumbling decaying islands crouched obscurely, a distant Burano just visible between two of them.

Stepping warily over hazardous gaps and unevennesses in pavements and roadway, Iris turned into her own street, where the tide-retreating weed-stained water in its bisecting canal carried surrealistic-shaped wedges of snow-white plastic, tins, papers, and other litter to their resting-place in the lagoon. As she opened the main gate, an elegant silver-tabby stray posed on the doorstep, a large grey rat half as big as herself gripped in her jaws, slipped away to shelter in the garden. Having extracted a letter from her postbox, Iris opened her own door, to be met with the smell of carpets still damp from a flood from a burst water-pipe three days earlier. Thumps and scrapings, silenced only in the few night hours, assailed her from the flat above: she had never discovered what could possibly be going on up there. Her sandy tabby eyed her languidly from the typewritten sheets she had elected to stretch out on.

She sank into a chair to read the letter in peace, only to be sat on in her turn by a solid furry cushion purring ecstatically and marking time vigorously with extended claws. Her letter envelope bore a foreign stamp and its contents informed her that a teaching job would be available for her in September: pay, conditions and other details on the attached sheet. With a sigh of thankfulness cut short by a wince as claws penetrated her knee, she viewed cat and carrying-basket in a corner of the room with some commiseration. 'But how will you enjoy the change, Liz?' she asked her supremely-contented tormentor. 'I do believe you actually like living here.'